THE DISTANT MARVELS

Chantel Acevedo

THE DISTANT MARVELS

Europa
editions

Europa Editions
214 West 29th Street
New York, N.Y. 10001
www.europaeditions.com
info@europaeditions.com

Copyright © 2015 by Chantel Acevedo
First Publication 2015 by Europa Editions

Library of Congress Cataloging in Publication Data is available
ISBN 978-1-60945-252-0

Acevedo, Chantel
The Distant Marvels

Book design by Emanuele Ragnisco
www.mekkanografici.com

Cover image: *El mantón azul*, pastel painting by Soledad Fernández

Prepress by Grafica Punto Print – Rome

Printed in the USA

For my mother, Marta,
and my grandmother, Maria Asela,
in gratitude for their strength
and for their love, which I surely felt before
I could even utter the words.

This Cuban woman, so beautiful, so heroic, so selfless,
a flower to be loved, a star to gaze upon, a shield to endure.
—José Martí

CONTENTS

Part II

Part III

THE DISTANT
MARVELS

PROLOGUE

An unexpected envelope was delivered to me two months ago, on the first day of August. The package it came in bore the address of the University of Havana, Department of History in blue ink and a symmetrical print. My name was written in a different hand, and my address in yet another, as if the package had passed from person to person, each contributing some element to its outward appearance. Unnerved by all of those invisible hands, I left the package untouched all afternoon. But I could feel its presence, like fingers reaching into my purse, or trying to lift my skirt slowly. Accustomed to being alone, I began to feel that the package was an intrusion, and I could no longer stand it.

So, I opened it. Inside there was a pair of letters. The first, new and crisp, the blue ink rubbing off on my fingers, explained the second, which was old and crumbling. *María Sirena,* it began, casually, impertinently, as if I were an old friend, *we believe this letter belongs to you. It has been housed in our archives, unopened, for many decades.* The letter, it was explained, was waylaid somehow at the turn of the century, had turned up in a collection of war-era correspondences sold at auction, and had been acquired by an alumnus of the university. An ingenious student, they wrote, had tracked me down as part of his thesis. And on it went, describing the historical effort to preserve what was most important, and find homes for the insignificant.

With one glance at the faded postal stamps, my heart began to pound.

I worked the brittle flap open, chips of paper falling like confetti. I pulled out an article from an American newspaper, so fragile that tiny parts of the paper crumbled to dust, etching out words and individual letters, as if the thing were censoring itself before my eyes. Another page, this one made of onion-skin, upon which a Spanish translation of the article had been written in delicate, old-fashioned penmanship, held my attention for a moment until a small square of stiff paper fluttered to the floor from within the envelope.

I bent down and saw that it was a picture of my little boy. My hands, holding the envelope and pages, curled into question marks, and then all of the contents of the package, those unwanted, insignificant things to the historians at the university, slipped to the floor.

That day, I sat on the floor and read the article again and again. I put the picture in my bra, close to my skin, until a corner of it bent, then, I wept for that small damage. I could not undo the crease, but I found a frame for the picture, one deep enough to contain not only the photo but also the article and its translation. I whispered the diminutive of his name, the only name I ever spoke to him, "Mayito," and wondered at the way the envelope had found its way to Maisí, and my little cottage by the sea.

PART I

1.

Waiting for the Sea to Come

My next-door neighbor, Ada, treads through the sand wearing plastic sandals that flap against her hard heels. I hear her before I see her. She's come to my back porch to warn me of a storm in the Atlantic. It does not matter to Ada that I can see for myself the ferocious churn of the sky, like a black mouth opening and closing, and the white, teeth-like caps of the waves. She has a television, and has become the ears of the neighborhood, watching reporters all day, then, broadcasting the news from house to house. She says the storm began off the coast of Africa, that they named it Huracán Flora, and that already, in Haiti, the sea itself had been wrenched away, revealing a sunken ship for a moment before the water came crashing back down. The storm is said to be bigger than all of Cuba, and Ada says I should be worried.

"You needn't have come," I tell her, and point at the sky. "I don't need a television to tell me what's coming. Cobbled sky," I say, but don't finish the old adage—*cielo pedrado, piso mojado*. Cobbled sky, wet ground.

The pregnant clouds race one another in the sky. In the sand, blue crabs scuttle towards rocks, forcing themselves into nooks and crannies. Ada and I watch them for a moment from my back porch. The movement in the sky and on the ground is disorienting, and I feel a touch of vertigo.

"They're opening the old governor's mansion in Santiago to those of us on the coast. For safety's sake," Ada says, reaching out her hand to me as if I would take it, come out of my chair, and abandon my house to the winds.

"Me quedo aquí," I tell her, and face the sea again.

"What would Beatríz think?" she asks me, her mouth pursed.

My eyes prickle, and I blink them hard. "I haven't heard from her in weeks. She's an Habanera now, didn't you know?" A small crab makes its way towards my foot, as if it wants to get into the house. It opens a tiny, cobalt claw at me. First Ada's outstretched hand, then the crab's claw. I am besieged.

"Déjame," I say quietly. The roiling surf is calming. I feel right by the sea. "And besides," I say then, completing my thoughts aloud. "I won't step foot in that mansion."

Ada groans and sits beside me. The wicker couch creaks and the wind whips her skirt about. She is seventy-three, nine years younger than I. But nine years seem to be just enough to make a difference. Ada's ankles have not yet begun to swell just from sitting. She has not yet discovered the disquieting tendency to fall over for no good reason, as if the earth has tilted suddenly, playing a child's practical joke on her.

"Beatríz will come for you," Ada insists.

"That is an old dream, Adita," I say, and lay my hand over hers. My daughter is a woman of the city now, or so she says. She has become the kind of person who sets foot in a house and immediately begins to criticize it. "That old rug has holes in it, Mami," or "Why don't you dye your hair?" Once, I asked if she was ashamed of me, and she waved her hands in the air as if performing a magic trick, and said nothing.

"It's coming here, to Maisí," Ada says. "We must go." She grips my hand hard, stands, and tugs, trying to lift me.

"Déjame," I say again, more forcefully this time.

"You want the sea to swallow you?" Ada yells. The crabs still at the sound for a moment, then resume their crawl across the beach.

"It might be preferable," I say, and Ada's eyes film with tears. Were she to walk into my bedroom these days with the kind of confidence she bears when in my house, as if every room were hers as well, Ada would see the dozen unfilled doctor's prescriptions on my dresser. But she only searches my face for an explanation I do not give her.

Once more, I say, "Déjame," and this time, Ada leaves without a sound, though I can tell, by the way her arms are moving, that she is wiping her eyes.

Ada will be back, I know. She will take the time to pack up her cottage. Her daughter-in-law, Panchita, will come over with her grandsons, strapping boys with piercing blue eyes. Ada, who never brags about her great-grandchildren, knowing that it would hurt me, will shuffle behind the boys, touching them on the shoulders to get their attention, her eyes swallowing them up. They will load her valuable things into their car (for Ada's son, Miguel, owns a bright blue '57 Ford Fairlane that roars up and down the street, startling me each time), and drive west, keeping inland, getting as far as Matanzas, maybe. I will watch all of this from right here, this seat.

I plan on not moving at all.

2.
The Mermaid's Daughter

Of course, I have to leave my seat by the sea sometime. I feel hungry, and fire up the stove. I chop up a ripe plátano and fry it in oil. There is day-old rice on the counter, which smells fishy, the way rice does after a few hours, but it is good to eat. I throw the rest of it out onto the beach, and the crabs, which are still mid-exodus, stop over the grains before trotting on. I can hear them under the house, scratching, digging, burrowing. I lie awake in bed listening to them.

I do not sleep that night, though it feels as if I'm dreaming. In truth, I'm merely remembering, and what I remember is a story my mother told me long ago about another storm.

Her name was Iluminada Alonso. Her friends in Santiago de Cuba called her, affectionately, Lulu. Lulu's water broke the morning of my birth, on a July day in 1881, on a ship named *Thalia* that had left Boston Harbor two days earlier, bound for Cuba. The dribble of her fluids mingled with the seawater that had splashed on deck. She had not told anyone about her pains all night, thinking that if only she ignored them, they might go away. After all, Lulu did not want to give birth on a boat, so many miles from Cuba.

But there came a moment when my mother could no longer pretend.

At dawn, Lulu had climbed above deck, gasping for air. She'd gripped the handrail, felt the water between her legs, and cried out. The crew, unaccustomed to women onboard their vessel, and paralyzed by the idea of a pregnant woman, shouted among themselves, calling to my father, Agustín Alonso, who emerged from below deck with shaving cream still on his face. He saw Lulu on the deck, alone against the sea and darkening sky, and understood.

Lulu said that three marvelous things happened at my birth. When she told me the story, she looked out beyond my face, as if she were seeing them again, and as if she knew that the days when wondrous things happened without explanation belonged only in the past. The first marvel was a storm that came that morning, suddenly, and with few clouds feeding it. A mass of darkness, from which lightning flashed, and rain poured down, hung above the ship. But around the edges of that murky mass was the blue sky of summer, so the sun shone even as it rained, and the water glistened as it came down. People still say that when it rains and the sun is shining, the devil's daughter is giving birth. They believed it then, too, and this gave the sailors pause, so they dropped anchor and scurried below deck. Lulu said that her pains came and went with the lightning, as if the heavens were delivering something, as well.

She remembered Agustín arguing with the captain, a Spaniard, who raised the Spanish flag each morning on his ship. When has saw his wife in labor, Agustín had run to his trunk, dug out a crinkled flag, and thrust it in the face of the captain. "My child is Cuban, not Spanish," he'd said. Lulu and Agustín had been in Boston that summer, meeting with leaders of Cuba's revolutionary movement. The flag was a new design, and meant a great deal to Agustín.

My father forced the flag into the captain's hands. It was roughly sewn, and made up of blue and white stripes, and a single star on a red field. The captain opened the flag, then crumpled it, and tried to shove it in his back pocket like a used handkerchief. "The authorities will hear of—" he began to say.

Agustín had no choice but to thrust his pistol under the captain's jaw.

Lulu remembered the sight of a skinny cabin boy climbing the mast without ropes, taking down the Spanish flag, and attaching Cuba's new colors above the sails.

"Put it down in the ship's log," Agustín had demanded, "that my child was born free."

There were no women onboard the *Thalia*, and so Agustín delivered me himself, on a straw mattress brought above deck because Lulu could not bear to go into the dark belly of the ship.

"¡Luz!" she'd yelled. "I need light!"

She'd kicked at Agustín, and scratched his face when he tried to drag her downstairs. He gave in at last. He peered between my mother's legs and yanked me out. He used the short knife he kept tucked in his waistband to cut the cord. That same knife had gutted a Spaniard during the first war, my father told me often, his eyes twinkling. The three of us cried out together into the thick, stormy air. Then, it was silent. The rain stopped. Later, the bloody mattress was thrown overboard, and Lulu says she watched it floating, following the ship for a while as if it were being towed.

Then the second strange, marvelous thing occurred: three gulls lighted on the mattress, picking at the afterbirth that clung to the fabric, clucking at each other as if in conversation about something important, then diving into the water. Only then, Lulu says, did the mattress sink. As for the gulls, Lulu watched and watched the sea, scanning a swath of water the length of the ship, but she never saw them emerge.

Lulu died believing that our blood and that of the three gulls mingled with the sea, becoming an offering that led to the third and strangest marvel.

My father had wanted to name me Inconsolada after his mother, who had died long ago. Lulu, having borne a long "I" name all her life, chafed at the idea. In addition, her mother-in-law had been a heartless woman. The name itself meant "inconsolable," and it seemed like a curse.

"Give me a few days," Lulu had said, as the *Thalia* sailed steadily alongside the eastern coast of the United States. Agustín did not press the matter. The ship's captain had threatened to have him arrested once we returned to Cuba, and so Agustín was busy bribing and flattering the man, getting him drunk on rum during his breaks, in the hopes that he would not remember whether Agustín had actually pulled a gun on him that frightening morning, or if he'd just imagined it.

Finally, one afternoon, the ship rounded the tip of Florida, and within a few hours, was in sight of Cuba. The island appeared like a low cloud on the horizon. Inspired, Lulu carried me unsteadily towards the ship's bow, to glimpse our homeland. The sea was calm and crystal clear. Dolphins played a few feet away, their polished backs breaking the surface again and again, like extraordinary fruit bobbing in the water. Lulu says that the dolphins dove deeply suddenly, and in their foamy wake, a ghostly white hand emerged, then another, then, finally, the dark, wet head of a lady rose from the water. Lulu could not describe the lady's face, or whether her skin was fair or dark, or if her ears peeked out from her long hair. She said the lady's features shifted as she spoke, so that her eyes would grow narrow, then large, her mouth would widen and reveal savage teeth, then the lips would soften, becoming plump and purple like a bruise.

The lady did not speak, though it felt to Lulu as if she had marked me, claiming me for herself. The lady had lifted her arms and beckoned with a small flick of her wrists. Lulu shook her head, and the lady seemed to frown with a mouth that changed its shape so often it appeared she was trembling. Lulu closed her eyes and when she looked again, the lady was gone, but my mother still did not relax her hold on me.

She had studied to be a teacher in Havana, could read and write better than most, and knew well the temptations of nymphs, and the dark dangers of sirenas, who sang to heroes and lured them from their ships. She thought, too, of la Virgen, who appeared to black slaves at sea near El Cobre, home to Cuba's nickel mines. Because she did not know what form of divinity she was dealing with, Lulu took no chances and named me María Sirena.

3.

The House on the Edge of the World

I t is dawn, and Ada has returned to my house. I don't think she slept either. I can hear her knocking on my front door. Beyond that are sounds of her great-grandchildren bickering over a trunk full of fabric scraps. "Leave it behind!" one of them shouts, while the other curses at his brother in colorful slang.

"María Sirena!" Ada yells between knocks. "There's still time!" she is saying. The wind has strengthened overnight, but the racing clouds have slowed their pace. Perhaps the storm is turning.

I rise from bed, cross myself, and open the door for Ada. She hugs me hard.

"Vámonos," she says firmly.

I stamp my foot, like a child. Why can't she understand it? I made this decision long ago, not to fight death a single moment more. I have an ache in my stomach that will not go away. When I touch the place just inside my hip, I feel a tender, warm knot there. I can feel the danger of it in my heart, which pounds whenever I let my mind linger on the pain. Ya. Basta. I am not brave enough to drown myself. I have had enough of guns during the war, and this latest revolution, and have no desire to see a gun again, much less shoot myself with one. But I don't fear death. I am ready to welcome the storm. Let the sea lady from my birth claim me as she'd threatened long ago.

"You want to die," Ada says at last, her eyes wide and horrified.

"I've lived too long," I whisper.

"You like playing the martyr?" Ada asks, her hands on her hips. I say nothing, and stare at her sandals.

Perhaps Ada reads the shame in me, because she says, "If you die in this storm, I will stand on this shore and tell everyone hunting for your corpse that María Sirena Alonso de Torres was a good woman who raised a smart daughter. And just like that," Ada says, snapping her fingers, "I will undo your martyrdom!"

Ada turns, walks out the door, and slams it closed behind her. A little puff of air strikes me, and it carries Ada's violet perfume with it. I will miss her. Most afternoons, Ada comes over with her crochet needle and yarn, and sits on the porch with me, her fingers turning purple with the tightness of her grip as she makes delicate rosettes for fabric corsages, which she wears on Sundays. I love listening to her stories, how her voice harmonizes so well with the soft murmur of the sea.

Lately, Ada has taken to talking about her childhood. It has been a nice turn from talking about the news, and the new revolution, and those bearded men, the Castristas, in charge of everything now. She and I had watched the executions of Batista's supporters on her television for only a few minutes when I begged her to turn it off. "Didn't we see enough of this during the war?" I said, meaning the War of Independence, to which Ada replied, "I don't remember a thing, Sirenita." She was only eight when the American ship, the *Maine*, exploded in the harbor in Havana, but she liked telling me an old family story about her elder sister, how the boom had shaken her inkwell right off her desk, how the ink had splashed her white leather shoes, and how her mother had beaten her that night with a switch of palm for ruining them. Apparently, they told the story at Christmas every year in Ada's family, and she laughed in the telling, as if it had been a great joke. I still feel sorry for Ada's sister, though the woman is long dead.

My memory of that day is altogether different. Just turned seventeen years old, I spent that winter day in 1898 holding my son and nuzzling the soft fuzz of his hair. I can smell it still, that baby smell, and my throat clenches at the memory.

The sky has blackened again, and the clouds are round and heavy and so dark that it feels like night. But it is still early in the morning. The neighbors are busy taping up their windows, marking the glass with big Xs out of duct tape, in the hopes that shattered glass will not get too far. Some have managed to find sheets of plywood, and are busy covering up windows, bringing in potted plants, and standing at the bus stop with their things in suitcases and plastic bags, waiting for a ride to the shelters in Santiago.

I watch them from my spot on the porch. My house, which sits catty-corner at the end of the street, has a partial view of the sea, and a partial view of the rest of the neighborhood. The original owners, who I never knew, planted the house in such a way for unknown reasons. Now here, in Maisí, the easternmost corner of Cuba, I am the first to greet the dawn. Of everyone on the island, I feel the sun first, and my house is positioned in such a way that the light falls across my face when I wake, and it feels like a blessing. Perhaps that beam of morning light is the reason the house sits at such an odd angle. I like to imagine the old owners in bed together, their cheeks warming at daybreak, turning to one another and saying, "Buenos días."

This morning it is too dark for the sunbeams to penetrate the gloom. The storm is coming our way, and my little house, on the very edge of the island, does not stand a chance.

I go about my day, ignoring the wind whistling through the pines now, making a mournful sound I have not heard before. After breakfast, I read from the *Song of Solomon* for a while. It is my favorite book in the Bible. There are no murders in it. No beheadings. No godly fury. There is only a boy and a girl, and it reminds me of the soap operas on the radio and of other, sweeter days in my life. I read until my eyes start to cross, and then I nap.

I wake to the sound of shattering glass, opening my eyes just in time to see the lace curtains in my bedroom flapping wildly, like a tethered bird, just a second before the curtain rod falls off the wall. The wind has sent a conch shell through the glass, and it has landed near my bed, its pink interior glistening with rainwater, its rough carapace snagged on the rug.

"Carajo," I mutter, and bend to pick up the shell. How heavy it is. I turn it over and water pours out. Outside, the surf is roaring. I put the shell to my ear and hear the sound magnified a thousand times. Slowly, I shuffle around the room, taking picture frames off the dresser and tucking them inside the drawers. The doctor's prescriptions have already fluttered away, and they float in the air like dry leaves. The wind whips about my hair, which I still keep long and which I usually pin to the top of my head. I tie it all in a knot, and go on putting the photographs away, aware that the rain is coming into the room quickly and that my housedress is already soaked.

There is a daguerreotype of my parents, Lulu and Agustín, set in a crystal frame. In the picture, my father's hair is short, and his dark beard and mustache are also neatly trimmed. He wears a sack coat, and a dark waistcoat, and he stands behind my mother, who sits in an upholstered armchair. Her deeply set eyes and brows are dark, a shade darker than her auburn hair. Lulu's face is a touch blurry in the picture. She must have moved during the long development stage of the photo. Had the image been sharper, I could have seen the freckles that dotted her nose and cheeks. She once said it looked as if San Pedro himself had splattered her face with mud before she was born, but I disagreed. The freckles made my mother's countenance sweeter somehow, as if she never grew into her adult looks at all. I sorely regret having inherited my father's smooth, pale skin. Lulu wears a white, high-collared dress with mutton sleeves in the photograph. Her hair is parted down the middle, and soft curls gather at her temples. I tuck the daguerreotype in my underwear drawer, under three layers of girdles.

There are a few photographs of my husband, Gilberto, may he rest in peace, and my daughter, Beatríz. In one picture, Beatríz is a toddler, standing on Gilberto's open palm, held high over his head. It was a terrifying trick, one they knew I hated very much. Up so high, Beatríz would call out to me, "¡Mamá, Mamá!" Meanwhile, Gilberto's arm would tremble with the weight of our daughter, who was always large for her age. A formal portrait of the three of us is framed in an ornate brass frame. My hair was short then, in the style popular during the First World War, and Gilberto was in his military uniform. Beatríz was about a year old in that photo, and held a teddy bear against her chest, her small mouth a fierce scowl.

There is one more framed picture, of course, which does not go in the drawer. This one stays with me, come what may. I tuck the small frame into the pocket of my housedress. The picture was lost to me once. I won't let it happen again.

Rain blows in horizontally, splattering the walls and drenching my bedcovers. I leave the room and close the door behind me. In the living room, another window has blown out. A seagull, dazed by the wind, has taken cover on my sofa. It looks at me with one dark, marble eye, and then turns its head, as if to say that it can't concern itself with the well-being of an old lady. Curtains flap all over the house, and it reminds me of sails at sea, swollen and full of life. On the wall, paintings rock on their nails.

4.
Compatriots in Grief

At first, I mistake the knocking on the front door for another shell, or some other debris, smashing into the house. But then I hear a voice calling, "¡Señora, señora!" I'm afraid it is one of Maisí's fishermen, caught outside and now stranded. I don't want one of those men in my house. Fishermen always smell like dead things, and they talk about the weather as if they are kin to the rain and the wind, and their certainty about everything bothers me. Maisí is crawling with fishermen.

But what can I do? Let the man be swept out to sea? I make my way to the front door, ducking the curtains that beat against the walls as if in panic. By contrast, I feel rather calm, as if I have swallowed the eye of the storm.

"¿Que quieres?" I ask, opening the door.

A soldier in olive green uniform scowls at me. Her dark hair hangs wetly in her eyes, which are heavily lined in black. Her lips are covered in a pale lipstick, the color of wheat. She wears enormous golden hoops in her ears. She is young, no more than twenty. A bright orange life vest dangles from her left hand. Without asking, she begins to wrestle me into it.

"¡Déjame!" I yell. My jaw aches as I speak, as if my body is tired of saying the word.

"I have my orders," she says in a very deep voice. She sounds like a man. Somehow, she manages to get me into the life vest. "Get the old people to safety," she goes on.

"I'm safe here," I tell her.

"Only together can we be safe," she says, and tugs on the straps of the vest hard, pulling the air out of my lungs.

"I'm not leaving my house," I say, gripping the doorway.

"That's what they all think," the soldier answers, grabs my wrists, and pulls me along. She is my height, but stronger than I ever was. Two thick veins crisscross on her forearms. Her damp skin gives off a lemony scent, and the fair hairs on her arms suggest vanity. This young woman douses herself in lemon to lighten her hair. I know. I once did that, too.

I follow, stumbling, freeing one hand at last and feeling in my pocket for the picture of Mayito. It is there, the frame's edge poking my thigh. She leads me to a bus filled with others, mainly solitary women my age. Where are all the men? Dead, I hear a voice say, and recognize it as my own, resounding in my head. Not newly dead, I think again, and can imagine the women suddenly, each in mourning, beside a grave. It is a bus full of widows. I look at them all in turn. I can tell, by the way they sit, that there are some women here I could never like. One, who has taken the first seat by the soldier, and has leaned over to whisper to her, seems too ambitious, as if she is ready to jump behind the wheel at any moment. Another, seated next to me, is busy chewing her thumb and staring out the window in terror. I've never liked fearful women. Yet I can tell we all have grief in common. There is that. Also, they all wear orange vests like mine. Where in the world have they found the vests? Did the soldier's commanding officer think a wave would wash the bus out to sea? I scan the horizon and look at the churning sea. There is one young woman among us. Her life vest rests under her feet, and she grinds her heels into it, as if she might punch through the thing. She has her head wrapped in a blue rag. I can see a slice of pale skin at the base of her skull, and it is clear she has no hair. A cancer patient, I think, and make a small cross in the air. Her countenance is angry. I have never seen such an angry face, and I can tell that she had wanted to drown in the storm, too.

I turn to take one last look at my house before the bus pulls away. At least the lemon-scented soldier managed to shut my front door. My house is the last stop, and I wonder if Ada tipped the government off about me.

Thunder booms fantastically, and a few of the women in the bus shriek. My heart pounds after the sound. Another flash of lightning comes on the heels of the first, followed by a sonorous crack of thunder. Again my heart beats wildly, and I rest my hand on my chest and watch the sky.

The soldier turns up the radio. On one station, they are playing Beny Moré's "Amor Sin Fe." She turns the dial and finds another clear station, which is broadcasting bulletins about Hurricane Flora. The voice is tinny, but audible, and the soldier leaves the report on.

"Five thousand dead in Haiti," a woman behind me says, parroting what we'd just heard the announcer say. "The eye is as big as all of Port-au-Prince," she says, repeating again. The voice strikes me as familiar. I turn to look at the woman, and my breath catches. There sits Mireya Peña, who listens as if the reporter is sitting before her. Her hands reach out as if she could touch him, and her eyes are wide, the whites visible all around her gray irises. This one, I know, does not want to drown. "Twelve foot waves, Dios mío," Mireya says, still replicating the announcer, when, finally, the young one with the cloth covering her head turns around and shouts, "¡Cállate!"

I am certain Mireya has noticed me, but she is pretending I am not here. She lives in Maisí, though I have not seen her this close in years. Whenever we spot one another in the market, we look away uneasily, each thinking, I'm sure, that she has bested the other in some unspoken duel. At times, my anger at Mireya runs molten. Mostly, I am filled with sadness at losing a dear friend.

There is silence. Then comes another boom of thunder that

makes us all jump. The soldier turns the radio dial again, and this time finds another Moré song, "Hoy Como Ayer." She punches the radio once more, and there is old Beny again, singing "Como Fue." Moré died that February, and all the stations pay him tribute by playing his songs for much of the day. With a savage punch, the soldier turns the radio off, and we listen to one another's breathing, and the thunder diminishing as we drive inland.

I can imagine the kind of music the soldier wants to listen to. Ada's grandsons have records of The Beatles that they used to play incessantly on her suitcase record player whenever they visited. I would sing along to "Love, love me do" when the wind carried the song to me. But The Beatles' music was banned by the government, deemed antirevolutionary earlier this year, and I have not heard a single note coming from Ada's house since. The soldier seems young enough, and bold enough, to prefer forbidden music to those dusty Beny Moré songs, in spite of her uniform. I can see rebellion in the way she grips the steering wheel, her knuckles white, and the way her thumb taps the stick shift, as if she were listening to a secret song in her head. There is frustration written all over her, and suddenly, the young soldier becomes very dear to me. I think, let her take me to safety, and I close my eyes.

Just then, as a reward for the thought, the pain in my stomach flares, and I have to press my fist against it for a long time until the feeling passes.

"Where are we going, huh?" the bald woman asks loudly.

"Casa Velázquez," the soldier answers quietly. "You're the last group to be evacuated." She wipes her brow with the back of her hand. "Maisí is in the middle of nowhere," she says. "I don't know how you can live in that backwater."

"It's on the edge of everything," I say, defending the little town that I've called home for so long. It was the first thing that came to mind, and for a moment I regret opening my mouth. But the soldier shrugs, and then, the women around me seem to relax. Some of them nod at me.

"Good one," the young woman says to me, and for the first time, she, too, seems to relax. She rests against her seatback finally, sneaks a long finger between the rag and her skull, and scratches her head.

5.
How Time Unknits Itself

I have a perfect memory. I remember nearly everything I've ever read or heard. When we pull up to Casa Velázquez, I know what it looks like on the inside, though I've never crossed the threshold of that place. I feel a cold wisp of air on my neck. The soldier has opened the bus doors, and I feel that the temperature outside has dipped considerably. Yet I can't help thinking that Agustín's ghost has touched me. I rise, stretch, and climb out of the bus. I feel my father's cold palm lying still against my throat.

Casa Velázquez is the oldest house in the island. The first Cuban governor, the Spanish conquerer Diego Velázquez de Cuéllar, was the home's resident, back in the sixteenth century. By the time he founded Santiago de Cuba, Velázquez had already sailed with Columbus, seen the deaths of a thousand Indians, and set his dark, Spanish eyes on the Mayans across the sea. In this house, he'd drunk tea and thought of gold and conquest, while all of Europe buzzed with the news that there was more to the earth, so much more. These days, the house is being converted into a museum of colonial history. The soldier lines us up in front of the building, the massive stone wall blocking the wind that has picked up again. Some of the women have thought to bring suitcases with them, and these bulge like overstuffed pillows in their arms and at their feet. I have nothing but Mayito's picture in my pocket.

As we enter I am struck silent with the force of my father's memory. He spent time in Casa Velázquez as a child. My grandmother, Inconsolada, served as governess in the grand house. Here are the painted scrolls along the walls. I squint at them, and see the faces he described. "Like furry demons," he'd said, and I see them, too, the patterns rising out of remembrance. We walk in single file past enormous mahogany shutters with a thousand Moorish cutouts in them. "Like a prison," Agustín would tell me, then show me the scars around his ankle, from the time the mayor's eldest son had tried to use the shutters as a stockade, forcing my father's wrists and ankles into those cutouts and leaving him there, dangling, for the better part of an afternoon.

We are led in silence through room after room. In one place, I look up and see archways made of stained glass, above a set of dark shutters. Light pours in through them, and we step in rainbow puddles on the floor. Where in the world is the light coming from? Clouds have obscured the sun for hours.

"Wait here," the soldier tells us, and walks through another door, which she props open with a brick someone has left on the floor for that purpose. I can hear her talking to someone. Beyond that are the weary murmurs of others. Another round of lightning and thunder come, darkening the room. The colors fade from the floor, and at once, I hear wailing, and dozens of voices singing, *oba 'ye oba yana yana*. I don't understand the words, but I understand the fear behind them. When the lightning flares again, and the room is bright for a second, they sing more loudly. *OBA 'YE OBA YANA YANA*. Somewhere, women are screaming. A baby in a diaper and bare feet clings to a long, cotton skirt. It raises thin ochre arms, hoping to be picked up. Hibiscus flowers, red and yellow, swirl on the ground, flapping like fish out of water. I hear a man's voice saying, *Por Dios, the storm is coming*, and then, more singing. I look to the open door through which our soldier has disappeared, and I see people laughing, raising crystal goblets to their lips, unafraid of the weather.

"Oye," I hear very close to me. "Oye, are you okay?" It's the bald woman. She is clutching my chin and shaking my face. "Wake up. I'll go get help, but first wake up for me."

I open my eyes, and the first thing I notice is that my hand is at my stomach again, and that my fingers ache from the pressure I've been putting on myself. The woman sees my hand. She pushes it away roughly, pats my stomach, and I wince. Only then do her eyes soften when she looks at me, as if I am an old friend, someone she has not recognized until just now.

"Where are they?" I ask her.

"Who?"

"The people singing. It was another language. They were afraid," I say, looking around. The old women are all staring at me in silence. Wary-eyed, they seem to fear me more than the storm. I cannot blame them. I would not want to ride out a hurricane with a crazy person either.

"In here, all of you," the soldier says from the doorway. The women start to file in.

"Up you go," the woman at my side says to me, holding out her hand. I feel strange, like a person whose heart stops for a moment before she is revived, as if I've been somewhere else for a while. Standing brings clarity. The chanting was a memory that didn't belong to me, but to my father.

"Me llamo María Sirena," I say, wanting to normalize this moment a little, keep the color from flooding my whole face.

"Susana Soto," she says in return. "Come on, they're leaving us behind."

I follow Susana through the heavy door. The soldier is giving us a bored look, as if she can't wait for this storm to start and do some real damage. I think again that she must be very young. Children always get excited about hurricanes. While their parents flutter about wildly, covering windows in wood and cardboard, children gaze longingly through the gaps in the shutters and see pictures in the shadowy clouds. I remember

Beatríz during a small storm, how she escaped Gilberto's grasp and ran outside, her mouth open, her tongue catching raindrops that whipped her little face and left red marks on her cheeks. The soldier reminds me of Beatríz just now. I catch her looking out the window, chewing her lower lip in anticipation, just before she shuts the door behind us.

Though the door is heavy and unwieldy, it clicks closed softly, the sound like a rumor of the past. The clatter of the rain is muted, and the thunder sounds far away, though I know the lightning strikes are close by.

Our soldier speaks. "Huracán Flora is expected to hit land by midnight. Orders are to stay here in Casa Velázquez until the entire storm passes Cuba." She looks at us all in turn as she speaks in that deep voice. She commands the room, and I feel another surge of affection for this girl. There is something familiar about her I cannot place.

"Yes, you," she says, pointing firmly at the nervous woman with her arm raised. Her name, I've learned, is Asela.

"Are we safe here?" Asela asks tremulously. Her arm comes down slowly as she speaks, and she clutches at her throat.

"Perfectly," the soldier says. She takes a deep breath, and I can tell she's ready to launch into something.

"Can you name another country in all the world that would allow commonplace women like us to take shelter in a national treasure such as this house?" our soldier asks proudly. Her back is straight, making her breasts seem larger. There is a gleam in her eye, as if she were trying to seduce all of us.

"Not one," she says. She turns around and lifts a very thin porcelain dish from a cabinet behind her that is missing its glass pane. "Eleventh century," she says, fingering the delicate green flowers on the edge of the plate. At its center is a dragon curling in on itself, its mouth touching its tail. "Very old Chinese ceramic," she says. "Perhaps Marco Polo himself brought it to Europe. From Spain it came here, maybe?" she suggests, then places the plate in Asela's trembling hands. "Here, to rest in your hands, compañera."

Asela pushes the plate away. "No, it costs too much. What if it breaks?" she asks. Around her, some of the other women eye the plate, and the cabinet full of others like it, with interest. I notice Mireya looking at me with the gaze of a hawk. When I meet the stare, she turns to look at the plate. My stomach hurts again at the noiseless confrontation with her.

"Cuba and her spoils belong to everyone, compañera. It's the 1960s, my friends. A new dawn is here!" the soldier says, urging Asela to pass the plate around. "Relax. We're safe," she says, fluttering her lashes at Asela.

Seduction, I think again. Despite her youth, our soldier is an expert at it.

"This place may be safe, but Maisí will be wiped off the map," Susana mutters beside me.

"If it is, we'll just come back here, move in, live in this palace of a place. Casa Velázquez belongs to all of us, doesn't it? Fidel won't mind," I mock our soldier in whispers so that she doesn't hear me.

Susana laughs throatily. Some of the women turn to look at us, and I know what they are thinking, that the sick one and the crazy one are conspiring now. There is mistrust in their eyes again.

We get as comfortable as we can. There is a large table with ten chairs in front of the cabinet full of china. Most of the women settle in those seats, and they look as if they are about to eat a sumptuous meal, as if servants will come through the heavy door bearing silver platters. A pair of wing chairs takes up a rounded alcove. Between them is a marble-topped table, with a brass candlestick on it. The candle is missing. Two other women sit there. Susana and I take up a couch that has been upholstered in gold velvet. The material is thin, and I can feel the wooden frame underneath the cushion. Still, it's the most comfortable seat in the large room. Susana and I both groan as we sit.

"Look at our soldier," I say, pointing at her. She has taken up a spot on the cold floor, just by the door. In her hand is a nubby pencil, and on her lap is a notebook. She has covered a page in intricate swirls, one after another. Her head is cocked to the side as she works. If not for the olive green uniform, she would look like any other girl lost in thought, keeping her hands busy.

"*Our* soldier?" Susana asks. The corner of her mouth is turned up.

"Don't laugh at me," I say. "I don't know her name, that's all."

"Ofelia," Susana says.

I consider the soldier now, newly named. Her hair is still wet from the rain, while the rest of us have all dried up. "Look at how the water sticks to her," I say.

"Destined to drown herself, maybe?" Susana says, testing me.

"Hm, perhaps a mad prince has broken her heart," I say. Susana laughs outright.

"You know *Hamlet*!" she says, slapping her thigh, which quivers underneath her hand for a bit. "I taught literature here in Santiago."

"And now?" I ask.

"Bueno," she says, steadying herself. "There's this." She points to the scarf on her head. "They are using chemotherapy these days on patients like me. They call it progress, but I get tired easily. I was diagnosed the day the school's directora told me I was only allowed to teach from a list of Soviet-approved books. It was the worst day of my life. Cancer gave me a good reason to quit without having to tell anyone what I thought of the new curriculum." After a quiet moment between us, she asks, "What about you? You've really read *Hamlet*?"

"I know it by heart."

Susana looks at me doubtfully.

"I was a lector," I say. I remember those days often and fondly, sitting above the men as they worked, the high wooden stool wobbly underneath me. I'd read for hours, entertaining them as they rolled tobacco. "Shakespeare was a favorite in the tabaquerías," I say.

"A cigar factory reader?" Susana says, suddenly breathless. She turns her whole body towards me, and I notice at once how her shirt hangs crookedly on her, and that she leans over what I know now is a missing breast, her right shoulder turning in, protectively.

"And you read Shakespeare?"

"All the parts," I say proudly, the voices coming to me at once—Hamlet's vibrating tenor, Gertrude's husky whispers.

"What else did you read?" Susana asks.

"Oh, whatever the men wanted," I say, seeing them in my mind now—the rows of men in that steamy room, their knobby hands rolling cigars, their fedoras sitting high on their heads. They were attentive listeners. "They liked Dumas," I tell Susana.

"*Tous pour un, un pour tous!*" Susana says loudly.

I laugh, and realize it is the first time in days. "No," I say, touching her knee gently. "They loved *The Count of Montecristo* best of all."

"Ah," Susana says, and a sleepy smile comes across her face, and I know that she's read that one, too. I tell her how the stink of tobacco leaves would get in my hair and clothes, and how even a good bath didn't remove the smell. "Sometimes, I think it's still on me," I say, and lift the back of my hand to my face, breathing deeply. All I smell is the sea.

Ofelia stands and stretches then. We all watch her. Even the women chattering at the large table stop talking and wait for Ofelia to say or do something.

Ofelia twists to the left, then to the right, and we all hear her spine crackle. One of the women says, "Ay," and the others laugh. Ofelia looks up then, realizing that everyone has been watching her.

"I'll be right back," she says, and leaves the room.

"Ten cuidado, m'ija," one of the oldest women calls out to Ofelia, and I smile at her worry, thinking that we've all grown fond of the girl. I wonder how many of the women here have daughters like her. The pain in my stomach feels like intense hunger, but I know that eating will not bring relief. I let out a weak sigh.

"Are you okay?" Susana asks.

"Sí," I say, and wave my hand at her, as if I could erase this sickness from the air between us.

Susana nods, understanding. She looks back at the door from which Ofelia left the room. "How old do you think she is?" she asks.

"I'd say she's twenty-three or four."

"Ah," Susana says. "I'm twenty-nine. Yesterday was my birthday."

"Felicidades," I say, and touch her knee again. I'm not sure why I'm taking such liberties with Susana, who is a stranger to me. Perhaps she reminds me of my Beatríz.

"Every birthday's a gift. I suddenly want to be old. I want to be as old as you," she says. Her cheeks redden. "Perdóname," she says, chastened.

"I am old!" I say. "I wish you old age, Susana, and time for the years to knit, then unknit themselves." Her eyes fill with tears, and she wipes them away roughly. I close my eyes against my own foolish sentimentality. Such language! Time unknitting!

"Tell me more about the cigar factory," she says after a moment. "What else did the cigar rollers like to hear you read?"

I don't answer right away. It feels as if Susana is very far away, suddenly. I tune my ears to the storm, and it is raging now, the rain pounding the roof of Casa Velázquez like rocks being thrown from heaven. I tug at my housedress, flattening the wrinkled fabric with my hand as I listen. I'm still wearing slippers. My sensible black shoes are in my house in Maisí. Are they still where I left them, under my bed, or are they floating in the middle of the room? Perhaps they are already at the bottom of the sea.

"Sometimes," I tell Susana at last, "I would only pretend to read to the cigar rollers. There I would sit, high in my lector's chair, five feet over the heads of the men, with a worn copy of something or other on my lap. Maybe a Jules Verne novel, or a copy of Cervantes, or some such thing. I would say, 'Now, I'd like to read a story from a not-so-famous writer. Perhaps you've heard of—' then I'd give them a false name, 'Carla Carvajál. She is stupendous!' I'd rave, and the men would nod, never looking up from their tobacco leaf, or their fat, brown fingers. Then I'd pretend to read from this so-called Carla Carvajál, but what I was really doing was telling my own stories, true stories, about my life." I say all of this in a rush. It is the first time I've ever told this to anyone. Not even Ada knows the extent of my vanity, for that is what I think I was doing—indulging my vanity.

"And they believed you?" Susana asks, incredulous. I nod slowly, my eyes closed. I can see them, sighing at all the right moments, wiping tears from their cheeks as I pretended to read, making sure to flip the pages of the book in my lap every so often, allowing my eyes to scan back and forth.

They would tell me that Carla Carvajál was a maravilla. "A woman, too!" they would exclaim, and I would smile at them and say, "It's a wonder the world hasn't heard of her yet." The men would nod, their teeth gripping new cigars.

I notice that someone has brought in a pitcher of lemonade and some sugar cookies while we have been chatting. Susana sees them, too, and she's up quickly, filling a plate with the treats, and clutching two full cups, which she holds deftly in one hand.

"Sustenance at last," she says, then, gulps down her drink. "They say that tumors love sugar. That they eat it up and grow larger." Susana shrugs, her eyes growing wet, and takes a monstrous bite out of a cookie. "You'll have to tell me one of the stories," she says, her mouth full.

I drink the lemonade in sips, in between pauses, as I tell her the story of my birth, of the mermaid that appeared to my mother, claiming me. I tell her that my parents were rebels, and how my father fought in all three wars of independence. I tell her of my connection to this house. I tell her about vengeance, and the tragic life of slaves, and a story about pirate's gold.

6.
Of Golden Opportunities Missed

L ulu always said Agustín's rage was inherited. An inherited rage! My mother suspected its source was an old family story about pirates and hidden gold.

Inconsolada, my grandmother and Agustín's mother, was born in Spain's Canary Islands and called herself an isleña, an islander, all her life, though she never meant Cuba when she used the word. Inconsolada was a little girl, tending her own grandmother's deathbed, when the woman, whose name is lost to history, began to mutter something about gold. Inconsolada brought a cup of water to the woman's parched lips, yelled for her parents, and waited to hear more, for they had found a scratched galleon coin wrapped in a corset among the woman's belongings, and had begun to suspect that she had had dealings with Portuguese pirates in her youth.

She spoke at last in the final moments of her life. There was gold, she said, many, many pounds of it, buried in an iron chest among the coral reefs, a league or so offshore of Las Palmas. I remember the details of the treasure's location because Agustín had been made to remember by his mother. He'd written it down on a piece of paper that he kept under his mattress, his body pillowed by that morsel of bitter hope.

I say it is bitter because they never found the gold, though they searched. A bull shark in those coral reefs ate a cousin of Inconsolada's during the treasure hunt. His name was Agustín, too. Another cousin, the first Agustín's brother, whose name no one remembers, drowned on the same day. Because Inconsolada was a girl, she was not taught to swim, and so she never trolled those colorful rocks for buried treasure except in her dreams at night.

The grandmother's deathbed confession haunted Inconsolada, and she hung the burden of this memory on my father's neck like a cross, or a curse, so that he grew up believing he'd been cheated by fate, by an old woman's poor memory, and by the force of tides that may have buried the chest of gold forever. In short, Agustín always felt like a rich boy made to suffer the life of a poor one.

Inconsolada married a laborer, a man named Eugenio. When it became clear that the sugar in the Caribbean was sweeter, and that no one wanted to buy the cane that grew in the Canaries anymore, Inconsolada and Eugenio immigrated to Cuba in an exodus of isleños in 1859. Spain, led by Isabella II, encouraged the exodus, thinking it best that islanders should populate the colonies in the Caribbean. The constitution of Spain's island folk, having been surrounded by water all their lives, was suited for places like Cuba and Puerto Rico, whereas uptight citizens of Madrid, knowing nothing of navigable waters, seemed to choke and wither in that hot, Cuban air.

That was the year Agustín was born, in Santiago de Cuba, in an inn where Inconsolada and Eugenio were staying. "Better than Christ!" Agustín would say, joking that his mother had delivered him in a room, and not a stable outside the inn. My mother, I remember, would cross herself vigorously when he said this, and then draw a rough "t" on my forehead, too. The story of the pirate gold came with them to Cuba, and Inconsolada, who had inherited the single galleon coin, would keep the coin tucked between her breasts, where its cold, hard shape kept her company.

Eugenio was cut down in a sugar cane field shortly after Agustín was born. The cane grows high at harvest, and Eugenio was a slender, short man. Another worker, blinded by the sun at noon, accidentally struck Eugenio with his machete. The two men screamed, one in pain and the other in horror at what he had done. Inconsolada, beautiful and well-read, for her father was a bookseller back in Spain, took a job as a governess to the children of Juan Carlos Medina, the mayor of Santiago. At last she'd found her mansion in which to live, though it wasn't an easy life for her or for Agustín.

It happened during a monstrous storm, a huracán like the one heading towards us now. Agustín was still a boy in Santiago, about nine or ten years old. The coming storm had destroyed part of Havana, and the winds were ripping eastward, towards Santiago. In those days, the mayor was staying in Casa Velázquez. Made of stone and coral, the house had weathered countless storms. So, Mayor Juan Medina invited his friends—Spanish magistrates, plantation owners, and other officials—to spend the hours of the storm in his safe home. There gathered a hundred or so finely dressed Spaniards. The men wore high-collared coats, even though it was the height of summer, and women came dressed in lace and taffeta, the fabric gripping their necks tightly, whalebone corsets crushing their ribs. Their slaves came behind them, carrying pots of paella, beans, stews, and enough food to keep them full for days. The slaves set the dishes and serving trays on an enormous cedar table in the center of the house, where there were no windows. Bright marble floors lent the space a light feeling, as if the sunlight was somehow getting in. There, with his sons, wife, and friends, the mayor intended to wait out the storm, barring himself in against the howling wind and battering rains. He kept only four of his closest servants with him, and locked out the rest, including Inconsolada, Agustín, and fifty servants and slaves.

"I hope the stained glass doesn't shatter." The Mayor's wife, whose name was, of all things, Cristál, said this to Inconsolada before Juan Carlos Medina himself shut the door. "Should it break, try to save the larger pieces," she called out at the last moment.

A few seconds later, the youngest of Medina's sons pushed the door open again, and begged Agustín, "Take care of my cat, will you?" He thrust a plump, white kitten into Agustín's arms.

Soon, songs and the clink of dishes could be heard from within that fortified party. The others pressed their bodies against the wall of the patio as the shutters bulged with the force of the storm. Inconsolada and Agustín watched in horror as a bohío, one of those thatched roof homes found in the countryside, blew past, tumbling like a dry, dead thing. The slaves began chanting in their Yoruban language, while the cat mewled incessantly against Agustín's chest. Inconsolada stood resolutely, her mouth a red line, her chest heaving. In her hand she held the galleon coin, and her eyes looked far away, perhaps all the way back to Spain, or deep into a murky sea where the possibility of another kind of life had been sunk.

Just at the moment that the eye of the storm passed, and the world grew calm and bright for a moment, Agustín heard the joyous squeal of Medina's son inside, followed by Cristál's tinkling laugh, which was, in itself, an homage to her name. Furious, Inconsolada whispered something into her son's ear, so that Agustín opened the patio door and let out the kitten. Later, as the western wall of the eye swirled towards them, Agustín laughed as he watched the cat cartwheeling in the air, head over tail, past the windows and out of sight forever.

The mayor would later order Agustín to stand in the blistering July sun for five hours, holding up three bibles stacked on his open palms. Inconsolada would say nothing about it, pretending she had not seen her son put the cat out in the middle of a hurricane.

Like a good tyrant, Agustín was a storyteller, so that he remembered things in great detail, and what he didn't remember, he made up. None of this may be true. But I recall it all with precision, as if I'd lived it.

What was I to learn from Agustín's story? What did he mean for me to take from it? First, that vengeance could not be left to God or fate. A person had to act on his own, decisively. And second, that punishment should be suffered without tears or complaint.

"What about love?" I asked my father once in the middle of a jungle in Oriente, as we trekked our way towards shelter in the midst of a war. "Did you love your mother, even after all of that?"

"I did love her," he'd told me. "Though I'm not sure she paid attention to any of that." Then, putting his palm on top of my head, like a warm hat, he whispered, "Pay attention. Be a person for whom love is not lost, child." It was a sweet moment between us, and I did try to mind the ways in which my father seemed to love me. But the truth is that I used to cry thinking about that kitten, and I prayed that its little soul haunted my father and grandmother, that he heard its tiny mewling in his ear like an annoying ring.

7.
A Minor Change in Scenery

When I finish, Susana leans back, exhausted. I realize she hasn't sat comfortably all through my story. She throws her head back and stares at the ceiling for a moment. "Ay, María Sirena," she starts to say, but is interrupted when the door to the room opens violently.

There, drenched to her core, stands Ofelia. Behind her, the world is alight in flashes of lightning, and water pours in around her feet, rushing towards us all. The women start to shriek, and Ofelia shouts, "¡Silencio!" We are quiet at once. Susana is standing at my side, clutching my hand.

"The first floor of Casa Velázquez is flooding. We are moving, in an orderly fashion, upstairs. All of you, line up!" she barks at us. Susana helps me to stand, and we keep to the back of the line. I hold my slippers in both hands, wearing them like mittens. Some of the women are holding eleventh century dishes, guarding them like babies against their breasts. We slosh through the water out the door, and up a narrow staircase that creaks with our weight. Susana climbs behind me, and behind her is Ofelia.

When we reach the top of the stairs, Ofelia yells, "To the left!" and the line snakes in that direction. Up here are a series of rooms; the doors are all wide open. There are people sheltering in all the rooms, and they stare as we walk past. I know what they are thinking. They are thinking that there are already too many people in Casa Velázquez. They are thinking of limited supplies in the kitchens, and of their homes floating away.

"In here," Ofelia says, pointing to a large bedroom. There is a bed in the center of the room, the mattress sunken and covered in cat hair. There, sitting in the dip in the mattress, is a gray cat, and it eyes us maliciously. One of the women in our group, the one named Asela, starts to sneeze and can't stop. "El gato," she says, pointing, and Ofelia leads her away to another room. We watch her go sadly. Already, we are bound to one another.

"We'll be fine here," Ofelia says, and her eyes fall on the eldest woman among us, who is weeping silently, her back curved like a sliver of moon, having seated herself on a corner of the bed.

"We'll be fine, compañeras," Ofelia says again. "I'll go find blankets and pillows. It's late, ladies. I suggest you all try to sleep." Ofelia leaves again, and we settle in the room. Some sit on the bed, others make their way slowly to the floor. I hear the creak of old bones in every corner of the room.

"There," Susana says, pointing towards a large window flanked by a pair of wingback chairs upholstered in midnight blue.

"But the window," I warn, thinking of the big conch that had flown into my room that morning.

Susana shrugs, as if to say, "Who cares?"

I dip my hand into my pocket, feel Mayito's portrait, and shrug, too. So, we take our seats, away from the others like last time. The room is dark and no one comes to bring a candle or flashlight. Ofelia does not return, having forgotten all about the blankets and pillows. In the corners of the room, and on the bed, the women huddle, and slowly, snores begin to break through the sound of rain and rushing water.

Susana has leaned her head on my shoulder, and her scarf feels soft against my cheek. She takes my hand in hers while her head jerks softly against me.

"No llores," I tell her, though I know she's been saving her tears for this moment, when all is dark and the room is noisy, so that no one notices.

"Another story then, Señora Carvajal," she whispers, "to distract a dying woman."

"Mañana," I tell her, leaning back in my seat. I close my eyes but cannot sleep. The weight of Susana's head on my shoulder reminds me of Beatríz, who would fall asleep beside me each night, her skinny legs thrown over mine, her breath sweet on my neck.

In the darkness I can pretend I am not here, in Casa Velazquez, among these seven strangers. Susana, Noraida, Estrella, I think, reciting their names to myself. Dulce, Rosalia, Celia. And Mireya, yes, Mireya. Except for Susana, they are old, like me. I don't care for the reminder that I am more fossil now than flesh. If I try, I can imagine that I am young again, my daughter close to me, safe beside me. But a memory comes unbidden, of Beatríz in the days after her father's death, weeping into my neck, and every once in a while giving me a hard pinch, as if to punish me for his death. I let her do it until my own anger got the better of me.

"Basta," I told her, peeling her arms away from me. Gilberto's heart had stopped one morning while he was cutting Beatríz's hair, a task he'd taken up because his hands were steadier than mine. The scissors had clattered to the floor, Gilberto uttered a small sound, like a sigh, and fell to the floor. It had been that fast. I'd been in another room, sorting laundry, when I heard Beatríz's scream. I found her sitting on the cool tiles, her father's head in her lap, saying, "Papi, Papi," as if she could call him back. She was small, no older than three. The first World War had finally come to a close and it all seemed like springtime. I've learned since that it is in those moments, when one is lulled into hopefulness, that the sword drops onto one's head.

Ay, Beatríz, how I wish she were here instead of Susana.

Her face blooms bright in my imagination. I remember her dressed in white at her First Communion, how she later admitted that she'd kept the Host lodged between her cheek and molars until it disintegrated, afraid to bite into the doughy body of Christ. I consider her at fifteen, bookish and romantic then, writing poems on broad hibiscus leaves and floating them in the canals behind our apartment. At eighteen, she fell in love with Mireya Peña's son, Alejandro, a poet, too, and her appetite for him was so crushing that he became all the food she needed; she lost the plumpness in her arms and dark circles shadowed her eyes. "He is the best poem I've ever written," she gushed to me one night, and I called her a little fool, and warned her about poets. I told her a story about a poet, who died facing the sun, and she laughed and called me ridiculous. She regained herself—her weight, her senses—when she left Alejandro the night before their wedding. I got my daughter back, but in trade, I lost Mireya's friendship and earned her dagger eyes for the rest of my life.

I cannot sleep. It is a restlessness of the spirit, and I start counting my breaths, a habit I've long had, and wait for that curious feeling of suffocation to descend, the notion that there is not enough air, and this, finally, crowds out thoughts of my daughter and Mireya. After a while, I drift off and do not dream.

8.
The Listeners Gather

I t is still raining in the morning. Ofelia has rejoined us. She is still wet, and now she is sniffling. I am sure she's going to catch a cold, maybe pneumonia if she doesn't get dry. The women are chatting like old friends now. I've learned their names. They, too, are worried about Ofelia. We've cast our fears out among us—fear for our homes, for our own safety, for faraway relatives—and found Ofelia on whom to anchor our worries. "M'ija," I tell her, "sit with us a while. Let your hair dry."

But Ofelia laughs at me, young as she is. "I don't shrink when I get wet!" she says. "Or melt, like a witch." None of us laughs, not even Susana. Good health, we know, is not guaranteed. Ofelia leaves, returning moments later with a basket full of stale bread and a pitcher of water. "It's all we have for now. The storm is stalled out over Oriente Province."

"And the flooding?" one of the women asks.

Ofelia fidgets with the basket. "We've lost the first floor for now." She says something else, but a sudden hammer of rain makes her hard to hear.

Dulce asks, "Are the waters still rising?"

"You're safe here," she says, and tries to smile.

So, we're trapped. I turn to look out the window, and see, through the wavy, leaded glass, that the water line is high. Yesterday, the tops of cars were visible here and there. Now, I don't see any. In the distance, an unmanned rowboat rocks on the water. In it sits a mangy dog looking north. A billboard erected across the street is peeling, flapping in the stiff breeze.

On it, a faded picture of Lucille Ball holds a box of cigarettes. I'm surprised the advertisement still stands after the triumph of the revolution. Perhaps it is because Lucy is married to Ricky, and, Yankee or not, Desi Arnáz is one of ours. My stomach goes sour thinking of the United States, and my lost son, and all that I've lost, so that I have to lean against the wall and take deep breaths to steady myself.

Soon, women, pushing to get a view of the outside, surround me. "Dios mío," one says, and then they're all talking, shouting at Ofelia, asking about the foundations of the house, the life vests, the rest of the island, whether anyone can swim, and making so much noise that Susana yells, "¡Cállense!" again, and they quiet at once.

"Con calma, por favor," Ofelia says more quietly. "We will be fine. They will take care of all of us. Worry not, compañeras." Ofelia's whole body is tense as she talks, and leaning towards the front door, as if she cannot wait to leave. She looks as though she needs to sit somewhere alone, quietly, listening to the rain. Her uniform has a small stain just above her left breast, and her frizzy black hair is wilder now, escaping her small olive-colored military cap. She crosses the room, placing a hand on Mireya's shoulder briefly as she walks past her, then peers out the window. Her nose touches the glass, and her breath fogs it.

I watch as she purses her mouth and brow. When she leaves at last without another word, she takes the basket of bread with her.

"Our bread," one of the women says miserably.

"She just forgot," Susana says, defending Ofelia.

"What do we do now?" asks a woman, whose name is Noraida. Her hair is dyed an unnatural shade of red, and it is so frizzy that she looks like she's caught fire. Her nails, too, are red and long, and they click together when she speaks.

"Keep busy," says Mireya, who has fished eyeglasses out of

her purse. They are so thick that her eyes look like dinner plates. When had her sight gone bad, I wonder. She used to have such clear eyes, could see ships in the distance before anyone else, pointing to them and saying, "Come get us! I want to see the world!" There was a spirit in the Mireya I used to know, the one who would bring over her little son, Alejandro, to play with Beatríz. How sour it had all gone. So far, we have been successful in saying nothing to one another.

"Pray to la virgen," says Celia. Her fingers have been knotted in a glass rosary since I boarded the bus.

"To San Judas Tadéo," says Dulce, who is the oldest in the room, bent over like a shepherd's hook. "He's the saint of lost causes."

"Changó. God of lightning," says another, Estrella, who is wearing white from head to toe. Her dark skin glows against the fabric. White shells, beaded tightly together, are wound twice around her neck. A few of the women nod knowingly at her. She's a Santera, that's obvious. Perhaps the African gods are most useful against storms.

"A story," Susana says, looking at me significantly. "María Sirena was a lectora. She tells wonderful stories."

The women look at me expectantly. They sit, arrange their dresses, and wait. I start to say no, but Susana squeezes my hand. I hear the faint rumbling of someone's stomach. Mireya sniffs, and pushes her glasses back up her nose. A fly buzzes in front of my face, and I wave it away.

"We don't have all day," croaks Dulce, and I know Susana wishes to grow as old as she is, older than one can imagine being, and I send up a quick to prayer to la virgen, San Judas, and Changó, for all of the women here.

"Bueno," I begin, then pause. Where to pick up the thread of memories? Should I start at the beginning, telling the story of the mermaid, or the gold? I feel my father's ghost again, cold on my neck, pushing me forward; I think of heavy bibles; the corner of Mayito's framed photo pricks my thigh from within my pocket. Like a crab, I think, I'll move forward. Never back. I plumb my memories for the first stories I ever heard, the ones my mother told me of her own youth and mine.

"This story happened just after the second war for independence," I say. "There is a man in the story named Agustín, who was a hero and a monster. And a woman, named Lulu, who loved Agustín sometimes, hated him other times, and loved herself more. To me, they were mamá and papá . . . "

9.
The Threats of Men

Lulu only remembered the two men conversing in the distance, far from the dock where the ship had come to rest. I was in her arms, squirming in the heat, my small cheek sweaty against her damp breast. The men were arguing, and both of them had dark manes that gleamed in the bright Cuban sun. One was Agustín. The other, the Spanish captain of our ship, the Thalia, had a whistle dangling from his neck. Lulu looked at me for a moment, dipping her pinkie into my mouth to quiet me. It was then that she heard the shrill whistle, and looked up in time to see the Spanish captain backing away rapidly, his lips puckered around the metal thing, trilling and trilling like a panicked bird. At once, men in uniform surrounded Agustín. Lulu screamed with me in her arms as they hit her husband repeatedly. The whistleblower went on whistling, but beneath that sound was the sick thud of fists on flesh and bones.

The captain of the *Thalia* sidled up to my mother later, saying, "When it comes time to inscribe this one," meaning me, "do yourself a favor and tell them she was born under a Spanish flag. Maybe name her María Cristina, in honor of the queen, eh?" he said, and jokingly nudged my mother.

"Her name is, indeed, María, Capitán," my mother said, leaving out the Sirena part. Already, she was thinking of survival, even while Agustín was being beaten.

"Good girl," the captain said. How much did he know about Agustín's role in the war against Spain? Lulu shook her head wearily, images of Agustín setting fire to the carriages of Spanish officers in Havana sweeping through her memory. She could see him still, torch aloft, his cheeks blazing. Did the Spaniards know that she and Agustín had met with Cuban rebels in America? That there were plans afoot to launch a third war for independence? Lulu watched the men as they dragged Agustín away, his body limp, his feet twitching, which she took as a sign of life.

"Viva España," she whispered as she passed the captain, and he smiled again. I chose that moment to sneeze for the first time in my life, and then I began to cry.

The captain said, "God bless you."

Later that night, the captain came to the small inn where we had been put. The place was near the prison where Agustín was being kept, and a few guests milled about. "How is the baby? Is she catching a cold?" the captain asked from behind the closed door.

Lulu jumped at the sound of his voice, and called out, "No, María is fine," leaving out my full name again.

"May I enter?" the captain asked.

Lulu contemplated her answer. Could she refuse? Agustín was in the hands of the Spanish. The enemies of freedom, as she thought of them. The captain knocked once more. Lulu heard him clearing his throat before speaking: "Please, may I enter?"

Nervous, she thought. And she recognized at once that particular, tremulous quality in his voice. The captain was besotted. Lulu knew, because she'd always been a great beauty, and because boys had sought her out even when she was very small. Her mother had noticed this about her, too. She'd watched Lulu among her friends, how they gathered around her, laughing at even her smallest jokes, seeking her eyes as if Lulu could bless them with a glance. Her mother forbade Lulu from visiting the homes of school friends who had brothers, or whose fathers were too young. "A person never knows what's in the mind of a man," Lulu's mother had warned, teaching her how to tell a man whose nature was simply fidgety from one who was falling in love.

Lulu cracked open the door, and the captain thrust his nose in quickly. It was a nice nose, Lulu thought. Long, but straight. His pores were small. He licked his lips a few times before speaking. "Are you well?" he asked. "Do you need anything?"

The truth was, Lulu did need a few things. She was weak from hunger, exhausted from lack of sleep; her breasts ached with too much milk and her ears rang from my cries. Furthermore, she was still bleeding, and had no little cloths with her. She'd torn her petticoat to shreds and tried to use that, but the material was too thin and scratchy. Lulu felt color rise in her cheeks. How could she ask this man, any man, for help in this regard?

The captain must have mistaken her sudden blush for coyness. Perhaps he imagined that he was well on his way to conquering the beautiful wife of the rebel. So, he treaded gently.

"Lady," he said in a soft voice. "Ask anything of me."

"Free Agustín," Lulu said at once.

The captain pursed his lips. A muscle twitched near his left eye. "It's out of my hands. I imagine you will see him soon enough."

A flood of warmth pooled between her thighs, reminding Lulu of her immediate need. "The inn owner," she said. "Surely he has a wife who can help me."

The captain raised an eyebrow, confused.

"The baby is only a few days old, capitán," Lulu said slowly, her eyes cast down. She didn't dare look at the captain, but could feel his discomfort even through the small crack in the door. "A woman has certain . . . things she must attend to regarding her . . . "

"Of course," he said too quickly. "I'll send the innkeeper up to . . . "

"No. I'll go to him, capitán."

"Aldo," he said. "My name is Aldo Alarcón."

Lulu let the name sink in, otherwise she knew she'd forget it. All names became Agustín in her head. Agustín. Agustín. Like a skipping record on a phonograph she'd seen once.

"Aldo," she whispered, and it sounded like a sigh, so that the captain smiled and relaxed a little.

"And you?" he asked. Still, his nose poked through the space in the door, which had widened only a little during their conversation.

"Illuminada," she said. The name Lulu she would keep to herself.

"It is a perfect name. I can barely stand to look at you without shading my eyes." Aldo chuckled at his own joke, then sighed. Lulu looked down at her feet. She began to bounce me in her arms, shushing me. I cried heartily. My face, which had been as pale as a star, grew red. "Shh," Lulu said and I stopped to listen. The wetness below gathered close to her skin. And still, the intolerable captain would not leave.

"I must see the owner," she said.

At last, snapped out of his reverie, Aldo Alarcón said, "Of course, after you," and drew wide the door.

Lulu walked out holding me, taking small, cautious steps. How mortifying, she thought. Then she remembered Agustín being dragged away, and the stream of blood coming from his nose and dotting the earth. A shudder ran through Lulu, so she held me tightly as she walked. Later, she told me that I had given her strength all through my father's imprisonment. "You were like an anchor. Or the railing of a ship. Meant for steadying," she'd said.

Aldo led her to the inn's modest lobby—an airy place, though the tiling on the floors and walls was dark and intricate.

A man in a cream-colored coat and matching waistcoat and trousers manned the front desk. His clothes were wrinkled all over, and the man's thick neck bulged at the black tie, as if tiny hands were strangling him slowly. On the wall above the man's head was a landscape painting of the mogotes in the Viñales Valley, all steep, round-topped hills that suggested another world. The painting was lovingly framed and kept dust-free, unlike the rest of the lobby. The man eyed Lulu and Aldo Alarcón nervously.

"La señora requires the presence of your wife," the captain said a bit too loudly. Lulu suppressed a sigh. Why did such men find the need to shout when giving commands?

The man, who happened to be the inn owner, stood up at attention. His lips worried over his teeth for a moment, then he stuttered, "I-I-I h-have no wife, capitán."

Aldo Alarcón slammed an open palm against the table in a show of frustration. Lulu was sure it was just a show. He'd wanted to startle everyone, impose his authority, but the wood was so thick that the sound was muted, and laughable. Besides, Lulu was fairly certain the captain had hurt his hand.

"Perhaps you have a sister?" Lulu asked, interrupting. "I require the help of a generous woman. I have heard," she said, calculating, "that the people of the Viñales Valley are the kindest in the world."

The man brightened. "It's t-t-true," he said, "Jesucristo should have b-b-been born in Viñales, not Bethlehem. Every home would have opened its d-doors! I'll fetch my niece at once." He disappeared through a narrow door.

The captain drummed his fingers on the desk. They were red and cracked, like salted fish. He scowled at Lulu. "No wonder all the sailors on my ship were sad to see you go," Aldo Alarcón said. "You were too kind to them."

"Only as kind as human decency requires." Lulu bit her tongue. She'd overstepped herself, saw Agustín again in her mind, bloody and limp, heard the captain's whistle, remembered where Aldo Alarcón's loyalties rested.

The captain had been leaning on the front desk. Now he stood away from it, drawing up to his full height. "Decency," he said, "What does a rebel's woman know of that?" Then, he ran his pinkie finger down Lulu's cheek, let it linger on her chin for a moment, then patted my head. "Sweet baby."

Lulu tried very hard not to huddle over me, but instead, she met Aldo Alarcón's eyes steadily. She could feel the cold wake of his finger on her cheek. This was not the kind of man who would kiss the inside of a wrist, or draw a woman in softly, a thick, protective hand on the small of her back, and nibble at an earlobe. Lulu knew because Agustín was not that kind of man, either.

The owner of the inn interrupted at just the right moment, halting what must have been Aldo Alarcón's dangerous thoughts in that instant—*Should this woman be free? What threats does she pose to Spanish Cuba?*

As for Lulu, she'd been thinking—*How far can I get if I run?*

"My niece, F-Fernanda," the manager announced, dragging a skinny girl in a baggy blouse and pleated skirt. Like her uncle's clothes, hers had the look of many wearings. The pleats were sad, flattened things, and Lulu's fingers ached to fold them down.

The girl approached Lulu confidently. Despite her clothes, she cut a figure far different from the inn owner's. Her hands rested on her slim hips. She eyed first Lulu, then me, and said, "My Tío Julio says you need a woman to help you."

Lulu nearly laughed. A woman. The girl before her was still a child, her chest flat. Did she even know what little cloths were for? "Fernanda," Lulu began, then stopped. "Is there anyone older about?"

"When was the baby born?" Fernanda asked, all business.

Lulu paused. There was something authoritative in the girl's voice and in her eyes, which seemed to patrol the room every so often, stopping on Aldo Alarcón for only a second each time.

"Less than a week ago."

"Do you have luggage? Any supplies at all?"

"Confiscated."

Fernanda stole a quick glance at Aldo Alarcón again, then tapped a finger against her lips. Her nail was chewed to the quick. "You need soup for your strength," she said after a moment. "And milk to drink. There's a bolt of linen in the back room. I can sew. Little cloths and diapers. They'll be ready by morning."

"Thank you," Lulu said.

"Your shirt, señora," Fernanda whispered, and indicated with a sharp thrust of her chin.

Lulu looked down and saw that her button shirt was partly undone, and a half-moon of swollen breast was exposed, the skin stretched and glistening.

"Oh," she said, shifting me in her arms to adjust herself.

"It was nothing," Fernanda said before Lulu could thank her. Then the girl was off again, as quick as she'd come.

"I'd be l-lost with-without her," the inn owner said, his eyes following his niece. He fiddled with his lapels for a minute, then turned to look at Lulu. Lulu felt a ping and snap in her chest. There was, she realized, goodness in him. Not saintly virtue, no. But a tenderness Lulu had not seen in a man in a long time. Fernanda had called him Tío Julio, and there it was, a nameplate on the desk that Lulu had not noticed before— Julio Reyes.

He must have caught her looking, because Julio turned the little brass plate for her to see before asking, "Is there anything else I can do for you?" without stuttering once.

T he captain had returned Lulu's luggage to her only after the Spanish authorities had ransacked it. Fernanda had made several linen diapers for me, as well as a few gowns of muslin, replete with a satin ribbon that tied at my feet. So, both my mother and I were well dressed for what Aldo Alarcón called our "outings among decent people."

Early in the mornings, when the darkness withdrew slowly from the sky, and the weak streetlamps dimmed one by one, Aldo Alarcón would come knocking on Lulu's door. "I remember this," she would tell me, "because you had not yet learned to sleep through the nights and I would stay up to wait for the dawn, staring out the window. As soon as the sun broke the horizon, like a fresh egg cracked open, the captain's knock would sound."

"Perhaps you'd like to take a walk with me?" Aldo Alarcón would ask, and my mother would nod. The captain would close the door softly, allowing her to dress herself and me, and then she would emerge, freshly scrubbed somehow, and perfumed, too, as if in that tiny inn room was a secret, unseen bathtub for her ablutions. The truth was, my mother always looked this way—clean, her face never shiny, her skin sweet-smelling.

At the start of day, Havana always seemed cloaked in mystery. The buildings, men setting up wares, women bustling children to school, suggested only the starkness of form, and not the rich details of that old city. This way and that, the captain and Lulu strolled. They would stop at a small bakery, and he would buy her warm bread and café con leche. He would watch her eat in silence, nodding every so often as she swallowed. Lulu said she felt a kinship with pigs and cows in those days—how it must have felt to be fed, fattened, the sound of a knife being sharpened in the distance making the food taste sour.

Not that Aldo Alarcón meant to kill Lulu—he wanted her for himself, and hoped that food and small gifts would turn her heart. It was the small death of his presence every day that Lulu feared. After all, she and Agustín had been among the Cuban rebels for so long that now the Spanish seemed to her unreal people. They were monsters with sharp claws in her dreams; men and women with terrible breath and rattling bundles of chains in their arms. What were dreams but the mind's way of preparing one for the day? So, Lulu hated the captain because he was Spanish, and because he, in turn, hated the Cuban rebels.

Every day, Lulu would swallow the last bite of bread, which she'd roll in her coffee cup, and ask, "When will Agustín be released?"

She asked it quietly, demurely.

He would respond heatedly, his hands flying to his jaw to rub the tension there. Lulu imagined claws at the ends of his fingers.

"The struggle for 'independence,'" he'd say, sneering at the word, "is over. Where is Macéo, that upstart negro? They offered him thirty ounces of gold and he ran. Where is Martí? Your great heroes? Cowards, run out of the island. Cuba belongs to Spain. It's been so since Columbus."

"Macéo never took the money," Lulu said.

"Cállate," Alarcón said, ending the conversation.

Lulu would sit and stare at her hands. Antonio Macéo, that great general, was a name the rebels murmured reverently. And

José Martí, the poet, had put their hearts into words, into lyric and song. But it was true—both men had been exiled after the war. In a way, it gave her hope. If such men as Macéo and Martí had been spared, perhaps a nobody like Agustín would not have to go before the executioner.

Just then, a very dark-skinned man trundled by them, his cart filled with malangas still dusty from the ground. He nodded sharply at Lulu, then returned his eyes to his viands. "He wouldn't have dared look at you in the old days," Aldo Alarcón said, gripping Lulu's hand as if trying to reassure her. "The negros are getting too bold."

"Even the Americans have outlawed slavery," Lulu said. "Decades ago."

"Gracias a Diós this isn't America," Alarcón said drily.

"When will Agustín be released?" she would ask again.

"Didn't I answer you already?"

"No, capitán."

"Aldo. Call me Aldo. I don't know when he'll be released. When he has paid for his crimes, I suppose," the captain would say, rising and helping Lulu to her feet.

This happened nearly every morning that Aldo Alarcón's ship was in port. On the mornings when he was at sea, sailing the *Thalia* around the island, or back and forth from New York City to Havana, Lulu was free to explore Havana on her own. Sometimes, she would go to the prison, stand before its façade, and peer at all the barred windows, hoping Agustín would send her a sign. And sometimes he would, thrusting his hand through the bars and waving. Or, at least, Lulu assumed that it was Agustín's hand. She couldn't be sure. Other days, she would spend the morning knitting baby clothes for me with Fernanda, who was always full of chatter and gossip. Meanwhile, Julio Reyes would watch from behind the inn's front desk, chewing his bottom lip or massaging his neck, his eyes never straying too far from Lulu.

Nights, Julio Reyes would tap gently on Lulu's door, and she would let him in. "Forget the war," he whispered to her on that first night. "Forget the d-dead you've seen. Forget that this is not really a inn for you but a kind of p-prison."

"I cannot forget what freedom tastes like. I have savored it. The Spanish are monsters, I can't forget that either," she had said. "And Agustín, he lives still," she had told Julio, though the gentle inn owner ran a finger slowly over her knuckles. In this way, Agustín was losing his definition in her mind's eye.

"No, you cannot forget any of it," he agreed.

My mother and I spent the next fourteen years at the inn, prisoners of Aldo Alarcón. As I grew, I learned to read and write during quiet lessons with my mother, wherein she bound my left hand with a scarf so that I might not use it, saying, "We compose our letters with our right hand. It's only proper." She taught me to sew, making sure I knew that it was bad luck to attach the left sleeve on a dress before the right. In the kitchen of the inn, I learned to quarter a rabbit. Julio Reyes pulled my baby teeth when they came loose, and took the best-shaped one and set it like a gem in a small gold ring, which I had outgrown by the time I was ten.

Some nights, when the inn was empty, Lulu would let me sleep in an unoccupied room, and I imagined I was a Spanish infanta, one of the beautiful, golden girls in a painting in the lobby of the inn, which I stared at often. "It isn't an authentic painting," Fernanda said to me once, but I had no idea what she meant. I touched the canvas just to make sure and found it to be as real as my own skin. On other nights, I pretended that the noises coming from Lulu's room were the sounds of a zoo at night, though I'd never been to one after dark, nor in daylight. I imagined the grievances of lions, or the snoring of a rhinoceros, or the clawing of a baboon trying to break free from his cage. Sometimes Aldo Alarcón came to the inn at night, and on those occasions the zoo in my head was dangerous and swarmy, an appalling prison. When it was just us—Lulu and Julio Reyes in my mother's room, and I, like a little infanta in her own quarters—the zoo sounded different. There was the soft padding of a gazelle's light feet on rushes, or the sighing of rabbits in a warm warren, and other tender noises rising like balloons.

Such was my life at the inn, and on that day when Fernanda came pounding up the stairs with two important messages—that a revolution had begun outside of Santiago de Cuba, and that Agustín was free—Julio Reyes was there, sleeping in the bed with my mother, while I watched the sky go from black to purple to pink to blue.

Julio Reyes always left my mother's room before the street-lamps began to extinguish themselves at dawn, one after another, like a promenade of lights in reverse.

The women sit in silence when I finish speaking. If not for the persistent whine of the wind outside, it would feel as if we were inside some cave, or a monstrous creature has swallowed us all. Anticipation blooms in my chest. I've always prided myself on my ability to tell a story. Hadn't the men at the cigar factory showered me with affection? Now, I am ready for it—the praise I am accustomed to.

But I've forgotten about Mireya, who is the first to make a sound. First, she coughs a little, then, she stands, smoothing her housedress with lean hands that resemble stiff palm fronds. They flutter and she touches her glasses as she struggles to get the words out. "How could you do such a thing to your mother?"

The smile on my face fades. I feel it go, feel my face freeze in a strange grimace. "I'm not sure what you mean," I say.

"She's your mother," Mireya says angrily. "And you air her shameful past as if it were a ten-cent novel." Mireya trembles all over. She fingers a locket that dangles between her breasts, and I imagine that inside is a Victorian picture of Mireya's own mother, who, no doubt, was free of all sin.

"Can't you tell us a beautiful story? One with hope?" Mireya stares hard at me. I've trespassed against her, not just because of the history between us, but through the story. Here is a woman incapable of any more sorrow than what life has already doled out. Lulu's tragic past has pushed her too far.

"We're on the brink of drowning here, or being blown away, and this is what we have to listen to?" Mireya asks the other women, looking at each of them wildly. The storm has done this, I think to myself. It's made us all a little crazy. Even now, the sound of the wind pounds in my ears. Drafts snake in and scratch my skin.

"Doesn't anyone have a less shameful story to tell?" Mireya asks at last, slumping onto the bed. A puff of cat hair and dust rise around her.

For a moment, the women stare at Mireya, then turn to me. But I'm remembering Lulu again, how she told me the story first. She had said there were names for women like her, who had loved as she had loved. She recited them for me—puta, sucia, descarada, sinvergüenza. She'd listed them slowly, watching as I mouthed the words, getting the shape of them right. Then, she'd said, "None of those are my name, María Sirena. I am a decent person. As are you, no matter who you love." I'd needed that advice at the moment, when the world had turned against me for loving a man I wasn't supposed to.

I am about to say something along these lines to the women when Estrella and Noraida start to laugh. Noraida has twirled a lock of her dyed-red hair around her finger so tightly that the tip of it is red, too, turning purple by the second.

"Sit down, Mireya, you righteous cow. Don't you know? These aren't real stories," Estrella says.

Noraida releases her finger from her hair and points it, now blue-tipped, at Mireya. "It was her *job* to tell stories like that. She's good, isn't she?"

"I know what she is," Mireya says. Of course she does. I told her about my work as a lector when we first met. But the stories? Those I kept to myself. Why color our friendship with that sad history? Better that my friends know me as a new creature, without a past. Now, it doesn't matter. Mireya and I are no longer friends. Let her know the truth. Let her know it all, I think.

A wave of vertigo comes upon me. I am dreaming. I'm certain of it. It's happening again, getting lost in a dream or a memory, like I did downstairs when I would have sworn I'd been surrounded by the governor's old slaves. I feel myself listing a little to the right, like I'm on a ship in rough water.

Susana is at my side at once, straightening me. "¿María Sirena, estás bien?" she whispers. I shake my head.

"A ten-cent novel, like Mireya said," Noraida says brightly, though it feels as if I'm hearing her from a great distance. The room is spinning now, and outside, the lightning slaps the sky.

The stories are as true as this room, as the storm outside, as the sharp edge of Mayito's framed picture in my pocket. I want to say this, but there are other words shaping themselves on my tongue, other pictures crowding my head—of a charred building and of footprints in blood.

Noraida has settled herself on a shabby divan at the foot of the bed, turning her back on Mireya, who is now chewing the nail of her left thumb, her cheeks red from embarrassment or rage, I cannot tell.

Now, she takes aim at me. "I bet I know how this one ends. The gentle innkeeper, Julio Reyes, kills the bastard Aldo Alarcón, doesn't he? Then he sweeps Lulu off her feet and they run away together," she says. "That's the way of romances. They're all like that," she says.

"Finish the story," Noraida demands. Outside, the faint sound of a siren disturbs our room. Noraida turns towards the sound, biting her bottom lip and squinting. The siren stops mid-blare, and Noraida leans back in her chair. "Go on then," she says to me, and the rest of the women lean forward, like palms in a strong wind. But only Susana speaks. With a hint of sadness in her voice she asks, "So, what's your real name?"

When I begin again, it is as if I am no longer doing the speaking. It's like I'm there again, sitting in the tall chair in the cigar factory, holding a book in my hand from which I do not read. But this time, I tell a part of the story I'd never meant to tell.

12.

A Story Unspoken Before Now

S omeone threw open the door to Lulu's room. Both Lulu and Julio Reyes sat up in bed at once, terror in their eyes. But it was only Fernanda, and her forehead was shiny with sweat, her chest heaving.

"They've done it. There's been a revolt in Baire!" Fernanda cried, not caring a bit about her uncle's bare chest under those thin blankets.

"Baire?" Lulu whispered. My mother had grown up there, a village just fifty miles from Santiago de Cuba.

"Casualties?" she asked, thinking of old friends perhaps, but Julio Reyes had spoken, too, asking, "What else has been reported?" so that Fernanda did not hear Lulu's question.

"They say Macéo and Martí are back!" Fernanda said, clapping her hands. Just as quickly, her face darkened. "But you must turn her out at once, Tío Julio. There's been a prison break. Her husband is surely on his way here," she said.

"Thank you, Fernanda. Give us a moment, please. Take María Sirena with you." Fernanda pulled me up by my arms and dragged me away from the room. Though I was fourteen years old, I still shared a room with Lulu. A small trundle bed had been put in by the window for me. Fernanda had pulled me out of bed, and I was still drowsy.

"Ay," I cried out, swatting at Fernanda.

"Be quiet!" Fernanda had urged me. "You're so much trouble sometimes." Fernanda was a hard girl, toughened by work in the inn, life without a mother, and having no siblings at all.

No young man had ever looked at her twice. She was twenty-six and practically ran the inn. What would she do were it to fall to ruin? Enter the convent? Fernanda was a young woman without choices, and it had made her rigid, her face frozen in a bitter expression nearly all of the time.

But she was also a gossip, and when I pressed my ear against the door to my mother's room, Fernanda had followed suit, and so we heard what we should not have.

"Mi vida," Julio Reyes was saying to Lulu, and Lulu had murmured something, then began sobbing.

"Agustín is not the man for me. He is my husband, but he was a brute. I married too young, too young," she was saying between gulps of air.

"Then we run away t-together. Tonight, we leave Havana, leave this w-war. I will bar the front door in case Agustín tries to f-find you."

"And María Sirena?" Lulu asked. My heart soared at hearing my name in my mother's mouth. She had not forgotten me.

"Of course. She is like my daughter, too."

Then, there was silence. There had been no mention of Fernanda's name, no one to form the syllables of it in her mouth. She'd been hoping to hear it, of course. A simple "F-fernanda" from her uncle's twisted tongue would have been enough to keep her from doing what she did.

But he had said nothing, and the sounds that followed were wet and revolting. Fernanda slipped away without a word. I watched her go for a moment, then decided to follow her from a distance.

"I will not go to a convent!" Fernanda said to herself out loud, and I heard her. The two of us stumbled as we made our way down the busy streets—Fernanda, because she was distraught, and I, because Havana was unfamiliar to me. I was not allowed out alone without Lulu or Alarcón. We were prisoners as much as my father was. Alarcón made sure of it. Once, when

Lulu and I had left in the middle of a cool night, Alarcón had met us at the train station, a cigar in his hand. He pointed the glowing red tip at us and it was as if the devil himself had spied on us, binding us to him.

"Do you think I'm stupid? That you aren't watched like a prize, mi amor?" he asked my mother, and pinched her hard on the arm, just above the elbow. "I love you so very much, Illuminada," he kept saying as he walked us back to the inn, pinching her harder and harder every so often, so that her arm would be black and blue by the morning. That was the last time we tried to leave. I spent most days in the inn with Lulu, who taught me to read and write and recite poetry. My childhood slipped by quietly, muffled by the warm wood walls of the inn's lobby, and made interesting by the many guests that streamed in and out on a daily basis. I learned a bit of German from a beautiful pianist who'd come to tour Havana. Many Americans came and went, and the little English I spoke was accented like theirs. It was as good an education as a girl could wish for when imprisoned.

Now, the city was a maelstrom of bodies, and I was a shy thing, still wearing little girl clothes, though the bodices of my dresses felt tighter by the day. I had not yet had a monthly bleeding, and Lulu treated me like a child. So, I acted the part. Naïve and vulnerable, I followed Fernanda through that hot maze of a city because I suspected she was up to no good.

There were people everywhere. Spanish police barked orders at everyone, warning that the prisoners were among them. But the people knew better than to pay it any mind. Most of the jailed, they knew, were Cuban rebels. This was cause for celebration. And so, music poured out of the inns and homes, despite the occasional gunshot or shout from a Spanish officer.

Fernanda led me up a sharp hill. The harbor came into view. There, docked and surrounded by dazed-looking sailors, was the *Thalia*, Aldo Alarcón's ship.

Fernanda ran down the hill towards the ship and onto the dock. Aldo Alarcón was standing on the bow, his eyes squinting against the brightness of the horizon. His back was to the city as he faced the open sea. It was as if he did not hear the gunshots at all. I hid behind a wooden container that smelled of fish. From there, I could hear and see everything.

"¡Capitán!" Fernanda called out to Aldo Alarcón. The captain turned at once, and when he saw Fernanda, he blanched.

He leaned heavily over the railing of the ship. I bit my tongue hard. I'd hoped for a second that the man would tumble and break his neck, but I chastised myself for the thought. Once, I had told my mother that Aldo Alarcón deserved to die, and Lulu had warned me never to wish ill on any person, no matter how awful he was. "That is what the Spanish do, and they will lose this island as a consequence. You will see."

"Is my Illuminada safe?" he shouted down.

"No," Fernanda lied. "Her husband is coming for her and she's afraid."

"I'll kill him!" the captain said, his hand going to the gun at his side.

"She asked me to come for you. So that you might rescue her," Fernanda said.

Aldo Alarcón's eyes widened. He pushed himself off the railing and nearly tumbled down the plank in excitement.

"Did she? Did she? She asked for me?" he demanded once on the dock, and Fernanda nodded gravely.

"Here, take this," she said, putting a heavy iron key in the palm of the captain's hand. "There is a back door to the inn, one we never use but is always locked. Let yourself in, rescue Illuminada, and take her away from my uncle and me. We want nothing to do with her."

Aldo Alarcón raised an eyebrow. "The daughter you can keep," he said, took the key, and turned towards his ship.

"Don't forget!" Fernanda called to him. "Come as soon as you can. And bring your gun!"

Aldo Alarcón waved the iron key in the air, dismissing Fernanda.

I crouched behind the box and took several deep breaths. It was no use. I burst into sobs. I cried for as long as it took Fernanda to disappear down the cobblestone road and get lost among the people on the street. My sobs made my whole body shake, and were the kind of cries only children can manage without hurting themselves. Even so, it felt as if my chest were being torn in two.

I could picture the inn and the street it was on, but I had no idea how to get there. The Havana streets were complex, and unnumbered, and an address was of no use to me. What I did know was that if Aldo Alarcón was going to the inn today of all days, someone was going to get hurt.

I must have wept for an hour. No one stopped to help me. Perhaps I looked like one of those raggedy orphan children of which there were so many in Havana in those days. But I was wearing shoes. Nice, polished shoes of black charról that Julio Reyes had bought me for Christmas. Someone should have noticed those, I remember thinking to myself at the time. I was not a girl set adrift. I was loved! And my mamá needed me. Who would sleep near her on cold nights? Who would twirl the ends of her long hair so that the tips fell into small ringlets? To whom would she whisper stories of the sea, of a mermaid that rose from the depths to name me? We weren't complete without one another, Lulu and I.

With these thoughts in mind, I stood and turned and surveyed the place where I was. To the left was the Cathedral of San Francisco de Asis.

Before me, the tall, gray convent rose in gothic spires to the sky. The apse hung long and low over the bay, and the bells started to chime loudly, making my ears hurt. I scanned the street before me. Fernanda had gone left at the intersection, I was sure of it. But we'd taken so many turns getting to the ship that I had no idea where the inn could be.

I asked three people walking past if they knew of the Reyes Inn, but they had a wild look in their eyes, and when I approached them, they'd flinched.

"Get somewhere safe, girl," one of the women had said, fanning herself with a rickety fan and hurrying off.

"I'm trying to," I called after her, but she did not turn around. No one I asked seemed to know in which direction to point me. One had said, "Go north." Another had suggested I go south.

I scuttled along the street, sticking close to buildings and keeping my nose in the air. Every so often I'd stop a stranger and ask, "The Reyes Inn?" but it was no use. Either I was ignored, or the person did not know of the place. I began to wonder if my life had been a dream, that there was no inn, that I was only a shadow of a girl, without substance. My nostrils flickered as I ran past a taxidermy shop. Shiny marlins hung in the windows, their blue scales picking up the afternoon light. Beneath them sat what I thought was a jaguar, or panther, one paw in the air as if waiting for a handshake. The whole place smelled of iron and, strangely, treacle. A few blocks further, I pinched my nose against the stench of horse manure, piled halfway up the wall of a building. Two brown horses clopped their hooves in place, the black carriages shiny behind them. Two more blocks and the light began to fade. Havana seemed a grayer place at once. Five policemen pounded past me. I shouted to them, "I'm lost! Help me find the inn!" but they did not seem to hear me.

So, I followed them.

Three more blocks and the policemen slowed. They'd reached the prison, and halted, their mouths open. I opened my mouth, too. A part of the prison's façade had been blown off, and I could see the cells where men once slept. It was as if someone had taken a giant butter knife and sliced the walls away.

"Papá," I whispered, for I knew my father was being kept in that prison. I had stood in that very spot with Lulu, where she commanded me to wave at the windows, not knowing which one held my father. "What if a murderer is watching me?" I had asked, and she'd pulled my hair and told me not to be ridiculous. Now I saw how one of the cells had watercolor paintings of yellow daisies on the walls. I had drawn them, each one, on paper I'd borrowed from the front desk of the inn. Lulu had mailed them to my father at the prison. Scores of my drawings flapped lazily in the breeze now coming through that comfortless room.

I cast down my eyes. There, on the pavement, were a dozen dead men in prison uniforms. Some had died in the blast. Their arms and legs stuck out like spider limbs. Others bore dark, wet holes in their foreheads, chests, and necks. Gunshots, I knew somehow, though I'd never seen such wounds before. I thought, surely one of these men is my father. I'd seen only one tintype of him, but it was a blurry, ruined picture. My eyes settled on a slender man who died with his eyes open, terrified and beseeching. His hands lay palm up. His graceful fingers were curled into a claw. I seemed to recognize his nose—jutting out beyond a weak jaw—and there was something about the hazel color of his eyes, with specks of yellow on green, that resembled mine. I had drifted *that* close to the bodies.

I was yanked away from the scene by the collar. It was one of those policemen whom I had followed to the scene. "¡A tú casa!" he yelled at me ferociously, a bit of spit leaving his mouth, making him look more like a wild dog than a man.

"The Reyes Inn?" I asked him, surprised to find my voice worked. "Where is the inn by the bakery? The one that makes the cinnamon cakes, señor. Julio Reyes's inn?" I rattled off what I knew quickly, afraid that the policemen would turn away from me.

"Two blocks that way," he said, pointing towards the sunset.

I ran, taking one last look at the man, who might be my father, there on the ground, and I realized that the sight of him like that would dwell in my mind forever.

The doors of the inn were locked, as were the windows. Even so, I hugged myself in joy. Sooner or later, Lulu would have to leave the inn, and I would be outside, waiting for her. There was even the smell of the bakery in the air to keep me company. I took giant whiffs of it, and my growling stomach settled a bit.

That's just about the time I heard my mother's voice, thin but sharp, like a blade: "I'll tear your hair out!"

"¡Mamá!" I shouted, and clawed at the front door until my knuckles were all scraped. I kicked at the door once, twice, then, on my third kick, I heard a gunshot. I thought of the prisoners at once. I didn't know it then, but I was steeling myself for what might have happened inside. The memory of those dead prisoners gave me strength, for they had faced their deaths with open eyes, and I would not flinch from it.

I ran around the building, trying all the doors as I went. Looking up, I spotted the small window that led to the kitchens. The smell of chicken and rice—last night's dinner— still lingered around the place. An old crate served as a step, and I pulled myself through the window, scuffing my charról shoes and tearing my stockings. Once inside, I could no longer hear Lulu, but I knew where she was.

I ran through the kitchen and burst out into the lobby. It was dark. The lamps were not lit, though the acrid smell of kerosene rested in the air. The lights, then, had been turned down recently. I slowed, listening for Lulu upstairs. It was frighteningly quiet, except for a rhythmic, muffled sort of sound, as if a horse were galloping very, very far off in the distance. For some reason, I closed my eyes against the darkness. Feeling safer that way, I felt the floor with my toe and made some progress. That's when I tripped on something large and warm.

A moan sounded through the lobby. "Señor Reyes," I said, bending down and feeling for the man with my hands. My fingers found his ankle, then his knee. He moaned again when I touched a bit of torn fabric on his arm soaked in something wet and sticky.

"Lulu," Julio Reyes croaked. "He has Lulu." I felt his heavy hands on my shoulders, and he pressed down on me as he raised himself up. It felt as if he might kill me with his weight, but I stifled my cries.

"I can go get help," I said. "Where are the other guests?" I asked. The inn was sometimes full with guests. Other times, it was like a haunted place, and we were the souls trapped inside.

"They've all left," Julio Reyes said. "Alarcón s-sent them away at g-gunpoint." Julio Reyes coughed wetly, groaning after each cough.

A piercing cry from upstairs sent me running through the dark lobby. I heard Reyes call my name, but I had slipped away before he could say more. I stumbled over a warm and oddly shaped something on the floor, and was up again quickly. At the top of the stairs, I stopped. All was silent now and I grew frightened. The thick floorboards had been laid lengthwise down the hall, and they seemed to point to the directions I could take—to Lulu's room, or back down to Julio Reyes.

That's when I noticed that the door to Lulu's room was ajar. I slid into the room and found that a single candle on the dresser lighted the space. The bedclothes had been thrown on the floor, and Lulu's trunk had been packed haphazardly, so that a slip stuck out from under the closed lid, like a tail caught in a trap. And though I heard a grunting sound, like someone struggling with a heavy thing, I saw no one in the room.

My first thought was of ghosts, my father's ghost specifically, coming back to haunt Lulu and me. Then, I heard a soft whimper coming from the other side of the bed, by the window. I climbed over the thin mattress and looked down. I met Aldo Alarcón's eyes, and held his dark gaze for a few moments before realizing that my mother was right there, underneath him on the floor, her legs bare and white in the moonlight, and that one of his hands was pressed against her throat.

"Lárgate," he said. It was the kind of thing a person said to an animal. "Get out," he repeated. "Or I'll kill you, too." There was a trace of blood in the air. Lulu whimpered again. I thought of Julio Reyes downstairs. Perhaps he was dying. I wondered where Fernanda had gone.

"María Sirena," my mother whispered, "run."

Aldo Alarcón snatched at me suddenly with his free hand, and I was surprised into action. Bolting off the bed, I ran out of the room and into the hallway that was suddenly lit by a single, approaching light. It blinded me at first, and I prayed hard. Not Fernanda, not Fernanda, I said to God and la Virgen and San Francisco de Asis—all of them at once.

The light was all I could see until it glided past me, and I felt a warm hand caress the top of my head for a moment. Turning around, I saw that it was Julio Reyes who had gone past, going into Lulu's room. In the clarifying light that spilled from his lamp, I noticed the bloodstains on the hallway floorboards, and the red footprints that were too small to be my mother's, and too large to be mine. I was about to measure my foot against one of the bloody prints when a shot rang out. The alarming sound sent me into tremors, and I cried out, "¡Mamá!"

Rushing to the room I had shared with her for so many years, I expected to see my mother's corpse. What I saw instead was the body of the captain, Aldo Alarcón, facedown on the carpet, his blood soaking the place where he lay. Either my mother or Julio Reyes had killed the man. I'd assumed it was Julio Reyes, but then I saw the pistol—the very one I'd seen Aldo Alarcón holding—drop from my mother's hand.

There on the ground it resembled a dead bat, so black and angular and still. Immediately, Lulu wrapped herself in a sheet. I noticed blood upon her, too, trickling down her legs.

"The baby. The baby," she was whimpering, and I thought, of course, that she meant me.

"I am here, Mamá," I said.

"He's killed it. Our baby," she kept saying to Julio Reyes, who watched her tearfully. "Oh," she cried, and doubled over, clutching her abdomen.

"Mamá, I am here. I am well!" I shouted at her, patting my body with my hands to prove the point. But when she spotted me, Lulu uttered two words that were garbled in her throat: "Get out."

The memory of her in that moment, ragged and hostile, remained a vague one for a long time. It became clear only a few months later, when I'd seen enough to make meaning of those blurry shapes. I cannot pinpoint the exact moment when the remembrance suddenly sharpened in my head, but it was similar to the feeling of putting on eyeglasses for the first time. Like a miracle, the images made sense. When I brought it up, Lulu would claim to know nothing of that evening. I would ask her about the baby, the one she'd lost after Alarcón raped her, and she'd shake her head and say, "Do not speak of such things."

Until now, I have not spoken of it.

My mother told me to get out, but I stood still. From outside the window came the sound of gravel crunching underfoot. Julio Reyes pulled on the sash and the curtain came open. "Dios mío," he said, turning to Lulu with frightened eyes. He tried to tidy the room, pushing a chamber pot under the bed, stepping over Aldo Alarcón's body to tuck stray clothes back into Lulu's trunk. But then he stopped, leaned against a wall, and held his arm tightly. His bloody fingerprints were all over Lulu's things.

Lulu had looked outside the window, too, and her chest swelled, as if the future itself had filled her at once. Things would be different now, she knew, and she closed her eyes tightly. Julio began to move again, trying to put the room in order.

"Julio, stop," she cried, and his hands froze over a kerosene lamp he was trying to light. "Just stop. You know what must happen next." She walked over to him, half-dressed still, sobbing, and laid her palm on his cheek. He kissed her hand.

From downstairs came a long, weak moan. "Fernanda," Julio Reyes said, and looked at me with pleading eyes. "Help her."

Confused, but determined to make some sense of everything, I took the candle that Julio Reyes had brought upstairs, and followed the sound of Fernanda's moaning down the burnished steps. I found her awake, and half-sitting at the foot of the stairs. She was holding one of her feet tightly with both hands, and when she showed me, I could see where the bullet had pierced her foot.

"All I'm good for now is a convent," she sobbed, wrapping her arms, bloody hands and all, around my neck. "Damn Alarcón forever," she cried through gritted teeth.

"It will be fine," I told her, though my spine had gone rigid at her touch. What was she capable of now that she'd lost everything? I caught sight of the two of us in a mirror on the other side of the room. I could just see Fernanda's face. She was crying in silence, her mouth open wide in the effort.

She held onto me until we heard the front door being kicked in. It gave way easily and a man in a prison uniform that looked as if it had been scorched in places stood unsteadily, gripping the doorframe.

"Is Iluminada Alonso here?" he asked.

"Upstairs," Fernanda replied, and I pinched her hard for giving my mother away to a stranger. She didn't seem to notice me.

The prisoner did not say gracias, but brushed past us roughly, knocking the side of my head with his knee as he climbed the stairs. He smelled like smoke.

"I knew he'd come. I tried to warn Tío Julio," Fernanda whispered.

"Who?"

"You little idiot," Fernanda said . . . "It's your father."

13

A Nightmare Within a Nightmare

The lightbulb overhead gutters, then burns out with a pop. We sit in semidarkness. The moon is full and things are cast in a strange, pink light.

"I've never heard a romance that goes like that," Noraida whispers. What is it about the dark that quiets voices?

The door opens and closes before I can see who it was that left. I try counting the women, but I realize that, despite the full moon, there are patches of darkness in the room so profound that it's as if the women have disappeared. We say nothing to one another. The wind has died down and the rain has all but stopped. I can hear the tinny sound of a radio playing next door, and we strain to hear if it's news of the hurricane. I catch snatches of advertisements for a movie called *Cuba Baila.* The rhythms of a mambo filter through the air, and an announcer baritone-voice proclaims the film a "delight" and "1963's premier event" and other such hyperbole. In a corner of the room, Rosalia begins to shift, and then, Estrella whispers, "Anda, baila," and the two of them shimmy as they sit, drawn to the music. The advertisement ends and a news report starts. But the voice is hard to make out. I catch only the word "flood," repeated a few times.

I wish one of the women would go and listen for us all. I wish one among us would be bolder about such things. But I know the women are afraid of Ofelia, though they seem to like her. We've grown accustomed to strange rules in this new Cuba—what we can buy or sell is decided in Havana, and we can't leave the island at all without permission. Rubber stamps have taken on the power of gods here. Even leaving this room seems as if it might be forbidden.

I'm afraid to leave for other reasons. So many secrets have poured out like spilled dirt from a broken pot. I feel a sudden closeness to the women in the room, even to Mireya, who can't look me in the eye. They know my mother's shame. What if I told them of our time in the Spanish reconcentration camps? If I told them about Mayito, of what I did to my own son, would they understand? It paralyzes me to think of it. Meanwhile, the radio drones on and on, meaninglessly.

Just then, Ofelia throws open the door to our room. She's carrying a flashlight in one hand. The light is sickly and yellow. Under her other arm, she's tucked several flat pillows, and these she drops on the floor.

"A dormír," she commands, as if we are children. I am surprised to see the women scrambling, faster than I thought they could move. The pillows seem thin, musty, and not worth the effort. Susana stops and turns to look at me, gesturing towards the pillows. *Later,* I mouth. Ofelia leaves again, and I wonder where she is sleeping at night.

With the door to our room open, the radio next door is clearly audible now, and the announcer is, indeed, talking about the hurricane. The final bands of wind are off-coast now. Damage is extensive throughout the island. There is no word of whether or not Maisí has been blown into the ocean, to become our very own Cuban Atlantis. Noraida gets to her feet and peeks out the front door. Then, she disappears. Nobody says a word. When she appears again, she is blinking hard, the darkness of our room suddenly unfamiliar. "The water is waist-high downstairs," she says. "I saw rats swimming in it." Then she sits alone, and covers her face with her hands. Next door, the radio blares on. It feels as if the entire house has gone still to listen to the reports. I wonder who is next door. Are they old women like us? Sick ones like Susana? Could they be orphans? A whole roomful of elderly men? People in wheelchairs? I have this sudden, ridiculous vision of a room full of clowns and dwarves—circus refugees who have lost their colorful tents in the storm.

I should have drowned in my cottage in Maisí. In my pocket, the picture frame with Mayito's small face in it has rubbed a part of my skin raw through the fabric. I touch my stomach tenderly in that place that bulges and aches. Yes, the hurt is still there. I pray that the end comes quickly when it comes.

When I get up at last, there is only one flat pillow left. It has no pillowcase, and rusty stains have made strange shapes on the fabric. I pick it up. The pillow smells like onions.

I settle into a corner of the room, away from Susana for the first time since the storm began. She's asleep already, in a moonlit patch of floor, her scarf crooked on her head. I want to be alone. I long for my little cottage, and when I close my eyes, I pretend I'm there again, in my own bed. I do sleep a little. Perhaps for just an hour or so. And in that sleep I dream, but it is more memory than dream.

I'm remembering the day my father escaped prison, how I'd left Fernanda at the bottom of the stairs, clutching her foot, and how I'd traced her bloody footprints back to the room where the adults were now arguing.

Agustín, his hands blackened with what appeared to be ash of some kind, was holding Julio Reyes up against a wall, those dark hands around the inn owner's throat. Julio Reyes's wounded arm bled onto Agustín's shoes

My mother was weeping openly, and the blood between her legs was still trickling in clots. The smell of iron was nauseating. "He saved me, Agustín. He saved me. Déjalo, por favor," she said as Julio Reyes's face began to turn purple under pressure from my father's grip.

"¿Y éste?" Agustín asked, kicking Aldo Alarcón's body with his foot.

My mother said nothing. But I found my voice in that moment. "That is Capitán Alarcón. He tried to kill us all," I said. I wanted my father's eyes to meet mine. I wanted him to demand something from me, too. After all, wasn't I his daughter? Hadn't I been waiting for him all this time? Hadn't I mourned his death at the prison, though clearly, I'd been wrong? That other prisoner had been a stranger after all.

Agustín looked at me intently for a moment. Then, releasing Julio Reyes, he flipped the captain over with his foot. A weak groan escaped the captain's lips. "That's a poor shot. The man is still alive," my father said, pointing at the wound in the captain's abdomen.

"I'm no good with a gun," Julio Reyes said without stammering.

Aldo Alarcón tried to speak, to accuse my mother of his murder, I knew. She stared at him wide-eyed, her own lips moving only a little, perhaps cursing him, or willing him to be still, or to die more quickly.

"I recognize this bastard," my father said, leaning low over the captain who'd turned him over to the Spanish authorities fourteen years earlier. A strange laugh burst from Agustín's throat. "A reunion!" he shouted, picked up the pistol that my mother had dropped, cocked it, and shot Aldo Alarcón in the face. "Now, no one will recognize you," he said.

My mother had screamed when the gun went off. I made no sound at all, and this seemed to please my father. He turned to Lulu and said, "Get yourself cleaned up. We're leaving."

"Where?" she asked, shakily, obeying him, wiping her legs down with a bedsheet.

"Away from Havana," my father said. He laid the pistol on the dresser. "Dos Rios, in Santiago," he said. "The rebels are amassing there. I hear José Martí is among them."

My mother's deep-set eyes fell upon my father, and she became very still. "Still a rebel?" she asked.

"Para siempre," he told her.

Julio Reyes must have been sure at that moment of having lost Lulu forever. For the first time in my life, I saw purpose in my mother's eyes. I saw fire.

Julio Reyes begged us to stay the night. He said it was safer to hide for now. Agustín's prison uniform was burned in the oven, and Julio Reyes gave him some of his own clothes to wear. As for Alarcón's body, they would stuff him in a laundry sack come dawn, and throw the remains into the sea. All was planned.

By midnight, Lulu and Agustín were asleep in the lobby, each on a different couch. Julio Reyes made a bed for me of blankets behind the counter, and I lay there and watched as he washed the flesh wound on his arm and bandaged it. Nobody wanted to sleep upstairs with Aldo Alarcón's body.

It is a wonder I slept. But when I did, I dreamed of fire. I dreamed of my mother and father and me huddled together in a prison cell. Around us, hundreds of drawings of flowers peeled off the walls and struck our faces. As they touched us, they burst into flames, so that we were left scorched in places. We cried out but no one heard us, or came to unlock the bars. One drawing lit upon a dirty, gray mattress, and that caught fire quickly, as if the mattress were stuffed with coal. We pressed against one another, our eyes stinging, all of us coughing, choking. "We are leaving, we are leaving, we are leaving this place," my father kept saying, and I could feel my mother nodding against me, holding my head against her chest.

I dreamt the same thing again and again, all night long. When I awoke, exhausted, my throat aching as if I had truly been breathing smoke, Agustín was sitting beside me. "Buenos días, niña," he said, and ran his fingers along my jaw and up to my cheek. They came away wet, and so I knew I'd been crying. I closed my eyes, and when I opened them, he'd shoved his hands into his shirt pocket, and pulled out a crumpled sheet. He opened it slowly, and there was one of the flowers I'd drawn.

"I haven't had the chance yet to thank you for these," Agustín said. "They led me back to you and your mother," he said, pointing at the inn address at the bottom of the sheet.

I looked at him. Mutely, I nodded.

"Is that all I get?" he asked, and leaned forward, presenting his cheek for me to kiss.

Slowly, I pressed my lips against his stubbly face. He smelled like burnt things.

"Bueno," he said, satisfied. "We leave soon, little rebel. Have some breakfast." Then, Agustín left, and my flower drawing stayed on the floor beside me. I would have touched it, folded it up again, reminded him to put it back in his pocket, but the drawing only reminded me of my nightmares.

14.
My Story in Other Mouths

I remember those April days of 1895, though not as clearly as what came before and what followed. We rode trains to Oriente province, headed straight to Dos Rios, where the delegados of the movement for Cuban independence were gathering. The trains were overloaded with people fleeing the chaos in Havana. There had been more bombs throughout the city, and now, half of the buildings had great chunks missing from them, like the prison.

What I recall is a press of hot bodies, my mother's arms tight around me, my father's occasional glare in our direction. I remember how the steam engine rattled so hard that my teeth knocked together and gave me a headache. I remember searching for young people like me, seeing none, and feeling as if I were the last girl on earth, fearing that the Spaniards had wiped us all out, like in the bible stories Lulu told me of Egyptian pharaohs who murdered children.

This is all I remember of the train to Dos Rios.

I'm thinking about trains because Ofelia has announced that the railroads are shut down, the tracks inundated. The roads, too, she says, and mentions something about supplies and relief efforts. "All of us are to stay put," she says. "It won't be long now," she adds without looking up.

"How long exactly?" Noraida asks.

"Yes, how long?" Mireya echoes.

Having sought me out in the morning, Susana sits beside me again. "The rain has stopped," she says. "Let us go home."

Ofelia's cheeks redden. She gazes levelly at us. "How many of you can swim?" she asks. "Because the water outside is as deep as the Cauto River right now."

She can't be right. I've seen the Cauto, swum in the torpid bends, fell in love on its banks. The river is so deep in places I've wondered whether there are underwater caverns, portals to the underworld, tunnels to the United States deep in the gloom.

Noraida has gone to the window, placing her hands against the glass like starfish in a tank. "I've swum the Cauto," she says to her reflection. Her shoulders rise and fall with her deep breaths. Estrella stands beside her and puts one of her fat arms around Noraida's waist. "Tranquila, mi hermana," I hear her say. "The waters will be gone soon."

Thoughts of water remind me I've had to go to bathroom for the last hour.

It's down the hall and to the right. I'm grateful for the privacy of the tiny space with the black and white tiles on the floor. The tiles are a renovation from a recent era, and clash with the thick beams of old wood overhead. I relieve myself and suddenly the pain in my side blooms, spreading outward until I'm holding my breath and clutching the edge of the toilet.

Gasping, I stand, clean myself, and pull the dangling string that flushes the toilet. I steal a glance at the bowl, knowing what I'll see—streaks of blood in the water. The waters swirl slowly. My heartbeat slows, too. The pain eases.

It won't be long now, I whisper, and send up a little prayer that someone, anyone, remembers me after I'm dead. I grab the beam overhead and steady myself. I can imagine so clearly the glow of kerosene lamps in the rooms of Casa Velazquez back in the days when this house was new. Like a vision, I can see my father as a boy, stomping up and down the stairs, his cheeks full and rosy. My memories mingle with the stories he and my mother told me, burrow their way into the present like a persistent, tiny mammal. I am grateful for them, for the stories, for a way of holding on to my parents. It is as if my father were still here, still a child, still putting that cat out in the middle of a storm, still leaving this place after his mother died from consumption, a boy of fourteen, alone in the world; I can see him meeting my mother in Santa Clara, see her bandaging a bite he'd received from the dog of a Spanish soldier, who'd turned the animal loose on my father.

Tears press against my closed eyelids. My legs and arms feel like they're manacled. The stories weigh so very much. Who will carry them when I'm gone? Beatríz? I hardly know my own daughter. She went off to Havana to become a stranger to her mother. And Mayito? I grip the beam harder.

There's a knock on the door. Someone calls out, "Apúrate," and I hurry to rearrange my dress, which is still tucked up under my arm. The pain strikes again and I grunt against it.

The person on the other side of the door calls out: "Are you well?"

I am dying. The stories will die with me.

I open the door and my head spins. My thoughts scatter like minnows in shallow water. Susana is there to catch me when I stumble.

"I didn't know it was you in there," she says.

"You have to help me," I tell her. She runs her hands up and down my shoulders.

"Anything," she says. "There must be a doctor here somewhere." Her forehead wrinkles in concern and a little divot appears above her nose.

"Help me," I say again. "Help me convince them."

15.
A Reluctant Witness

When we return to the room, the women are huddled by the window, their breath fogging up the glass. Their chatter sounds like a hive of bees.

"¡Ay!" Mireya cries out suddenly, breaking through the buzz. "Miren," she says, tapping her finger against the lower left corner of the window.

Susana and I hurry towards the group and see a flash of red in the water below. It is Noraida, swimming in the debris-filled water, her brightly dyed hair like streamers in her wake. We watch as she pushes aside a plastic cup, a sheet of plywood, an umbrella floating upside down and bobbing along. Noraida is a fine swimmer, and every so often, she does something with her legs to lift her out of the water, up to her waist. She scans the horizon, then dips down again, stroke after stroke taking her away from Casa Velázquez. We watch as she swims into a sheet of plastic, invisible in the water like a jellyfish, watch as it wraps around her face and she fights it, ripping the plastic away at last and beating against the water with her long arms.

"I can't look anymore," Estrella says, and sits on the bed.

"Estúpida," says Dulce, and a few of the women nod in agreement. We watch Noraida until she's only a speck of red in the distance. She swims up a side street, sticking close to an apartment building. On the balconies, people wave at her. She rests for a moment on the roof of a huge truck, running her hands over her face and neck. "She's stuck," Dulce says.

"She looks like an island out there," Mireya whispers. But Noraida kicks out once more, slipping into the water. She waves back at the onlookers, and swims on, disappearing from our view.

"Por Dios, I hope she doesn't drown," Mireya says solemnly.

We are still by the window, watching the swamped world come to life bit by bit. Every once in a while, a person floats by on a raft. I wonder whether the owners were planning on taking to sea, leaving Cuba on their own terms, visas and government permissions be damned. Overhead, the fat, black clouds roil away quickly, headed to some other place in the Caribbean. The sun is peeking out of the east dimly. I'm reminded of something my mother used to say, that should I ever feel afraid for my mortality, I should look up and remember that the sun, vast as it is, is dying, too. "None of us are alone in death," she'd said to me, even as her own light was extinguishing. Where she picked up that information I could not guess. My mother knew a great deal somehow, especially how to charm others into giving her what she wanted.

What I want at the moment is an audience. There's another story that's come to mind about my mother and her gifts. I want to tell it so badly and preserve it in the memories of these women that my skin itches.

I clear my throat. "Perdón," I say, and they turn to look at me. "I have a proposition for you. A way of passing the time and helping a sick woman." They steal glances at Susana, who looks hurt at once. Her hands fly up to her scarf, as if to make sure it is still in place.

"No, no," I say. "I mean myself. I am not well. Not long for this world. I want to tell you my story, the story of my life."

"We all want our stories told," Mireya says with a nervous laugh. "Vamos, who else has a story to tell?"

Rosalia starts looking through her purse, while Estrella picks at her nails.

"Dulce, come, it's your turn to tell us a story," Mireya insists, and turns her back to me.

Dulce sits slowly on the edge of the bed. She sighs loudly, lets out a quiet, "Ay," and flexes her feet before speaking, as if her every word takes preparation of some sort. "I was a girl of seventeen on the day I accompanied my father, a sergeant of the military police in Havana, to El Malecón, where two fishermen had fished the corpse of a man in a laundry bag, using enormous hooks meant for sharks. I may not remember whether or not I've brushed my hair on any given day, but I do remember my father, que en paz descanse," she said, crossing herself, "cutting open the laundry bag with a knife, rolling the body out of the bag the way one undoes a bolt of fabric, finding the man's wallet in his pocket and exclaiming, 'There you are, Capitán Alarcón. We've been looking for you,'" before stuffing the body back into the sack. "What was left of the corpse's face was unrecognizable. His lone eye was bare in its socket, and that is all I remember of him.

"You see, I don't doubt the truth of your story," she said, lifting a gnarled and spotted hand up to stop me from interrupting. "But that doesn't mean I want to hear the rest of it."

It feels like a weight has slipped into my throat. I cannot speak.

"But Señora Dulce," Susana begins. "She's dying."

"So am I," Dulce says. She's old, but her voice carries. "So are you," she tells Susana, who crumples next to me. "We all have stories to tell. Who will remember mine?"

"Go on, then," I say.

"¿Cómo?" Dulce asks.

"Tell us your story. I'm eager to hear it." If my own stories are an itch beneath my skin, driving me mad, then the need to hear other stories is like a thirst.

But Dulce blushes and her eyes grow wide and startled. Put on the spot, she quavers, waves her hands in front of her face and says, "Deja, deja. Do what you like, María Sirena." She busies herself with her purse, pulling a painted fan from inside. It makes a crackling sound as she opens it, and I can tell the fan is from Dulce's youth. The fan depicts a war scene in faded colors—farmers carrying machetes crawl over a hill studded with palm trees. The sky is painted gray, or, perhaps, age has faded the blue. In the distance, tiny horses stand in line, with even tinier soldiers painted atop them. The fan, too, tells a story, and when Dulce moves the thing back and forth to cool herself, it seems as if the illustration is moving, coming alive in minuscule.

The fan mesmerizes me for a moment only. Beyond this room, those taking shelter in upper stories of homes all over Santiago de Cuba are wondering when the waters will recede. The drowned are beginning to wash up against buildings, bumping lifelessly against coral walls. Beyond Santiago, out to sea, other islands are in the path of the storm, and people are nailing up thin sheets of plywood over windows and praying to God. Out past the Caribbean, our stories are short clips on the radio and television, reduced to a few seconds of information. Our lives are diminishing ripples in vast waters.

I catch my reflection in the window and it startles me. I don't look much like myself. I test it, purse my lips and watch my reflection do the same, but still, I do not recognize the gesture. Perhaps I am looking at another me, a doppelganger come to prod me into telling them all of it, even the stories I've kept to myself.

A deep crack resounds throughout the house in that moment, as if a beam somewhere has given way. "Ay!" a few of the women shout. I sit very still, bracing for a collapse. But none comes.

Mireya eyes the ceiling fearfully, her purse clutched to her chest. "The roof is going to come crashing down on us, I know it," she says.

"Don't be so negative," I tell her.

"Aren't you afraid?" Mireya asks. It's the first honest question she has asked me. I see a glimpse of my old friend in her look.

"I'll tell you about fear," I say, leaning forward. When no one stops me, I begin again.

PART II

1.
Lulu and the Poet at Dos Rios

We arrived in Dos Rios at the end of April in 1895. Agustín had rifled through my mother's trunk for something valuable to sell. But she had nothing but her clothes and mine, and the pistol she'd used on Aldo Alarcón, which Agustín did not want to part with.

"The galleon coin," Lulu told him, indicating where in the trunk's lining to cut. With a small knife, Agustín made a precise incision in the green-striped lining, shoved his fingers into the hole, and drew out the old coin that his mother had brought from Spain. I watched as my father clutched the gold coin. He kissed it and said, "Our salvation," disappearing with the coin into the village of Dos Rios, while Lulu and I waited for him.

When he returned, it was with a horse—a huge, speckled, pregnant mare.

"She'll be slow," Agustín said, "but she can carry us all."

We spent the day scavenging what we could from the trunk and our surroundings. There, on the outskirts of town, were plenty of fruit trees—mango and ciruella—though they were often choked in vines. We gathered what fruit we could. Lulu dressed me in many layers, and did the same for herself. Every once in a while I'd catch her wincing and clutching at her stomach. Sometimes, a tear slipped down her cheek. But she said nothing to Agustín about it. When he was a few feet away, I asked, "Mamá, what's wrong? Are you hurt?"

She clutched my face hard, her fingers digging into my

cheeks. "Not a word to your father about Julio Reyes, entiendes? If he suspects that Julio and I—" she said, stopping short. "He'll kill me, María Sirena. He's capable of it," she warned me.

Finally, when night fell, Agustín loaded us onto the horse. We rode through the dark. I sat sandwiched between my parents, and fell asleep with my forehead against my father's warm back. He smelled of copper and blood. In the morning, Agustín stopped at a small, thatch-roofed house, a bohío. The country people fed us some leftovers of arróz con leche, gave us a large hammock to use at night, and wished us well. "¡Viva Cuba libre!" they shouted as we rode away. My father lifted a fist in the air without turning around.

"The country people are with us," he said, his voice choked with tears.

He stopped in several places, and in each small bohío, Agustín learned more about the insurgents in the area, and where to find them. At dawn, we came upon a place in the woods that had been recently scorched. The grass was blackened beneath our horse's hooves, and the trees were gnarled and ashy. Here were several hammocks dangling from the enormous ceiba trees that had survived the fire.

Men were seated in a circle on the ground with maps laid out in front of them.

"It's him," Lulu said breathily at the moment that Agustín pulled hard on the reins. "José Martí," she said to me, whispering in my ear. My breath came short at the name. I followed the trail of my mother's gaze, but could not pick the man out from the group.

"Patriots," my father said, dismounting. The men rose, brandishing their rifles and machetes. My mother clutched me hard.

"Name yourself," one of the men said.

"Agustín Alonso. An insurgent like yourselves," my father

said, stepping closer to the men with each word. "I was in Havana just recently. Rotting in a prison for flying our flag."

"We heard the western rebellion was thwarted," one of the insurgents said. "There were supposed to have been two—one in Havana and another here, in Oriente."

"As far as I know, the chaos in Havana was a reaction to what you men accomplished here," Agustín said. The one who'd asked the question threw his hands up in frustration.

"Do you have supplies?" another asked.

"Hombre, nothing but a pair of strong arms and well-placed cojones," Agustín said, gripping his crotch for a moment.

Some of the men laughed. Then, another spoke: "Sí, and you've also brought two women to slow us down."

I felt myself beaming. I'd never been called a woman, though I knew it was dark, and that in the light of day he would have called me a girl.

"I can fight." My mother spoke quietly, though all the men heard her.

Remembering that she'd killed Aldo Alarcón, I shouted, "She can! I've seen her!"

More laughter. My father turned and scowled at me. The look on his face frightened me, and I remembered the story from his childhood that he'd told me on the train to Dos Rios, about the time he'd left his shoes in the middle of the hallway in Casa Velázquez, and how his mother had taken all of his things—shoes, shirts, books, toys, what little he had—and flung them in the Cauto River. "I may be a servant in this house, but I am not your maid. Learn to take care of what's yours and you'll secure a better life for yourself," his mother had said. Agustín had looked at me intently when he finished the story, saying, "My mother was a tremendous woman." I read a warning in his look and in the memory. My mother had held my hand too tightly during the telling of the tale, and I read a warning in that, too.

I felt my mother dismounting. She held onto me to steady herself. Her hands trembled.

"Señores," she began. "Compatriotas. You hope to found a free nation here, do you not?" She spoke animatedly, her delicate hands dancing before her, as if she were doing a floréo in a flamenco dance. The men watched, mesmerized. Even Agustín stopped scowling, the grimace falling from his face at once. "A nation is made up of men, sí, and women, too. As well as children." She pointed at me, and my face felt warm. I looked away, unable to bear so many of the insurgents' eyes fixed on me at once. "Then, let us fight. Let us learn to defend this new nation. We Cuban women can be midwives to this great birth, if only you'll let us."

There was silence. I wanted to applaud, shout, "Bravo, Mamá!" I didn't, of course. I sat in the saddle while the pregnant mare shuddered beneath me, huffing and snorting in that way of horses. The animal was the only thing making a sound. I ran my hands over her pelt to calm myself, and the horse settled down, too.

That was when I noticed the poet for the first time. He parted the group of men and approached us, a heavy pack still on his back, as if he expected to have to leave the modest campsite at any moment. "It's a pleasure to meet a family so brave," he said, extending a hand to my father, and then kissing my mother on both cheeks, like a European.

Lulu looked away demurely, whispered, "Gracias," and returned to the horse.

"Who is that?" I whispered to Lulu.

"That is the man who called the war," she said breathlessly. Later, I'd learn all about José Julián Martí, the poet and patriot, who had inspired Cubans on the island and abroad to rise up over Spain. But in that moment, all I saw was a slender man, with a large forehead and a thin mustache that curled up at the ends. His eyes were small and brown. There was something of the rodent about his features, though I liked him at once. Lulu and Agustín were struck dumb by his presence. They had seen him give a speech once, in New York, but familiarity had done nothing to diminish Martí's aura in their eyes.

"You may camp with us tonight, and ride with us tomorrow if you'd like," Martí said. My mother had charmed him, I knew. While my father had gripped his balls to show his strength, my mother had said a few words to the right man. I took note of the difference.

Another one of the insurgents, a bald man with a gleaming machete dangling from a rope around his waist, spoke up, "Oye, you have no military experience, poet. Perhaps it's best if you—"

"Cállate," said another insurgent to the bald man. "This is Martí you're talking to." Then, facing my father, Martí's defender said, "Make yourselves at home."

There was no more arguing against our presence that night.

Later, after we'd eaten a meal of roasted rabbit, my mother introduced me to Martí. "Señor," my mother said, holding me tight against her thighs, "mi hija, María Sirena." She presented me to the poet by caressing my cheek with her hand. I leaned into her touch, hungry for it still, though I was fourteen years old.

The poet cocked his head to the side. "I can tell already that you are your mother's muse," he said.

When Martí left us, my mother said, "Take a good look, María Sirena. There goes a man without equal."

"Papá?" I asked her, and she laughed.

"No, mi cielo, Martí. There would be no rebellion if not for the poet." Her gaze lingered long after the man, even after he'd lain down in his hammock, the only part of him visible a bony knee.

"The poet is handsome, too, isn't he?" she asked me, though she didn't expect an answer and I did not give her one.

I realized two things that night. The first was that Lulu admired my father in direct relation to his status as a rebel. She'd left Julio Reyes in Havana without much of a thought once Agustín returned, bloody and smelling of smoke. Now, at Dos Rios, another man threatened to trump my father's allegiance to the cause, and hence, take his place in my mother's estimation.

2.
Little Storyteller, Little Rebel

I imagined myself riding with the insurgents forever. Perhaps they'd find me a white horse like Martí's, I thought. One of the insurgents, a man they called El Blanco because of his fair skin and freckles, had a heavy whip that I'd studied from afar. It was braided and glossy, and I longed to carry a weapon like that. Another was a redheaded man, and they called him, not very creatively, Rojo. There was a pair of very young insurgents my age, brothers, no more than fourteen—Antonio and Francisco—who lisped like Spaniards and kept to themselves, which I was glad for. People my own age made me nervous. They seemed to be nearly grown when I still felt so small. There was a man named Toledo, who had a knife in his hands at all times. It had an ivory handle and the tip of the blade was rusty. He'd balance it on his knuckles and make it seesaw, to my delight. When my mother saw me laughing with Toledo, she dragged me away at once. Later, I noticed that Agustín and Toledo liked talking to one another, their faces tight grimaces as they discussed the most humane way of killing a downed man, and the least humane way, too. In the light of the cooking fire, which fell to my mother and me to stoke and tend, my father and Toledo looked like devils. There were others, but either I cannot remember their names, or I never knew them.

What I do know is that by the end of that spring, most of the men in our group were dead or missing.

We rode the countryside during the day, sometimes getting

into skirmishes with Spanish soldiers. I always knew there would be a fight on the days Agustín led Lulu and me to a stranger's bohío. The country people, who we called guajiros, would let us stay in their house and share their table. More often than not, we ate jutía and rice. The large rodent's meat was surprisingly juicy, though there was something of the swamp in it, as if I could taste the green muck of the jutía's home. I could taste something sour, too. Perhaps it was the fear that must have flavored the creature's body at the approach of a caimán, or in the end, a hunter. On those days, I knew the insurgents would find a narrow passage in the woods, where the trees were tightly grouped on either side of a trail, and hide, muddying their faces to blend with the forest, and wait in ambush for Spanish soldiers. They always seemed to know where the Spaniards would be, and I guessed the guajiros were relaying messages to the insurgents.

When Agustín returned for us, he'd be the worse for wear, his skin scraped, his clothes torn, the creases by his eyes caked with mud. But he was alive, and Lulu would embrace him silently, hold his face still as she studied it, and bury her head in his neck. All of this Agustín would endure as stiffly as if my mother had wrapped herself around a statue. He'd thank the guajiros who took care of us, settle us on the mare, and lead us to the next campsite without a word. Once, when Lulu caught me staring at my father on one of these rides through the woods, she told me, "It's a great burden to be a patriot." My expression must have given away some of what I was thinking, that my father's coldness on such days frightened me. Underneath us, the horse would sometimes buck and pull away from Agustín. I sympathized with the creature.

The mare had given birth to a sandy-colored foal early that spring. I'd watched the birth in fascination and horror. The horse's flared nostrils, her white, blocky teeth bared, the grunts of her labor, and then the messy slippage of the baby as it slid from her—all of it was burned into my memory. The foal died that morning, and the men butchered it for food. Though there was a great swelling of emotion regarding the cause, for the most part the insurgents we rode with were unyielding men who ate the foal with relish, waving pieces of charred meat around our horse's face and laughing. My father joined in on the fun while I watched, refusing food, pulling stinkweeds out of the earth with both fists in frustration, for I had wanted to keep the foal for myself and I'd been the one to discover its stiff little body in the morning, which had been hard on me. The men had laughed at my tears, at my furrowed brow, and Agustín said nothing in my defense.

Yet, the poet was of a different sort. On the days when we'd ridden our horses to exhaustion, and were forced to camp, the poet isolated himself with sheaves of creamy paper and filled them, line after line. Only once did I approach Martí. It was out of boredom, honestly. The others had no interest in me, and, more often than not, shooed me away. It was a point of contention among our group. Every few days, the insurgents would demand that Lulu and I be taken away for good. Always, Agustín's eyes would flare with anger, Lulu would say something about patriotism and courage, and the poet would raise a slender hand and say, "I'd like them to stay."

Why my father wanted us around, even as he seemed to ignore us at every turn, was something I did not understand. As for Martí, his attachment to us was equally mysterious. On the day I spoke with Martí, the first and only time I exchanged words with him, I asked him directly why he came to our defense, time and again.

The poet did not answer my question, and I wonder now if that's the way with poets. Instead, he redirected me, made me think of other things, occupied my imagination so thoroughly that I forgot what I'd come asking for in the first place.

Martí drew a sheet of onionskin paper from his pile. It crinkled prettily as he lifted it. So thin and glossy, the paper reminded me of moth wings. I longed to throw the sheets from a height to watch them flutter down to earth. However, Martí laid the paper over a book he was holding and handed me a carbon pencil.

"Do you ever tell stories?" he asked softly, and watched as I made circles and sharp angles and a crescent on the page. When I was done, I'd drawn a giant moth. "It can speak," I told the poet. "And it will answer any question you ask of it. The moth is so large it can carry small children across the island. It chases the moon from one side of Cuba to the other, with children on its back so that they can enjoy the nighttime without having to sleep." My understanding of astronomy and geography was limited, of course. Cuba was my entire world, and though Lulu told me often of my birth, of how the coast of a place named Georgia could be seen on the starboard side when I was born, I could not yet imagine anywhere but my island.

"Little storyteller," Martí said, gave me another sheet, and sent me on my way. I climbed the nearest tree, folded the page in half, and dropped the paper, quenching my desire to see it fly like a moth. I did this again and again until the page tore on a branch. As for the moth, it was the first story I remember telling.

Once, Lulu and I stayed a week at a bohío very close to the Cauto River. The river's murmur helped me sleep, and I hoped Agustín would not return. But return he did, with a limp and his knee swollen as big as his head. We left the peaceful little hut only to return to a camp whose numbers were cut in half. Rojo had been killed, and El Blanco mourned him with great sobs that resounded through the woods. The brothers, Antonio and Francisco, were gone, too, though when I asked my father about them, he shook his head sadly, and said,

"Don't ask, don't ask," so that I knew that either one or both of them was dead.

That night, the mood in the camp was solemn. Lulu and I stewed a jutía that one of the men had trapped in a snare. I watched my mother through the glassy waves of heat coming from the fire. Her cheeks were flushed, and her eyes were locked on something beyond the edge of the camp. I turned to follow her gaze. There, in the moonlight, stood the poet, his hands locked behind his head, his eyes turned up to the stars.

Lulu rose and handed me a wooden spoon dripping with hot stew. She whispered, "Keep stirring," and picked her way around the resting men until she reached Martí. The two of them talked a long time. It was not the first time Lulu and the poet had talked in the moonlight. I had never been privy to what they'd said to one another, but the two had always chatted out in the open, though at a distance from the others, and always when Agustín was away from the campsite. That night, I noticed the way pine needles poked out of her hair and her dress hung crookedly on her frame. The effect was charming, as if my mother were a wood nymph, and could, at a moment's notice, bolt into the forest never to be seen from again. Once or twice, the poet would point at the sky, and my mother would lift her chin and gaze at the stars. I could tell from the way her shoulder blades moved that she was taking big, deep breaths, and I, watching her, began to breathe in the same way. So it was that I didn't notice Agustín until he was right behind me.

"Where is your mother?" he demanded, an empty bowl in his outstretched hand.

"With the poet," I said, dipped the spoon into the stew, and drew out a full serving to give my father. But he was gone before I knew it. I watched as he walked up to Martí, his brimmed hat in hand as if he were approaching a priest. My mother jumped at the sight of him, then she composed herself, straightening her dress and crossing her arms. I could not hear what they were saying, but the conversation was short. They took their leave of Martí. Agustín and Lulu strode past me quickly, he gripping her upper arm and she taking short steps, unable to keep up with him. I stole one glance at the poet, who had his back turned to us all, his hands back behind his head, stargazing once more.

For a moment, I watched as my father led my mother deep into the woods. Then, I realized what was happening. They were leaving me alone with the insurgents! Fear gripped me quickly, and I abandoned my post at the fire and trailed after my parents. My feet caught on something on the ground at the edge of camp. I bent down to take a look. A machete in its sheath had been dropped there, and I picked it up and held it with two hands before me, sheath and all, as I followed my parents into the thick of the trees.

They walked fast, and at first, I could only hear their murmurs. Then, they stopped. Dawn was fast approaching, and weak sunlight was seeping in through the canopy, dressing my parents with a ghostly luminosity, so that they appeared unreal versions of themselves. I crept as close as I could to them, longing to be safely near them, and also afraid of what was going to happen. Agustín's face was a mask of anger. Lulu's was one of terror.

My father peered into the woods, looking past me. He seemed to be making sure he and Lulu were alone. Swiftly, he lifted his hand and brought it down hard against my mother's cheek. She clutched her face and bent low. The only sound she uttered was a single, high-pitched, "Ay!"

"You think the poet wants you? Like that stuttering innkeeper did?" Agustín asked her in a fierce whisper.

Lulu was quiet. She did not move from the position she'd placed herself in—hands to her face, bent at the waist.

"Did you hear me?" Agustín asked. When my mother did

not answer, he forced her to stand and pushed her up against a palm, growing spindly and ugly in the dense, lightless woods.

"Don't take me for a fool, Illuminada. From now on, you stay where I can see you," Agustín said through gritted teeth. He'd held her close to the tree with his knee and a single arm barred across her chest. He fumbled with his belt.

Of course, I knew little of jealousy then, and of the ways between some men and women. Agustín nearly had his heavy belt undone. All the while, my mother stood quite still, her eyes closed and her cheek pressed against the spiny bark of the palm tree. Imagining that Agustín was going to strike Lulu with his belt, I bolted from my hiding place, raised the machete in the air, and shouted, "¡Basta, Papá!"

He froze, and my mother's eyelids fluttered open.

"Don't you dare," I said out loud, mimicking what I'd heard him say to me when he thought I was about to do something naughty. "Don't you dare," I repeated, waving the machete.

Agustín released my mother. He approached me slowly, as if he were really afraid that I might strike him. When he was before me, he wrenched the machete from my hand.

"Little rebel," he said, unsheathing the knife and handing it back to me. "Do your worst." He closed his eyes and waited. I waited, too, for a few seconds that felt much longer. "Mátame," he commanded, his eyes closed.

I dropped the machete.

Agustín did not laugh at me, as I thought he would. Instead, he held me by the shoulders and said, "Save your killing for the Spaniards." Without looking at Lulu, he said, "María Sirena, take your mother back to the camp. Don't sheath that machete until you get there." Then he left, buckling his belt again.

As for Lulu, she'd slid down the length of the palm tree and drawn her knees up to her chin. She cried silently for a long time before I could coax her up and back to the fire and the stew.

"How hard it is to hate a person you've once loved," Lulu remarked to me later that night. She and I slept apart from the men, under a makeshift tent of muslin. I always slept cold while she ran hot, and so she placed my cool hand on her cheek to alleviate the sting of my father's slap.

"I cannot hate him, María Sirena," she said, meaning Agustín. "In loving him, I've left pieces of myself behind."

"Like when I caught my dress in that trap the other day?" I asked, having done just that earlier in the week, tearing one of my only dresses in a spring-loaded trap I discovered in the woods. I'd been lucky not to lose a finger or toe.

Lulu laughed softly. "Something like that."

"I want to marry a man who is nothing like a spring trap," I said.

Lulu nodded. She said something that I couldn't make out. Cicadas chirped incessantly outside our tent, and my ears rang a bit. It was not a night for whispers.

After a while I said, "I can't sleep," and so my mother told me a story.

3.

A Love Story

I will tell you, María Sirena, about the day I met your father. Come closer. Así, así. Don't move that cool hand of yours an inch, bien? Bien.

When I was young and unmarried, my parents, your abuelos, decided to leave Baire and move to Santa Clara. There, my father opened a zapatería, making and selling fine shoes and boots for men and women. Working with the leather and the waxy thread, his arm would pump up and down, a shoe coming to life in his hands. Shoemaking was like breathing for my father. It was a trade he'd learned from his father before him, who'd learned from his father, and so on. Whenever someone called him a cobbler, my father would grow angry, and say, "A cobbler only patches holes. What I do is an art!" and stomp out of whatever room in which he happened to be. The shop was small but well stocked, and soon, the business was doing fine, in spite of Spanish taxes. I worked the register, measured insoles and foot widths, and took orders.

I was about seventeen years old then, and unmarried. I'd begun my studies with a tutor—an old Spaniard who smelled like cedar—and hoped to become a teacher someday. My girlfriends were all beginning to pair off. Several had babies already, sweet, chubby things I loved to hold, huffing their wispy hair and dreaming of my own children. But my father had put a stop to each and every boy who had come courting. He would show his revolver to the insistent ones, pointing out that the gun held six bullets, "But I only need one." This he'd say meaningfully, his soft voice a whisper. Usually, the boy in question would leave, never to glance my way again. Without a single boy courting me, I knew what the neighborhood gossips were saying about me—that Illuminada Puentes would be una solterona, an old maid.

My parents kept me busy, hoping to occupy my mind with something other than young men. "There's time for all of that," my father would say, dismissing me with a wave of a ruler, strip of leather, or whatever he had on hand.

"He just wants you to be his little girl always," my mother would say, then, she would promise to talk with him about the permutations of my heart.

During the day, I had my hands wrapped around customers' stinking feet, the measuring tape I used coiled around my wrist like a snake. At night, I helped my mother sweep and cook and do laundry. I studied with the tutor twice a week. My hands were beginning to grow rough and thicken, like a farmer's. What man would want hands like that on his face, his back, caressing his shoulders? Not a one, I can promise you that.

So, when the first war against Spain broke out, I was happy. It meant that the shop filled with soldiers looking to resole their boots before heading out to battle. I learned their names, promised I'd pray for them, and, once or twice, wiped fat tears off the faces of these boys who had never held a rifle before. Of course, the soldiers were mostly members of the Spanish army. My understanding of the cause was minimal then, I'm ashamed to say. The fact that my parents were born and raised in Madrid didn't help the matter. Once, Spain had encouraged its citizens to leave the mother country, to spread its culture broadly, taking that Spanish lisp to every corner of the world. My parents were devoted disciples, and came to Cuba, Spain's most beautiful colony, with a mind to recreate their own little corner of Madrid amid the palmas reáles.

The truth was, I was proud to be a daughter of Spain, albeit in sentiment only. I was born in Oriente, at dawn. I was told that the midwife gave me a bit of sugarcane to suck on shortly after I was born. "For strength," she'd said. Encouraged by the superstitious nurses, my first clothes were yellow, the colors of la Virgen de la Caridád, Cuba's patron. So you see, María Sirena, I was Cuban from the start. But at the onset of the war, I would have given up my liberty to be the wife of one of those Spanish soldiers, so much did I fear becoming a solterona.

I imagined the soldiers that came into the shop as they might look in battle, their faces a rictus of terror, eyes bloodshot, hands trembling around their weapons. I imagined them sleeping on the hard ground, their long lashes touching their cheeks. Boys are at their best when they are sleeping, and I envisioned each of them in turn, beside me in bed, clutching me, seeking solace from nightmares.

The truth is, I had a wonderful imagination then, but I misplaced it the day the battle came to our street in Santa Clara. Rebels had come into the city, machetes in the air, rifles on their backs. They wanted to take Santa Clara back in the name of a free Cuba, and began by raiding each store down la Calle San Pedro for supplies.

I was alone in the shop, hiding behind the counter, when Agustín rushed in. He ran the length of the store, knocking down shoe samples from wooden shelves that lined the walls. He turned over tables and tested the wood of the table legs with a thump of his fingers. Finding them unsatisfactory (they were made of cheap pine after all), he vaulted over the counter next, and found me there, crouched, my hands over my head.

I heard him breathing hard as he stood over me. I feared the worst of this rebel, whom I hadn't looked at yet. Where were my Spanish soldiers? Where was my rescue?

I felt a soft touch on my hair and heard a whispered command: "Levántate." I did what he asked, rising slowly. When I looked up at Agustín for the first time, a curious feeling came over me. It felt as if someone had shaken me hard, like a doll being played with by a spirited child. My limbs, my cheeks, my eyelids, all of me felt looser, pliable. Dios, we were so young then. Agustín's dark hair was long, and it hung across his left eye, giving him a dangerous, half-hidden look. His plump lips were pink and glossy, as if he'd just been kissed. A thin mustache lined the top of his mouth, but his chin was shaven. Dots of dried blood here and there told me he'd shaved recently.

All of this I noticed at once. By the time Agustín opened his mouth to speak, I was already half in love with him.

"Do you have weapons in the store, mi vida? Anything I can use against those Spanish bastards?"

I swear I only heard the part where he'd called me "mi vida." It was a sweet nothing, a way of getting me to do what he asked, and it worked wonders. I flew to the back of the store, found my father's revolver, and handed it over to Agustín.

He whistled when I presented it to him, then he spun the cylinder only to find it empty. "Bullets?" he asked.

"Follow me, and help me look," I said, gripping his warm hand and leading the way to the storeroom. Together, we emptied drawers and upended boxes. Twice, Agustín's arm brushed mine as we worked. Once, he pulled a bit of cobweb from my hair gently. We found a half-empty box of bullets underneath a pile of invoices, and these Agustín loaded carefully, holding a bullet between his teeth while he slipped each one into the cylinder. The gun full, Agustín put the weapon in the waistband of his pants.

"No, here," I told him, pouring out the two remaining bullets from the box into the palm of his hand. "Just in case." These, he slipped into his pants pocket.

"Gracias, mi vida," he said, then kissed my cheek softly. It was a whispery kiss, but he pulled away so slowly that I could breathe in his coppery smell deeply. Then, he left, running back into the fray in the street. I could hear the popping of gunfire, the slap of revolvers and rifles going off like lightning. Unafraid suddenly, I stood outside the shop and watched Agustín's slender form as he ducked and dashed down la calle, disappearing from view.

I hid in the storeroom for the rest of the day. At night, my parents finally arrived, shaken and happy to see me alive. My father searched for his revolver for a long time before I burst into tears and made up a story about a rebel who had come and taken it, and had threatened me with a knife until I showed him where the bullets were.

"Animales," my father said, his voice a growl. "If I ever meet that scum of a man I will cut off his balls with my sharpest shears," he said, shaking a trembling fist in the air.

"Calma, calma," my mother murmured into his ear, rubbing his back in that way of hers that I still miss.

Methodically, with patience only a shoemaker knows, my father began to cover the broken windows with sheets of leather. It was all we had on hand. Outside, the street was quiet. Here and there, a shout would traverse the air, startling us before it went silent again. At one point, the sound of dogs barking and growling and the sharp cry of a human being pierced the night. There was the sound of two gunshots, then nothing. My mother and I held each other, but my father kept working at the window, tapping the leather in place with short nails into the wood molding.

Someone knocked on the door a few moments later.

"¿Quien es?" my father called.

A weak voice said only, "It's me."

My father faced us in confusion, but I *knew*. Tearing away from my mother, I ran to the door, wrenching it open. Agustín fell forward into my arms, his own arms scratched and bleeding. His legs were worse. His pants were torn to shreds and the skin beneath was shredded, too, reminding me of butchered animals.

"Mi vida, help me," he said, before losing consciousness in my arms.

"Papá!" I cried, staggering under Agustín's weight. But my father did not move from my mother's side. His eyes were on the pistol that had fallen from Agustín's hand.

"Mi pistola," my father said. Then again. "Mi pistola." Disbelief was plain on his face—his mouth was open and his eyes were wide as he looked from me to the gun again and again.

"Papá, I can explain," I began, but my father was upon me, shaking me hard so hard that my brain rattled in my skull and my mother was yelling at him to stop. My father pushed me away in disgust.

"Helping the enemy," he muttered, and left my mother and me alone in the room. Without a word, she helped me drag Agustín into the shop.

"What do we do?" I asked her, meaning about Agustín's injuries. My mother said nothing, and left the room. I laid my head on Agustín's chest and listened for his heartbeat. It knocked away reassuringly. Still, he was bleeding all over the floor, and his lips were starting to turn purple.

My mother returned with a bottle of rum, and a needle from my father's toolkit. The needle was slick, a clear substance dripping from the tiny tip. It smelled like rubbing alcohol. She took my hand and forced it open, then dumped the needle, already threaded with fine, waxy string, into my hand.

"I can't," I said, shaking all over.

"This is your mess," she said. "Your father and I did not choose this boy for you. You chose him." She eyed me steadily. "You want him? Then save him."

My mother must have known what I was capable of. After all, my father had taught me to have a steady hand, to make neat stitches so that a shoe would not fall apart anywhere—not on limestone, not in swamp water. I took a few deep breaths and poured some of the rum on Agustín's wounds. They looked like bites, and indeed, once the blood was washed away, I plucked a yellow incisor from his calf.

Agustín moaned, and his back arched off the table. "Calma, calma," I said, repeating my mother's mantra. Cupping the back of his head, I had him drink some of the rum. I waited until he grew sleepy again. His eyes stared towards the ceiling, but it was as if he looked past it.

"Even their dogs are cruel," he muttered, and tears fell onto his cheeks.

"I know," I said, and shushed him, running my hand over his lank hair. Then I gave him the rest of the rum.

"All we want is liberty. It is the right of every man," he said, groggy now. He smacked his chapped lips together slowly, savoring the drink.

"I know," I said again. "I feel that way, too," though I didn't really understand what I was saying at the time.

"Mi vida, you and I will see a free Cuba. Our children will be free," he said, his eyes half-closed.

My heart beat faster. I steadied my hands. "Of course," I whispered. When he finally slept, I began stitching him up. Every so often, Agustín would wince, but exhaustion and rum had worked their magic, and he slept through the worst of it. When I was finished, I put my head back on his chest and fell asleep, too.

In the morning, I woke with a pounding headache, and Agustín nowhere in sight. I looked around and wondered if it had been a dream. But there was the leather sheet flapping against the window. The empty bottle of rum lay at my feet, and my hands were rusty from blood.

"Mamá," I cried out, afraid to call for my father. But it was he who emerged from the back room of the shop, trailed by Agustín, who limped carefully.

"You have a choice, Illuminada," my father said. He was a soft-spoken man, and there was no edge to his voice. "This man wants to marry you."

I couldn't catch my breath. I didn't even know his name.

"You may go with the traitor if you wish," my father said, and now there *was* an edge in his voice.

"Manolo," my mother said, calling my father's name in warning. She was in the back room, and she peeked her head out.

"He's a rebel," my father called back to her. "He is not what we wanted for Illuminada." All the while, Agustín stood by, his eyes narrow and perceptive.

My headache intensified, and my vision grew strange—everything was limned in a thin black line, like a drawing. The floor swirled beneath my feet, and I found myself falling. Agustín was at my side at once, running his knuckles tenderly across my cheek.

"So, it's settled," my father said, angry with me I knew, though I hadn't said a word.

Agustín's eyes glittered as he looked at me. "Do you believe a man can fall in love in an instant?"

"I don't know," I said honestly. "It seems so in fairy tales."

"You saved my life. Those bullets, the ones you urged me to put in my pocket, killed the dogs that attacked me. One bullet for each savage dog. Then, you sewed me up, better than any surgeon could have, not that any of the Spanish doctors here would have treated a rebel like me. Courageous. Skillful. Beautiful. Men have fallen in love over lesser qualities in a woman." Agustín sat back on his heels, wincing, holding my hand.

I could feel his pulse through his skin and imagined that my own was racing to meet it. My mother had her hand on my father's shoulder, and I could see him softening. He, too, was a romantic, leaving fresh flowers for my mother, usually gardenias, on his pillow when he left for the zapatería early. He called her "mi belleza," even though deep lines marked the contours of her face, and her belly had gone soft and protruding. María Sirena, how I wish you'd known your grandparents. But they died within a month of one another—Papá from a cancer of the throat, Mamá from a failure of the heart. They loved each other so much they could not bear a life apart, and I believe that is the kind of love they wanted for me.

They thought I'd found it in Agustín. After all, I'd never disobeyed them before, and this—handing my father's revolver to a rebel—seemed to suggest an intensity of feeling on my part. They weren't wrong. Not at first.

I closed my eyes and nodded my head. "Sí, I'll marry you," I said to this boy, a stranger to me, though his blood was still caked under my fingernails, and I could hear his heart thumping in my ears still. Already, a part of him was left in me, and, I'm certain, a part of me was bound to him.

"Bien, bien," he said, kissed my forehead, and held me.

I cleared my throat, felt my headache start to fade, and asked, "Pardon me, but what is your name?"

4.

Requiem for a Poet

W e woke up to the clacking sounds of rifles being loaded and cleaned. We heard shouts all around the camp, and the heavy thump of footfalls around our tent, as men ran to and fro. Lulu and I looked at each other sleepily. Her story had taken much of the night to tell, and I had stayed awake for all of it, trying hard to imagine my father being chased and attacked by dogs, my heart aching for the grandparents I never knew. I would hear the story again, many times, but I would always remember this first version, which was so full of longing for those days. My father's handprint, which had been so red and angry on my mother's cheek last night, was now just a blush of color. Her other cheek looked wan in comparison. Lulu touched it tenderly, and I knew it still hurt.

Agustín burst into the tent suddenly, his skin drenched in sweat already, though it was early in the morning. "They're here," he was saying breathlessly. "The Spanish cavalry. Ambush!"

"Here?" my mother asked. "Here? Now?"

He gripped my hand and Lulu's. "A mile away. We don't have time to get you to a safe house. You're to stay in the tent, you understand?"

Lulu shook her head. "How many? Are we outnumbered?" Agustín nodded. "Then let me fight," she pleaded.

"What about María Sirena? Would you have her carry a machete to battle?" my father asked.

"She's old enough," Lulu said and I gasped. My mother gave me a forlorn look, making me feel very much unwanted, like a breathing obstacle to her desires. But she hugged me suddenly, fiercely, and the feeling vanished. "Of course not," she said at last. "We'll stay here."

Agustín leaned over and kissed my mother. His lips parted hers and they held each other a long time. It seemed as if he were saying goodbye. When they separated, my mother's face was wet with tears.

"After today, Dos Rios will be ours, I swear it," he said.

"Be careful," she whispered.

He eyed her reddened cheek and nodded.

Agustín hugged me next, kissed the top of my head and said, "Se obediente," and I nodded, promising I'd do whatever my mother asked of me. Then he left, and we watched him and the rest of the insurgents go on their skinny horses, their rifles slung across their backs.

The poet was the last to leave. He turned his horse around, a white stallion, and waved at Lulu. He was radiant in the rising sunlight, and seemed full of purpose, as if he were just now realizing the man he was meant to be—a warrior poet destined for greatness.

My mother blew him a kiss, and the poet smiled, then he kicked at his horse and trotted away. Lulu sighed softly beside me. "Now we wait," she said, and lay back down, her eyes staring at the top of the tent, her teeth worrying her bottom lip.

The heat of our nerves made us sweat. Outside, the woods were cloaked in silence. Not even the sinsontes were singing. After a while, Lulu and I left the tent, our ears primed to hear returning voices, or, worse, gunshot. Twice, a rustle in the woods sent us scrambling back inside the tent. When I said, "I thought you weren't afraid of them," meaning the Spanish, my mother grew bold, her eyes flashed with life, and we stayed outside of the tent for the rest of the morning. The pistol she'd used to end Aldo Alarcón's role in our lives rested on her lap, and it gleamed in a patch of sunlight as if it were coming to life.

We stayed that way the better part of the day, eating leftover stew for lunch. It had gone cold, the fire having gone out, but was still good. Later, I explored the campsite. The men had taken nearly everything they owned on their backs, in case they were stranded in another part of the woods. In one place, I found a box of matches. These I shoved into my underwear, for my dress had no pockets. There was some beef jerky in a mess of blankets. I rolled up my sleeves and hid the dried meat in the fold. Stumbling across an old nest, I picked it up and put it in my other sleeve. The nest would make good tinder, I knew. I made my long hair into a bun, and tucked a sharp letter opener I found into it, holding the bun in place. Lulu would recognize the letter opener as belonging to the poet, the initials J.J.M. on the handle.

"With you, we can survive anything," Lulu said to me as she appraised my small hoard. She laughed a little and held me close, rocking me. I was too big for it, of course. Still, I snuggled into her neck as best I could, trying hard to remember the days when this was easy for us. It was, I believe, my first moment of nostalgia, and perhaps the most painful instance of it. When Lulu peeled me away, she noticed my tears and asked, "¿Porqué?" In answer, I only wept harder for my mother, loving her so very much, knowing, for the first time, that we wouldn't be together always; one day, I would be too grown for even these kinds of embraces, too big to live by her side.

This was how my father found us—holding one another and in tears, for Lulu had picked up on my burst of emotion and began crying, too.

"You heard already? So many tears for the poet?" Agustín said harshly, his lip torn so badly that he was slurring his speech.

Lulu looked up and put me aside gently. She moved slowly, as if through deep waters. "The poet?" she asked. "Did something happen to Martí?"

Agustín nodded, and his eyes began to glisten. Martí may have been a rival for Lulu's attention, but he was the father of the insurgency, the one who had brought together a dozen disparate groups under one banner—that of Cuban freedom. And now, before the war had really begun, he was gone. Agustín knew all of this, and I could tell that the loss was like a punch in the gut. He could barely stand straight as he looked at us. Thick tears ran down his cheeks. He looked like a boy in that moment.

"Ven," my mother said, and guided him into the tent. There, she cleaned his lip and saw that the injury wasn't as bad as it looked. Agustín was tired. Even as she assessed his hurts, his eyes were closing. He looked at her, heavy-lidded, for a long moment before waving her hands away.

"I have a safe place for you both. Not far from here," he slurred before falling asleep. I noticed that his front tooth was chipped, and his tongue touched the jagged edge as he slept.

Lulu and I kept watch that night, guarding the tent. I put my head on Lulu's lap, my cheek pressed close against the pistol she still held. The stars whirled above us, the Milky Way in a different place in the sky each time I happened to look for it. I couldn't sleep, not after such a long day of waiting, not with the possibility that the Spanish would come for us at night. As for Lulu, she was thinking of the poet, I knew, because she kept murmuring snippets of poems, like prayers. Mainly, she was trying to remember the poems, I think, picking them up halfway through, then stopping and clicking her tongue in frustration.

"Cómo el amigo sincero . . . ," she'd begin, looking up to the stars as if they might jog her memory.

"Mamá," I said, interrupting her, "what did you and the poet talk about all of those times?"

"He wanted to hear my life story," Lulu said.

"Did you tell it to him?" I asked, wondering if there would have been poems about Lulu had the poet lived to compose them.

"Some. He was a good listener."

"Did he tell you his life story?" I asked, thinking that Martí probably didn't have a story like mine, including a father in prison, a mother who shot a man, or a mermaid rising from the depths to claim him.

"Some," she repeated. We were whispering, afraid of waking Agustín or attracting unwanted people to the campsite. So far, Agustín was the only insurrectionist to return.

"Tell me," I urged my mother, hugging her waist as tightly as I could.

Lulu adjusted her shirt and sighed. A breeze kicked up around us, smelling of urine from the latrines that the insurrectionists had dug up a few feet away. She closed her eyes, as if trying to recall Martí's voice, and it seemed as if it took some great effort. I've noticed this myself, how the voice of the deceased is the first thing one forgets, and I've often felt a double grief, for the dead and for their way of speaking, both torn from this world.

"There is a poem I asked him about. There are two women in it—one impudent and icy, the other disgraceful in the way she presents herself to the world, all red-lipped and brazen. I asked him, 'José, which of the two is worse?'

As Lulu was speaking, an unpleasant image came to mind of my future self, a grown woman in a dress cut too low, too revealing, while my face was frozen, an eyebrow arched sharply, my lips red and pursed. "What did he say?" I asked, clasping my hands to my chest.

"'They are both accursed, because both are capable of betrayal,' he said. A thick vein pulsed in his forehead as he spoke, so I knew, María Sirena, that the poet was angered by the question somehow. But I pressed on, because his answer did nothing but make me feel poorly about being a woman. 'What about the man who strays?' I asked.

"His look softened. He sighed, took my hands, and told me a story about a woman he loved who was not his wife. She'd died young, having bathed in a river that was too cold. She'd stayed too long in the water, and they'd found her there, floating faceup on the bank. Her lungs were clear of water, but her skin was blue as the sky. The poet says he bribed the sexton to let him into the mausoleum where her body lay, late on the night of her funeral. He kissed her cold hands, and he kissed her white shoes before leaving that horrible place. He felt frightfully unhappy, he said, and still mourn the girl.

"'Was she that special?' I asked him, and he said, 'She died of a broken heart. She killed herself over her love for me.' Ay, María Sirena, what a tortured expression he carried! Still, I can be cruel, and I pressed him further:

"'But what of your wife?' I asked, and he only said that the man who strays pays the price of his error with every breath. He said he'd written a poem about the girl, which helped his unhappiness a little, but I've not read it." After a while, Lulu said, "I think the poet was clearing his conscience Perhaps he knew he was going to die soon." Her voice cracked a little, and she cleared her throat.

Lulu grew quiet then, and her hand tugged at my hair lazily. We were both lost in our thoughts, my own imagination running wild with the thought of the poet in a dark mausoleum, the walls dank and mossy, his high, white forehead pressed against a slender, dead hand. My skin broke out in goose bumps at the thought.

Agustín sighed noisily and turned over, startling my mother. "I've made mistakes, too," she said. "And I am unhappy."

"Mamá," I said, and cuddled against her breasts.

Lulu went on as if she were speaking to herself, as if I weren't there, stealing her warmth and hearing every word. "I chose Agustín. No one forced me to take him for a husband. My decision . . . " she said, trailing off, her hand growing soft against my head. In a short while, she was asleep, and I followed her into dreams afterwards.

It was morning when the three of us woke. No other insurgents returned to camp, so Agustín, Lulu, and I packed up what we could, loaded up my father's mare, and headed off to a new site. We walked in silence. When the sun was high, Agustín broke the quiet and said, "The poet died facing the sun." It made my parents smile for some reason, and they held each other by the waist as we made our way through the densely wooded countryside.

5

Another Poet Mourned For

S usana slips a glass of water into my hand. It is cold, and the ice tinkles against the crystal. My throat is raw. In my days as a lector, I could read for eight hours and not feel any kind of discomfort. But I am unused to it now, and my jaw aches from talking. Still, the rest of the story bubbles in my throat, and I don't want to stop for long. I'm afraid of losing the thread of it, and of the quiet in this place, punctuated by shouts from outside and the sloshing of water against the walls of Casa Velázquez.

But right now it is not quiet at all because Mireya has begun to cry. She starts out softly, but her sorrow builds until she is hiccupping and gagging into a dusty doily she has grabbed off of a side table, sending plumes of grime into the air.

"¿Qué te pasa?" the women are asking her, patting her hair and drumming her back, as if she is choking on a piece of tough meat and not on a morsel of grief.

When Mireya answers them, I know what she is going to say before she says it. "Mi hijo, Alejandro. He was a poet, too. He died. Ay," she says, kisses the palms of her hands, and lifts them up over her head, as if blowing kisses to the dead.

I remember the exact day I learned of it, July 27, 1953, and how the news of Alejandro's death had been obscured by the news of the attacks on the Moncada Barracks the day before, and the arrest of the rebels who dared defy President Batista. All over Maisí there was talk of revolution, and people asking, "¿Hasta cuando?"—how long would we have to wait for a lasting peace?

So it was that Alejandro's death barely registered for people, and his funeral was poorly attended. Beatríz, of course, did not even come home for it. He had been her first love, and she told me in a letter that she could not bear to see him so still, his face garishly painted by the funeral director in Maisí who was infamous for making the town's dead citizens look clownish in their coffins, nor could she stand to look upon the hands that had once held hers folded over his hollow chest. She wrote all of this in a letter, and I thought that Alejandro would have appreciated the poetry of the missive.

Mireya and I had grown apart in the years after Beatríz and Alejandro broke up. Yet she would stop and chat in the market when we saw one another, and offer me her cheek when sitting near me at Mass in that moment when congregants offered one another a sign of peace. We would kiss one another, say "Paz," and return to our places on the pew, content with a cold friendship that had turned us into polite acquaintances.

At Alejandro's funeral, however, just as I was kneeling by the coffin, observing that, indeed, the makeup on his face was not the right shade at all, Mireya sent her sister, an imposing woman who had come to Maisí for the services, to ask me to leave.

"¿Porque?" I'd asked, confused, my eyes drawn towards Alejandro's narrow face, lingering long on his neck, which was swollen and too fat for his body in death.

"Mireya does not want you here. You must go. Now," the woman said, and so I left. Later, Mireya would run from me in the market, at church, anywhere we crossed paths.

Susana is holding Mireya's hands in hers, and asking about the cause of Alejandro's death. "An infection," Mireya says, and Susana sighs, shaking her head. Her scarf is off-kilter, and her eyes glisten. I know she feels relief, is glad the man did not die of cancer, happy that Alejandro's tale, at least, is not an example of her own path.

"I am sorry, Mireya," I say from across the room, because I am not brave enough to rise and attend to her.

Her mouth tightens at the sound of my voice. "You never liked him," she says softly. "Spare me your condolences." But there is no fight in her tone. Only defeat.

"He wasn't right for Beatríz," I hear myself saying, wishing I could stop even as I speak. What's wrong with me? I feel like a record player that has been left on even though no one wants to hear it. "But he was a good boy, a devoted son."

"The best son a woman could ask for," Mireya says.

"Que Dios lo tenga en la Gloria," I add.

"Amen," the other women say.

Ofelia comes in with a cardboard box balanced on her hip. Inside are plates of congrís and plátanos and a jug of water that looks brown when she pours it out into paper cups for us.

"Ay," Estrella says. "I'm not drinking that."

"It's just iron from the pipes," Ofelia reassures us. "The storm has damaged the pipes."

Even so, not one of us drinks the water. Earlier, we had seen a corpse floating past Casa Velázquez, facedown in the water, his clothes puffy with air. Who knows what is in the water? The rice, of course, was probably boiled in brown water, but at least it was boiled. We reason this out between swallows.

Ofelia eats with us, still in her sodden clothes. She chews slowly, her gaze far away. "This is good," I tell her, patting her arm.

She comes to life a little, and smiles at me.

It is a solemn meal, with Mireya sniffling as she eats. It has been a decade since Alejandro died suddenly of a bacterial infection, but a mother never stops grieving. I know this intimately, but I will not cry out my own sorrow and diminish Mireya's mourning. Whatever I did to offend her can't be undone. God knows I tried, visiting her house in the days after Alejandro's funeral, and being turned out by her sister.

After we eat, Rosalia sits beside me and asks me about José

Martí. "We all learned his poems in school. Recitations and such. I was terrible at it. Muy bruta. What was his voice like, I wonder? Do you remember?"

"It was a high voice. High for a man, but not feminine. Razor sharp. Precise," I say, surprised I remember it so well.

"Ah, I would have liked his voice to be the booming sort," Rosalia says, disappointed in me, as if I fashioned José Martí myself.

Estrella goes to the cardboard box Ofelia brought in and asks, "Is there more food?"

"No," Ofelia says, and picks up her own empty plate.

Susana asks, "No more for lunch, you mean?"

"Of course there is more," Celia says. "Isn't there, Ofelia?"

Wordless, Ofelia goes around the room and gathers all of the empty plates. She does not look at Susana, and I take it to mean that there may not be any more food at all.

Dulce is still eating, grain of rice by grain of rice, when she says, "Don't wait for me to finish," waving Ofelia off. "I eat like an infant these days. Go on with your story, María Sirena." Ofelia leaves with the cardboard box and the dirty dishes.

"The congrís was hard," Rosalia says.

"Food is food," Estrella responds. "That may be the last congrís we see for a while." We are all quiet, save for the sound of Dulce's fork against her plate.

"Go on," Susana says to me.

"Might as well," says Rosalia. "We have nothing else to do."

I look at Mireya. She swallows thickly and shrugs. Outside, someone is shouting the name "Fernando!" again and again. It is a woman's voice, and at once I think of a small boy, lost in the storm, perhaps, or a husband gone missing or even, a large dog that has run off in fear of thunder. She is anguished in her calling, and the name Fernando gets shriller each time she says it. I pick up the pieces of the story where I left off, and her voice fades.

6.

The Workshop

I t's a safer place for you both," Agustín explained, describing the workshop in the hills where we would live and work. "There are horses to tend, guns that need repair, machetes to sharpen, clothes to mend."

"A tallér? You want me to work in a tallér?" Lulu asked, her voice going shrill. I knew she dreamed of battle still. And why not? We had seen them, the women fighters, the mambisas, wearing pants like men, with rifles slung low on their hips instead of babies. My mother eyed them hungrily when they made their way through the camp, and on those days, she would refuse to cook or wash, but rather would sit with Aldo Alarcón's pistol in hand, picking dirt out of the gun's crevices with a fingernail.

"I do," Agustín said. "The talléres are run by women and children. They keep the Liberation Army in shape."

Lulu was silent afterwards, and did little speaking in the three days in took us to get to the nearest tallér. Instead, Agustín and I chatted, he telling me stories of his childhood in Santiago de Cuba. It was on that walk that I first learned of his time in Casa Velázquez, of his mother's gold coin, and other stories that revealed the patterns and permutations of his life. It was a good three days, and Agustín did not lose his temper once. In fact, he seemed jolly, hoisting me on his shoulders so that I could pick mangoes off the high branches for our lunch, teaching me how to kill a snake with a machete and how to use the skin for carrying water.

Every so often, Lulu would cough lightly, and a few times, she asked that we stop so she might rest. A thin line of sweat ran over the top of her lips, and she refused the food we brought with us, but seemed to drink more water than our horse. "Is Mamá sick?" I asked Agustín, who did not even turn to look at her.

"She's fine," he said, though later he forced her to ride the mare even when she wanted to walk.

By the time we reached the tallér, I was happy, and loath to part from my father. I knew would not see him again for a long time.

The tallér was hidden in a valley made shady by towering trees of all kinds. Tucked between the trunks were tents, which had been draped with palm fronds and other green detritus. Camouflaged this way, the tallér wasn't easy to spot. When Agustín tied up the mare, I thought we were only stopping to rest or eat, but my father led us down a steep, rocky path and right into the first tent in the tallér.

Hanging lamps lit the large tent inside. Women and children worked at tables, on the ground, or standing. In their hands were all kinds of weapons in different states of repair. The soft clink of tools filled the space, as did the murmurs of those working there. The place smelled of iron and chicken shit. A few moments later, a dusky hen scurried past me.

Agustín spoke quietly to a thin woman wearing a calico kerchief. She watched us as he talked in her ear, and nodded every so often. When she came over, she extended a hand to Lulu, saying, "Me llamo Bernarda. Welcome to the workshop."

Lulu did not shake the woman's hand. Instead, she wheeled on Agustín. "I am not staying here," she said between her teeth. Her cheeks were brightly lit as if from a fire within.

Agustín tipped his hat, a broad-brimmed, floppy hat made of straw, saying, "I'll be back soon," and just like that, without even a kiss to my cheek, my father was gone, and we were left in the tallér among strangers.

Lulu ran after him, and I followed. By the time the two of us reached the top of the hill, all we could see of Agustín was the back of his head, high atop the mare. "He took the horse," Lulu said, disbelief in her voice. "He took the horse."

Back down the hill we went, hand in hand, and into the tent. Lulu looked around, clicking her teeth together. Her hand crushed mine. Before I knew it, Lulu was sitting on the ground and weeping openly. Then, she beat her fist into the earth. Slowly, the tallér grew quiet as the women and children stopped to look at her. Even the chickens, which were allowed to wander the place, ceased their clucking. When Lulu began to scream, the women closed in like a human blanket, wrapping their arms around my mother, helping her to her feet and away from the tent. I heard her screams diminish as she went, then it was my turn to fall to the ground, afraid and alone.

The women were all gone from the tent. Only the children had been left behind. There were three girls, all a bit older than I was. Two were twins, and they wore their hair in long braids that touched their waists. Another was a very blond child, the kind of blond I'd seen infrequently, white as the sun. A smattering of boys, including a few in diapers that sagged, sopping wet, as they chased each other, occupied the space, too. They didn't seem to know what to do with me, and so they stared for a long time.

"My name is María Sirena," I said at last. My scalp was itching, but I would not scatch it, not now, in front of all these people.

"Stupid name," one of the boys said.

"Fausto!" one of the twins reprimanded him.

"I'm Marcela," the other twin said. "She's Graciela," she added, pointing to her sister. "That's Fausto, she's Veronica, but we call her Blondie, the little ones are Luís, Carlos, and Leopoldo, but we call him Polo."

"I'll never remember all of that," I said, and the children shrugged and shook their heads.

Then, another voice spoke out from the mouth of the tent. The figure was hard to see in the glaring sunlight, but I could tell he was a boy about my age. "You forgot to introduce me," he said, stepping into the tent. "Me llamo Mario," he said, and reached me in two quick strides. He held out his hand and lifted me to my feet.

It was the first time I had ever touched a black person that I could remember, though I didn't think of it until later that year, when the shade of Mario's skin became a threat to us both. "I was new here once, too," Mario said, his head cocked to the side as he spoke to me. His hair was uncombed, and his shirt was missing the two top buttons. He gave the impression, at once, of a boy without a mother. But his eyes were quick and bright, and turned up at the corners just a notch. His ears poked out a little from his head. On his chin was a deep scar, which I at first mistook for a dimple. When Mario smiled, the scar flattened to nothing but a patch of shiny skin. When he frowned, it became a tiny well.

"Come with me," he said, still holding my hand. I followed him out of the tent and around it. There, I saw that the valley was little more than a hollow, and that there were only three tents in total, plus a small enclosure for a couple of horses, both of which walked slowly enough to suggest that they were hurt animals. A pair of goats wandered among the horses; there were chickens everywhere.

"It isn't much," Mario said. "There are other talléres much bigger than this. They've taken over sugar plantations that the Liberation Army have burned and razed. They're proper factories for weapons. But this place? This place feels like home."

"You've seen those places? Those other talléres?" I asked.

"Sí. My father left me at one in Matanzas before coming here."

"Matanzas? My mother says that's where the fighting is

fiercest," I said, leaving out the other things Lulu had said, how she'd begged Agustín to head west, to Matanzas, to the thick of the battle, and how it had frightened me so much.

"She's right," Mario said. "My father is Ricardo Betancourt. He's the captain of a company. He's in Matanzas province now." Mario bent down to pick up a hen that had hobbled up to him. "Brinquita, I call her," he said, and held out the hen's left leg, which was mangled, like a dried bit of grapevine.

"How'd she get hurt?" I asked, petting the animal that had snuggled up against Mario's chest.

"Hawk," he said. "She's my pet, now." The chicken cooed in response. It would be like that always with Mario—animals seemed to respond to him. The horses were his to tend, as well. This he told me with pride, and said he wanted to lead a proper cavalry one day. "Negros like me are in charge of companies and battalions in the war, like my father is. Once we win independence, you'll see María Sirena, that there will be no more negro o blanco, just people." Mario had a faraway look in his eyes, and so I said nothing, but I thought of how Lulu and Agustín had referred to los negros mambises, the black insurrectionists, with such pride to have them fighting on our side, and I thought that perhaps Mario was right.

"So your father is a captain," I said, and whistled. "What about your mother? Is she a mambisa? My mother wants to be one, but Papá won't allow it."

Mario was about to answer me when I heard Lulu scream from inside the other tent, the one I hadn't seen yet. I ran as hard as I could, drew open the flap, and watched in horror as my mother brandished a machete and swung it to and fro at the women of the tallér.

"Illuminada," one of the women called my mother's name, her hands up in front of her. "Basta, basta. We won't force you to stay. But consider leaving the girl. A war is no place for an innocent."

Lulu screamed again. She caught sight of me and beckoned me to come to her. I stood still, unable to move even a toe in her direction. "María Sirena," she said, a warning in her voice, "we are leaving. Ven."

Still, I did not move. What was she thinking? A garbled noise came from my mother's throat then, and she pointed the machete to her stomach. "Even my daughter abandons me," she sobbed, closing her eyes. Her knuckles went white as her hands gripped the machete handle. I launched myself towards Lulu, but Mario held me back, and did not let go, even when I kicked at his shins with my heels.

Luckily, the women in the tent, watching this horror show, were quick. They subdued my mother, and before I knew it, had her bound to a cot with rags knotted together. They even muffled her mouth with a blue bit of cloth. She eyed them wildly, like a nutría in a trap. Her hair hung limp and wet around her head, long swaths of it wrapped around her neck like a noose.

Mario managed to drag me out of the tent, and dumped me in a slender stream that cut through the valley, for I was hysterical now, and it was said that cold water could sometimes help a person in shock. The coolness of the splash did the trick. I shut up at once, and looked at Mario standing above me, his brow tight in concern. "Are you well?" he asked.

"She's mad, Mario. My mother has gone mad," I whispered, as if it were a secret, as if everyone in the tallér hadn't seen her lose her mind.

He lifted me out of the stream and led me to a patch of sunlit grass. "Sit," he said. "Dry off." In the distance, I could hear the women talking in the tent, deciding, I'm sure, what to do with Lulu.

"You asked about my mother," Mario said. "I'll tell you, but you must promise to keep it a secret. ¿Me lo prometes?"

"Sí," I said. Already the sun was doing its work, and I felt warm to the bone.

"It starts with me, the third Mario Betancourt to be born," he said, and touched the scar on his chin.

Mario told me the story in pieces, some on the day that I thought Lulu had gone mad, more that night, my first night alone without my mother. Mario had sat by my hammock, holding my hand, whispering his sad story. He told me more of it when I learned that my mother was not mad at all, but had begun to show signs of a particular kind of meningitis, which we called "horse fever," or la fiebre del caballo. The doctor was called, and he said she wouldn't survive the night. I cried at her side through it all, dipping my fingers in water and letting the liquid drip into her dry, foul-smelling mouth. Many weeks later, when she had recovered, and remembered nothing of her madness on our first day in the tallér, Mario finished the story.

I have wondered since if his story was too awful to tell all at once, or if, like Scheherazade and her thousand tales, he'd wanted to prolong the telling on purpose, to be near me. A romantic notion, perhaps, but one I cling to now, when I have nothing left.

7.

Of Mothers and Madness

The first Mario Betancourt was born in a thatched hut on a sugar plantation in Sabanilla, Matanzas province. The hut, a small dirt-floor home in a section of the sugar fields no longer cultivated, housed four other members of the Betancourt family—Mario's parents, Margarita and Ricardo, Ricardo's bedridden mother, Lidia, and Lidia's mother, whom they called Cuquita, an ancient woman well past one hundred years of age, who tended to her ill daughter day and night, murmuring in Yoruba, so that no one understood. She still venerated the old African gods, remembering that place, and had refused baptism, even when she was whipped for it. They were all slaves on the plantation, and were some of the very few slaves who were allowed to stay together as a family. The plantation owner, Don Peregrino Calderón, lived in the big house with his wife, the docile Doña Encarnación, who bore two children—a handsome son named Roque, and an underweight girl who could not hear or speak. It was said that Don Peregrino Calderón was too softhearted, and possibly a homosexual, despite his wife. Those were the accusations thrown at a man whose slaves lived so long—to the landowning Spanish, he was as weak as a freshly whipped meringue.

Such were the witnesses to the first Mario Betancourt's arrival, who died only six hours after his birth, his tiny heart fluttering to a stop under his mother's hand. The second Mario Betancourt died the same way, outliving his brother by only nine minutes. To Margarita, it felt as if she were the only one who mourned the baby boys. Ricardo toiled each day cutting sugarcane alongside his wife. He had no energy for grief. She cut the cane with a ferocity that she'd lacked before her babies had died. But still, had anyone asked her, she would have said that she felt as dead inside as her children were. Ricardo and Margarita came alive only at night, when their rough hands would trail over one another's bodies like blind, groping things. Meanwhile, Lidia and Cuquita were lost in their own conversation made up of the sick woman's moans and the ancient one's muttering. During both labors, Margarita had walked herself to the plantation house where the doctor tended the slaves (it was, he'd said, more sanitary in the big, wood-shuttered house). She had returned on her own, empty-handed, carrying the thin receiving blankets she'd taken with her with such hope in a tight bundle.

Upon both tiny bodies, Margarita had made sure to leave a mark before the doctor came to take them away. She'd dug her nail into each baby's chin just hard enough until a half-moon line of blood appeared. It was meant to be a physical token, a signpost, a portal, for the spirit of this child, and the one before him, to come back someday. When Margarita's next baby was born, the third Mario Betancourt, his chin bore a bright red crescent mark that faded to silver by the time he could talk. The doctor claimed it was damage done to the child with forceps at birth, but inwardly, Margarita disagreed.

Aside from that scar, there was no indication that Mario Betancourt harbored the souls of his brothers within him, and there was no way of proving that his soul was on its third try on earth. But Margarita believed it wholly, would sometimes tell the young Mario stories set during the days of his past lives. The child would come to know three sets of birthdays, each celebrated meagerly, but with joy. He was named for the three saint days of his three births—Mario Juan Damian Betancourt.

Margarita tried for another child in the years after Mario's birth. Because Ricardo had told her he liked women with long hair, Margarita refused to cut hers, in the hope of enticing her husband into bed more often. By Mario's fourth birthday, his mother's hair reached her hips in a tangle of curls, and her dress was so torn that it flapped at her ankles, making her seem like a ghost that floated to and fro on the plantation. When a baby did come, at long last, another boy, he too died a few days after birth. This time, Margarita settled both the baby and Mario in her arms. The two of them watched as he shuddered, as a white ring developed around his mouth, and the room filled with the scent of his passing—a smell like diluted nutmeg. "Do you smell it?" Margarita asked. "His sweet soul?" And Mario had nodded, sí, mami, sí.

Margarita wasn't the same afterwards. She began talking to herself in the small hut, adding to the steady trickling of voices in that place. One day, a little over a week after the baby's death, when she was still bleeding from it, Margarita disrobed and stood in the middle of the cane field, naked to all of the plantation, her hair whipping about her, Medusa-like, in the stiff sea breeze, howling like an animal in a trap, blood running thick down her leg.

Mario watched it happen, and claimed that he dreamed of her that way, in nightmare upon nightmare. Sometimes, too, he'd dream of his infant brothers, with hollowed-out eyes and tiny mouths that chanted all of their names in a horrific chorus. But those deaths, and his mother's madness, were not the worst of the story. The plantation overseer, a man named Rubén Oviedo, was on horseback the morning Margarita stood naked in the cane field. Mario heard the galloping horse before he saw it, and knew it could only be Oviedo, a figure who had taken on monstrous properties in his imagination. Surely, thought Mario, Oviedo had fangs instead of teeth, and that whip of his, coiled at his waist, was a stinging tail. Ricardo, Mario's father, had urged Mario to stay away from Oviedo, and should he ever come upon the boy, he advised Mario to stare at Oviedo's feet and check for cloven hooves, but never, ever look up at the overseer. Mario and Oviedo had crossed paths twice—once without any repercussion, for Oviedo had just trotted past Mario without so much as a glance in the boy's direction, and a second time, when Mario had been digging in a mud puddle and Oviedo, horseless this time, had snuck up behind him and said, "Take a bath in it, negrito," then, left, chuckling at a joke Mario did not understand.

This time, Mario watched as Oviedo swooped down and pulled Margarita by her long hair onto his horse. He'd wrapped the dark curls three times around his forearms before yanking her up, and she'd flown, it seemed, over the saddle, landing on the pommel with a thud. Oviedo paused only to look around, and his gaze caught Mario's, who only whimpered where he stood. Then, Oviedo galloped away with Margarita, naked and helpless, deep into the cane field.

Later that night, Ricardo took Mario with him to the house, to beg for his wife's life. Don Peregrino himself had ushered Ricardo into the sitting room, a large space with low tables and chairs upholstered in gold velvet. White shutters graced each window, and the light poured through the slats like beams from a lighthouse.

"We cannot have a mad woman on the plantation, Ricardo," Don Peregrino said.

"Sí, señor," Ricardo answered, his eyes staring directly at Don Peregrino's feet.

"She's a liability," Don Peregrino said.

"She's my wife, señor," Ricardo answered. "And the boy's mother," he added, patting Mario's head.

Don Peregrino shook his head. "She may yet recover," he said. Ricardo looked up with eyes wide. His lips parted, but he did not speak.

"Recover?" Mario asked, and his little voice was a like a whip cracking in the room. The adults looked at him sharply. "But she was not hurt when she was taken," Mario persisted. That was when Ricardo grabbed the boy and clamped his hand over the boy's mouth.

"Cállate," Ricardo whispered fiercely.

"If she recovers from her injuries, we shall return the woman to you. But hear me, Ricardo, another disruption to the peace we have here will not be tolerated." Don Peregrino said all of this without taking his eyes off of Mario, the way a person talks when in the presence of a dangerous creature, like a toxic snake or caimán.

Ricardo waited a full year to see Margarita again. Certain she was dead, though Don Peregrino insisted the woman was still recovering from whatever wounds she'd incurred that day that Oviedo took her away on his horse, Ricardo began to shape a new life for himself, which included meeting secretly with other slaves from plantations all over Matanzas, men who would later stage slave rebellions, and, after that, join the insurrectionists in the war of independence. When at last Ricardo and Mario saw Margarita again, she arrived in the hut carrying a baby girl.

"Our daughter," she'd said, though the child was fair-skinned and her ears fanned out like a carriage with the doors open.

"Peregrino's ears," Ricardo remarked, turning his back on Margarita.

As for Mario, he was smitten by his baby sister, and asked to hold her again and again. When Margarita returned to the cane field it was Mario's job to care for the baby, whom Margarita had named Regla. At night, Mario slept next to little Regla, his body curved like a sickle around hers. The baby learned to walk holding onto her brother's fingers. She would eat well for him, opening her mouth to the spoon like a fledgling bird. Her skin was the color of driftwood, and her nose had tiny freckles all over it. Mario would run his fingers on her nose, tapping the dots and counting them. Regla would laugh as if she knew what he was talking about.

By 1886, Ricardo had helped organize two unsuccessful slave rebellions deep in Matanzas, on another plantation. No one connected him to the events, though the rebellions made life on the Peregrino plantation more difficult, as Peregrino gave Oviedo a freer hand in disciplining the slaves. Ricardo and Margarita were spared punishment, for they knew never to look at Oviedo, but to stare only at his feet. But the sound of the whip whizzing through the thick, tropical air could be heard at all hours of the day. Margarita was allowed to abandon her work in the field to care for the hurt slaves. Mario sometimes went with her. He would snap off aloe stems from the small garden his family kept, and rub the plant's glossy sap onto the slaves' small cuts. The long, burning lacerations were up to his mother to tend, and these she packed with clean cloths soaked in salted water.

Mario was six years old when he was freed, along with all of Cuba's slaves. The whole enterprise of carting humans across the Atlantic, breeding them, killing them, and starting over again had become an embarrassment to Spain. Even the Americans had washed their hands of the practice. Besides, the slave rebellions were becoming increasingly intolerable. "Just look at Haiti," the landowners would say to one another, fear bubbling to the surface of their skin, nearly cracking that stoic, Spanish façade these men seemed to have perfected.

When the news of their freedom reached them at last, Ricardo ran around their hut, shouting for joy. Cuquita got down on her ancient knees and prayed to her gods, and Margarita held up Regla and Mario and twirled them around, both children crying out joyfully.

That very night, three men arrived at the hut looking for

Ricardo. They were former slaves of the Requejo sugar plantation nearby. Mario could not remember their names, but swore
he would recognize them anywhere, for one of the men had a
scar on his scalp that ran from one ear to the other, parting his
hair like a line on a map. Another was the tallest man Mario
had ever seen. He'd had to duck to get into the hut, and the
top of his head scraped the ceiling. The third man's ears were
like two tiny seashells. At the time, Mario had wondered if he
could hear at all.

They carried unlit torches in their hands, and machetes
were tied to their waists with frayed rope.

"Tonight," the one with the small ears said, "is for paying
them back."

Ricardo seemed to know at once what they meant. "Where
will my family go afterwards? We cannot stay here."

"East, hombre. To Oriente. There are safe places to stay
along the way," the very tall man said. His voice seemed to
shake the very earth under their feet. Mario could not help
himself—he crept closer to the giant man.

"Bueno. Pack light," Ricardo said to the women in the
house, and left with the men, arguing over who had the flint
and which place might take light the quickest.

Margarita waited until Ricardo and the men were out of
sight. "Say nothing," she told Mario, handing the baby over to
him. Then, she ran into the night, in the opposite direction
from the one Ricardo had taken.

Mario stayed in the hut as he was commanded, feeding his
baby sister a bottle of goat's milk, and listening to his grandmother tell a story in Yoruba, which he did not understand
save for a word or two. A large crack, like a massive tree falling,
caught his attention at one point, and when he threw open the
door of the hut, he saw the plantation house in flames, bright
tongues of fire licking at the windows on the eastern side of the
home. On the west, the fire did not yet rage, but smoke, black

and billowy, poured from the windows there. Whoever was inside, Mario knew, was trapped.

Mario could not have known then that one of those people was his mother.

It was Peregrino's deaf-mute daughter who told them, after the fire had consumed the entire house. She'd run into the woods, sooty-cheeked, her eyes wild, coughing and gagging when she saw Ricardo, Lidia, Cuquita, and the children hiding. Ricardo had meant for them to go east with the three men, but Margarita was nowhere to be found, so they waited for the conflagration to gut itself out in the hopes that she would appear. Peregrino's daughter threw her arms around Ricardo's neck and cried. When he peeled her off of him, she clutched his face and mouthed the word, "Perdón," a few times before Ricardo understood. "Your wife," she mouthed, and tears filled her eyes. The girl held her arms out to Regla, who thrust pudgy hands in the girl's direction. Now, their faces so close together, it was clear that the two were sisters. No one could mistake it.

"Margarita tried to warn you? About the fire?" Ricardo said slowly so that the girl could read his lips. She nodded, and nuzzled Regla's hair.

"She loved us," the girl mouthed. Her bottom lip trembled and an odd, grunting sound escaped her, as if she were trying to say more.

Mario remembered the fury in his father's eyes most clearly, how that fury turned to tears, and how his face reshaped itself into a grimace. "Keep the baby," he said to Peregrino's daughter. "She's none of mine."

"No, Papá!" Mario cried, tugging on his father's arms, which had gone limp.

"You must choose, Mario," Ricardo said, his voice flat, his lip curled as if he'd tasted something that had gone sour. "Stay with the women, or come with me."

In the end, Mario chose his father, who did not even give him a chance to kiss his grandmothers or his sister goodbye, or to weep for his mother. They wailed in the woods, left behind with Peregrino's daughter, who joined the chorus of cries after a while, grunting like an animal, which was all she could do. Soon, Mario and Ricardo, heading east as planned, could no longer hear them.

8

Thoughts on Cosmic Justice

N o puedo mas," Mireya says, standing and marching to the door. She wiggles the handle and finds that we are locked in. She pounds the wood, shouting, "Let me out! I can't stand another moment!"

Of my stories? I wonder. Or of this confinement?

"Why is the door locked?" Susana asks, and joins Mireya, twisting the crystal knob hard. Then, she too starts knocking on the door.

Soon, a few other women have begun shouting, including Rosalia, who squeaks, "¡Auxilio!" as if she's being physically hurt.

It looks as if Dulce is struggling to control her breathing, so I sit beside her. Estrella runs to the window, throws it open, and starts to shout, "They've locked us in!" She does this for a bit, then stops midsentence. "I don't see anyone outside," she says in a small voice.

Celia fishes a piece of paper and a pen from her purse, scribbles a note on the paper, and slides it under the door. Then, she sits very quietly on the bed and closes her eyes, her lips moving a little.

"What if they've all left? What if they've locked up the house and forgotten us?" Dulce is asking me, and I am telling her, no, this is not possible. I tell her to listen carefully. There are the sounds of wood creaking, and pipes knocking.

"Casa Velázquez is full of people," I say. I imagine this place back when it was new, and the ladies of the house walked about in full skirts that swept the floors. I imagine that the sound of lapping water outside is actually the noise their dresses must have made against the floors and walls.

Mireya is jamming a hairpin into the lock of the door, while Susana, pale all of a sudden, sits down on the floor and clamps a hand over her mouth.

Finally, the doorknob turns, and Ofelia pushes her way inside.

"You've locked us in," Mireya yells at her, jabbing a thick finger into Ofelia's shoulder. Fear washes over the soldier's face for a moment, but is then replaced by anger.

"Of course I locked the door," Ofelia says, her voice booming. The women take a step away from her. "There are looters in Santiago. It was for your safety."

"The Marco Polo dishes?" Estrella asks.

"Gone," Ofelia says. "As are the Tiffany lamps that were in the dining room downstairs. Animals, I tell you. The country is overrun with animals." She runs her hands through her curly hair.

"They didn't get these!" Estrella says, her laughter a bark as she holds up two of the dishes from the dining room.

Ofelia smiles, her shoulders relaxing a moment when, suddenly, a gun goes off on the floor beneath us. Ofelia spins and leaves, closing the door and locking it behind her. We hear two more shots before there is silence. The fearsome noise has set a few of the women to weeping, and all but Mireya have pulled away from the door and huddled in the corners of the room. But Mireya continues to slam her fist into the wood, shouting for someone to let her out.

"Please, calm down," Susana is saying.

Mireya begins to kick the door, and when her shoe goes flying off her foot, she pounds the door with a calloused heel.

"Stop it, just stop!" Rosalia says, shuffling towards Mireya. "Get away from the door, you could be shot." Rosalia tugs at Mireya's arm.

"Miren," Estrella says, and opens her purse to reveal a

series of small photo albums with pictures of her twin sons in them. "A distraction," she says, handing the albums out to the women. Her boys are dark-haired and pout-lipped, with curls atop their heads like little rooster combs. "They're fifty-three years old now, can you imagine? You all must have pictures, yes? Let's see them. Come, come," Estrella says, and she points at our purses.

"I have some, too," Celia says. "Just a few I could grab at the last minute." She shares photos of her own twin boys. Suddenly, Estrella and Celia are talking animatedly about things the rest of us don't understand. "The boys grew up together," Celia explains when we ask. "Four boys, two sets of twins, all living on the same street in Maisí."

How hadn't I noticed the two of them, Estrella and Celia, clearly old friends? I look at Mireya and wish I could turn back the clock, reverse the damage done to our friendship. It would be good, I think, to have a dear friend in this place.

Now, more of the women are sharing photographs. The little frame with Mayito's picture stays in my pocket. I finger it gently and close my eyes, remembering my own little boy, and the way his tiny fingers curled around my thumb.

I overhear Susana describing a picture she is holding. "My great-uncle," she says. "He died laughing."

"Lucky man," Rosalia says, and then giggles herself.

"Mireya, you must have a picture or two in this giant purse of yours," Dulce says, tugging at the straps of Mireya's bag.

Mireya leaves the door at last, opens her purse, and pulls out a yellow envelope, fat with photographs.

The pictures are going from hand to hand, and I hold each of them. Here are Celia's twin boys—one blond, one dark, both with narrow eyes set close together, so that they appear to be conspiring some strange deed. Here are Dulce's grandchildren and great-grandchildren, all sitting about the Malecón in Havana, a stiff breeze blowing their curls. I ponder the frozen motion of it, the gravity-defying trickery of a camera lens, before Susana snatches the photograph away and another lands in my hands.

This one is of Alejandro. It is a professional portrait of a young man in a suit, his face made smooth and glowing by the camera's soft focus. He peers to the left of the lens, his red lips parted just a touch, his long fingers folded together in his lap. This was the boy my Beatríz loved, ten years before he died. I run my thumb over his face.

"Don't you dare," Mireya says, startling me. Then she takes the picture from me, shouting, "Your fault! Your fault my Alejandro is gone from this world!" She shoves me hard in the shoulder. I start to take one of my slippers off, thinking to strike her with it, the way mothers spank children when they've pushed their limits of patience.

"What's wrong with you?" Susana says, holding Mireya back. Mireya falls to the floor, sobbing.

I join her on the floor and wrap my arms around my old friend. "I don't know what you mean," I whisper to her. "I don't know what I've done to hurt you."

Mireya looks up at me with distant eyes, so red and swollen that I think that she has not felt any joy in a very long time, and I am awash with sympathy. We are alike, so very alike, I think for the first time, and feel my eyes filling with tears too.

Mireya is about to say something when Ofelia returns to us. Her hands are trembling, and her hair is wild, as if she has been running her fingers through it again and again. Her eyeliner is smeared and her pale lipstick is long gone. She no longer looks like a woman of the times, but like the pictures of ancient Egyptians in books and museums—dark-eyed and haunted.

"What happened?" Rosalia asks.

"We caught someone shooting at an ibis that had perched on a windowsill. He could have killed someone," she says.

"Ay," Dulce says, crossing herself.

"He's just a boy," she says, still trembling and damp. "He's been arrested." She pauses again, looking off into the distance. When she speaks again, it is as if she is talking to herself. "Skinny, shirtless boy. Using a military issue gun, too. God knows where he—" Ofelia says, but her gaze falls upon Mireya and me on the floor. In an instant she composes herself and is all action again.

"Ven conmigo," she says to Mireya.

Mireya shakes her head. "No, it's fine. I just wanted the door unlocked. I'm better now."

Ofelia rubs her eyes, kneeling beside Mireya. "I need to make sure we don't have any leaks. I could use the help," Ofelia says.

"Bueno," Mireya says, and allows herself to be helped to her feet. Ofelia struggles a bit until Estrella offers a hand. Then, Ofelia ushers Mireya out the door. Mireya has left Alejandro's portrait behind, and I tuck it into my pocket to sit with Mayito's frame. Our two lost boys, I think, will keep each other company.

Susana helps me to a seat next to Dulce again, who is toying with her painted fan again. Even though she keeps her watery eyes trained on her fan, she speaks to me softly, and I can feel my nerves calming as she talks. "I am sorry that bad things have happened and are happening to you."

"I'm fine—"

"There is no cosmic justice. This is just life, me entiendes?" I take Dulce's papery hand in mine and squeeze a little. Perhaps she is right, that there is no reason to suffering, no fair dealing when it comes to meting out bliss and pain. There are just choices, and the echoes of those choices.

The photos go around until they have returned to their owners. They are put away carefully, tenderly.

"We never saw any of your photos," Celia says to me.

"I didn't bring them," I tell her, adjusting my dress.

Celia's brow furrows, and she opens her mouth to say something when Dulce interrupts her. "Tell your story, María Sirena. Go on."

When I resume the story, the women fall quiet, and I think that my voice has come to resemble the sound the rain makes—a feature of the current landscape, broken up by passing flashes of light by which we see more clearly.

9.
Gestures of Inheritance

My mother's recovery from the fever went quickly, and the months since Agustín left us at the tallér came tumbling by like river water. Not all of those days were unhappy. Every woman and child there had a role to play. Lulu took charge of the children's schooling, and she taught the little ones to read and write and to manipulate numbers, the older ones to recite poetry and compose clear letters. We also learned how to polish and sharpen machetes, and how to clean rifles and pistols. We kept a small garden and raised chickens and goats. In the shadows of that rich valley, the tallér was a secret place, the kind of green and lush corner of the world one read about in books, where duendes and adas flitted inside flower blossoms, granting wishes.

As for Mario, his fingers were meant for weapons. Dulled machetes became deadly again in his hands. His father, Captain Ricardo Betancourt, helped Mario set up a smithy during one of his return trips and taught the boy simple blacksmithing. The tools the captain brought with him all bore Spanish insignias, and he'd laughed, saying that at least one Spanish cavalry unit would have to go without equipment.

As Mario worked in that furnace of a place, Marcela and Graciela, the twins, would loiter to watch, sweat collecting on their upper lips and under their arms. It was worth it, they'd said to me, to watch the boy work, shirtless, whistling as he labored.

"What are you talking about?" I'd asked them.

"Don't be stupid," Graciela said. She was the rough-tongued one, often in trouble for cursing. "He's a beautiful specimen."

"There's no one else worth looking at," Marcela added. They were sixteen that summer, and had outgrown their girl-sized dresses. Graciela had become, overnight, all hips. And Marcela, who was her fraternal twin, was all chest. I'd overheard one of the boys say that each was half a woman. I'd blushed and run away from the conversation, understanding what the boy meant. I didn't need to learn about sex from the older children, or at least not the mechanics of it. My mother had shared her bed with Julio Reyes for years while I had tried very hard to sleep. And yet, discussions about boys among the girls in the tallér suddenly gathered a different meaning. Bodies became something I noticed—who was hairy, who was fit or fat, whose hand I wanted to hold.

To hear the twins talk about Mario in this way, to know that they dreamed of doing things with him in the dark, caused a curious feeling in me. I was unsettled around the girls. Once, I pulled a chair out from under Graciela just as she was about to sit down. She rose and slapped me hard for the prank. When her mother asked me why I did it, I could only shrug. I had no idea myself. I would try to make it up to the twins by picking flowers for them, or offering to braid their hair, but then I'd see them eyeing Mario and it was like a small furnace had been lit in my chest, and I'd pull their hair too hard while I braided, yanking out a strand at a time until I was slapped again.

Lulu arched her eyebrows at the twins whenever she saw them sweaty and breathless, returning from a trip to Mario's smithy. "Have some pride," she'd said to them once in the middle of a history lesson, when she'd caught the twins writing their names alongside Mario's, encasing their fine calligraphy inside hearts.

It all ended when their mother, Bernarda, learned what the girls had been up to. "¿Un negro?" she'd shouted again and again, her voice growing shriller each time. She'd dragged Marcela and Graciela away by the hair, a twin in each hand, and we could all hear how she beat them, and how they screamed, "¡No, mamá!"

Later, the women would sit down with Bernarda and reprimand her. They would say that the spirit of the revolution was one of equality, that Mario was one of them, despite his color. But when Bernarda turned on them, saying, "What if one of your children took up with a negro? I don't believe you'd be so idealistic then," the others said nothing.

As for Mario, he seemed not to have noticed any of it. At first, I thought that perhaps he was slow. I remembered the story of his mother, and I wondered if that sad past hadn't affected him in some way, so that he lacked perceptiveness. How could he not have noticed the twins, the way they prepared his plate during mealtimes, presenting it to him as if it were some terrific gift, when all we seemed to eat was eggs and white rice, with an occasional bit of chicken and a glass of goat's milk?

Later, I realized that he had not paid attention to the twins because he was busy watching me. I learned this the day he was brought to the tallér half dead. He'd gone off to war the day of his sixteenth birthday. We'd said goodbye in the morning, outside of the tents, by the river. It was a long, dark moment for us, for I was imagining Mario shot and killed, and he read the anguish in my face at once. "Don't worry," he'd said. "I'll be back. I'm fast. I'm good with a gun, you know that." I'd nodded, and he'd pinched my cheek playfully, then was gone, disappearing into the thick woods in search of a regiment he might join. He'd return several times that year, and with each return, he seemed more grown, the contours of his face hardened a bit more, the veins in his forearms more distinct. I noticed all of these things simply at first, the way one notices a change in the weather—Look, it's raining. Or, look, Mario's hair has been cut. Later, I noticed the details of his face and body with a consuming attention. Lulu always said that a person in love loses her appetite, and that was the first indication to me of the condition of my heart. When Mario was in the tallér, meals made me nauseous. The very smell of that rare bit of meat cooking, which once would have made me shake my hips happily and dance around the kitchen, now made me clutch at my stomach. Mario was all the food I needed, and I fed my eyes and ears with the sights and sounds of him. At night, I dreamed about him, so that I was exhausted at all hours and my mother began to suspect that I'd caught dengue fever. She'd hover around me, clamping her palm to my forehead to check my temperature every so often, forcing me to down glass after glass of manzanilla tea, the fragrant plant growing in abundance in our garden.

I've often asked myself why I loved him so. Perhaps the answer is simple. Fausto and the other boys in the tallér were unattractive imps, always playing practical jokes and speaking in crude riddles whenever one of us girls happened to pass by. Coddled by their mothers who did their work for them, the boys became spoiled. Mario, motherless, knew no pampering. So he toiled unafraid. He was patient. He was handsome. And I was utterly lost in his presence.

At last, Mario was brought to the tallér in a makeshift stretcher, stitched together from Spanish uniforms. He had taken a bullet in the calf, and it had bled so much that the men in his company thought he would die. The tallér was sometimes used as a field hospital when a battle was waged nearby, and on that day, we had five other men brought to us, all of them bleeding, some of them calling for their mothers, for they were very young; another raved, "whip, whip," and twitched as if he were being lashed; and Lulu said something about the tragedy that was slavery and the courage of men in a company such as this one, made up of so many of Cuba's black sons.

Lulu set me to watch the men for fevers. She taught me how to lay my fingernails flat on their foreheads. "If you can feel heat through your nails, they're feverish." She taught me how to lay a wet cloth gently over a wounded man's eyes, shushing him as I did so, lest he think that the sudden darkness was death coming for him. She showed me how to air the cloth so that it would cool, then lay it down again. Meanwhile, the women tended to wounds. Lulu, in particular, was good with the needle and surgeon's thread. Around me I could hear the sound of shrapnel being plucked out of bodies and plunked onto the tin plates we used for eating. The men's moans became background noise, the way thunder goes unheard when a storm lingers too long.

I had not known at first that Mario was among the wounded. I did not learn of it until I'd laid my fingernails on his forehead, so intent was I on doing my job. Here was a man who felt as if he were on fire. A bloody shirt had been wrapped around his head, obscuring part of his face. As I turned to get a fresh cloth, his arm shot up, and he grabbed my wrist hard.

"María Sirena," he whispered, "is it bad? Do I look too terrible?"

"Oh," I said, and got a good look at Mario. My stomach rolled over. The shirt wrapped around his head was soaked red. His upper lip was swollen, as if he'd shoved his head into a beehive. The scar on his chin was crusty with blood, too. I gripped his hand in mine and said, "You are as handsome as ever."

He could not laugh for the pain, though his eyes crinkled at the corners. Then, he started murmuring something about wooden boxes and rusty machetes, and here and there he said words in a language I did not understand. Sometimes, he said his own names—Mario, Juan, Damian—and I grew afraid that the souls of his brothers were trying to claim him, to make him one of them.

"¡Mamá!" I cried out for Lulu, who came running and began to work on Mario's injuries at once.

"Go, María Sirena," she urged me when Mario bit through his lip, slamming his fists onto the table where he lay. The injured had been laid on our worktables, and in the hurry to put them there, tools were strewn on the floor, which we tripped over getting around the wounded men.

I was backing away when I heard Mario say, "No te vayas, Sirenita." The anguish in his voice froze me to the spot. He held out a trembling hand, which I took. I put my head on his chest as my mother worked on his leg, listening to his heart-beat, making sure it kept pounding. Mario's breath came out in rough gusts, and I could feel it warm on the back of my head. All along, I was thinking of the story Lulu had told me about falling in love with Agustín, how she'd mended him, and put her ear to his chest just this way. Her tender gesture had recurred with me, like an inherited thing. At one point, I noticed Lulu looking at me, and her eyes were full of tears. Later, she'd tell me that that was the moment she'd known that Mario was for me, and I was for him, and that she'd started grieving right then and there because she knew that our love would amount to tragedy.

The soldiers were moved to a shady spot in the valley and rested on hammocks strung between thick silk-cotton trees. I would sit on the ground, my legs crossed beneath me, and read to Mario in that perpetual twilight, for the trees obscured the sun at all hours. It took Mario a month to heal. In that time, I brought him meals, and read to him from the scant books we'd acquired over the years. His favorite was a biblical story, the *Song of Solomon*.

Whenever I read the line that went, "Do not stare at me because I am black, because I am darkened by the sun," my voice would quiver. I was sure Mario had caught me staring at him more than once, though my stares had nothing to do with the color of skin.

"You're a good reader," he'd remark, putting me at ease. It was a compliment that proved meaningful later in my life, when I made a living reading stories to men. Back in the tallér, Mario's kind observation made me blush, and I'm afraid I went too far, offering to read to him all day. Surely, I must have bored him, but he always agreed to listen.

Mario never once laid a finger on me, though, occasionally, he'd ruffle my hair and I would tingle all over, as if all of my limbs had gone to sleep at his touch. But when Mario was healed at last, he left to join a new company on a damp summer morning, without so much as an "adios" in my direction.

I was newly fifteen when he returned again. It was my most beautiful year, just as the saying goes. It was always said of ugly women that they were never fifteen years old. I'd gained weight in the right places, so that I wore some of Lulu's dresses. Occasionally, we would leave the tallér, risking riding by rail to Havana to visit the shops there. Lulu and I would return with bolts of cloth to make clothes for the women and children of the tallér, using money that Agustín and some of the other returning soldiers brought us. I began wearing shirt-waists and bell-shaped skirts, though I'd looked at the tight bodices and the enormous mutton-sleeved shirts in the shop windows with longing. I stuffed the shoulders of my shirtwaists with newspaper to create that little ruffled bump I'd seen on the more fashionable clothes in Havana. Lulu called me ridiculous, but I didn't care. Sometimes, I stuffed my shirt, too, and I'd walk around the tallér like a peacock, my chest thrust out, my hips swinging side to side.

It wasn't as if I had a reason to show off in the tallér. I knew I was approaching the age at which many young women married, but there was work to be done, a Cuba needing liberation, Lulu always said. "A man will come later into your life. For now, Cuba is all the man you need." She always uttered these patriotic sentiments with a lifted chin. Sometimes, she recited a snippet of a poem appropriate to the moment. Often, the poems were those of Martí, and her eyes would water as she recited. Then, she'd make the sign of the cross for the repose of Martí's soul.

I had gotten into an argument with Lulu that morning over one of these patriotic moments of hers. We'd been eating breakfast with the others when one of the children, a new boy named Sabino, complained about having to eat the same eggs and plantain tortillas we ate every day. "Where is the toast?" he whined. His mother, a small-boned young woman whose husband was a lieutenant in the Liberation Army, said nothing to reprimand Sabino. It was clear the boy commandeered his mother.

"Toast is a small sacrifice to make, young man," Lulu said in her haughty voice. "Imagine what your father has given up, the dangers he is facing in order to secure your liberty from the Spanish tyrants." While she spoke, she pointed her fork at the boy, a bit of egg dangling from one of the tines.

For some reason, that tiny speck of egg stirred my adolescent fury. How uncouth my mother was, I thought. Such patriotic airs she puts on. My whole body felt overheated. Embarrassed by her, I blurted, "Ay, be quiet for once, Mamá. No one wants to hear another lecture."

Everyone went silent at once. Forks and knives were set down gently. I had gone too far, and I knew it the moment that last word left my lips.

"Do you think you're grown, María Sirena?" Lulu asked calmly. "Do you think you know anything at all about the world?"

I shouldn't have said a thing. I should have apologized at once for my impudence and eaten my food in silence. But I could not. My tongue twitched with a response, my cheeks flooded with heat, and before I could stop myself, I said, "Sí, I'm grown! And I know better than to bore people with ridiculous poems and long diatribes."

Lulu was on her feet in a flash. Before I knew what she was doing, she'd thrust her hand into my shirt and drawn out the crumpled newspapers, deflating me on the spot. "Atrevida, who is the ridiculous one now?" she yelled, throwing the balled-up pages onto my plate.

I ran from the table, out of the tent, and past the pens where the goats and chickens were kept. It was raining, and now and then, thunder boomed. Somewhere, I left a shoe behind, like Cinderella, but didn't care. When I reached the banks of the River Cauto, I stopped, out of breath, crying in great jags. We were both ridiculous; that was the truth. I've seen it before, what mothers and daughters can do to one another during those terrible adolescent years. Grief must be at the bottom of it, for what is sadder for a parent than seeing her daughter shedding girlhood drop by precious drop? And what is more terrifying for a child than to doubt her mother, to begin to see her as a human with faults instead of as a goddess?

Mindlessly, I began to shed my outer clothes. I was already soaked from the rain, so I left my dress in a wet heap by the shore. I was so angry that I was chewing the inside of my cheek and drawing blood. I stepped into the water in only my underthings. The currents swirled around my legs, unsteadying me. The waters roiled, mingling with the rain. The drops on my head felt heavy, and it made me feel better. No one would come looking for me here, I knew. Lulu, especially, who disliked the rain, would stay indoors and wait for me to appear, contrite and pliable again. I would not have it! Convinced that my mother was at the root of all my problems, I began to catalog her sins in my head. My mother was a show-off. That was clear in the way she recited poetry all the time, as if to let the other mothers know that she would have been a teacher had it not been for the patriotic spirit that had consumed her. She was a disgrace. I could recall with precision the way her face would soften in the presence of handsome men. Closing my eyes, I could mimic the expression. It was a sleepy look, one that called to mind beds and dark places and skin smooth like the inside of an almond.

Before I knew it, I was in the middle of the river, which wasn't very deep in that place. I splashed my face with the cool water and tried to recall more of my mother's faults. The thoughts wouldn't come. The truth was, I admired Lulu a great deal. Whenever anyone suggested that we looked alike, I beamed with pride. I would purposely sit out in the sun in the hopes that freckles, like the ones Lulu had, would appear on my nose. I would squeeze lemons, rubbing the juice on my arms and head to lighten the hair on my body. Lulu was auburn-haired and I wanted to look like her twin. My anger began to fade.

What happened next may have been a hallucination brought on by anger or injury. I loathe admitting that. But I have not seen this vision since, nor hope to see it ever again, for it was terrifying, and yet familiar. Lulu had had a similar vision years earlier. Perhaps it was a delusion. Even as I tell it, I'm wondering if delusions, like gestures, can be inherited.

There, in the river, I saw a flash of silver in the water. At first, I thought it might be a fish. It appeared again downriver, and I tried to get closer. Rain got into my eyes and I blinked it away. The silver thing was too big to be a fish. Perhaps it was a sunken canoe, I thought, but I wondered why the current hadn't pushed it away. I drew closer. The silver thing, shaped like an enormous guitar, twitched then, swam farther away. Red, hairlike streamers seemed to follow in its wake. I say they were hairlike because I wasn't sure at the moment what in the world I was looking at. It wasn't until I remembered the story of my birth, of the mermaid who had spoken to my mother, that I had an inkling of what the silver thing could be. I swore I saw a pair of hands, white like milk, and the streamers were actually wavy strands of hair, and the silver, guitar-shaped thing was a body with a tail fin, scales sparkling in gray. She turned in the water a few feet ahead of me, beckoning me with pointed fingers, thin and crooked like twigs. I took three steps towards her, thinking that perhaps she would grant me a wish. "I wish my mother would understand me. I wish Mario would love me," I said under my breath as I approached her. The mermaid's face was placid, her rosy lips parted as if she were about to speak. When my feet got tangled in a net caught between a pair of heavy rocks, I fell into the water and got a good look at her. Under the surface her beauty slipped away, revealing a dry, brittle thing, like a scarecrow, like a felled tree. I screamed underwater and swallowed some. I tried to stand, coughing, managing to get my head above water. There was a great crack of light, and the sound was deafening, as if I'd been slapped with a pan. Down I went again, and this time, the mermaid was only a fallen tree, the bark coming off in long strip that scraped my face. Then I felt the burning of water in my lungs, and the water blackened around me, as if someone had poured a bottle of ink into the river that bloomed and spread, choking the air from my body.

When I woke, I was on shore, and Mario was hovering over me, his hands on my stomach, pressing down on me with all his might. I rose up as if pulled by strings, and vomited on his shoes.

"Gracias a Diós," he said, scooping me up in his arms and kissing the top of my head.

"I'm dizzy," I said. Water fell off the top of Mario's head onto my face. The rain sounded like a million drums being played at once. Lightning lit the shore for an instant, and I cringed against Mario. My head throbbed, and it felt as if my shoulder were burning. When I reached to touch it, Mario held my hand.

"The lightning. I saw it strike a tree above your head. It knocked down a branch that fell on you." His face was tight with concern, which made me afraid. My right arm had gone limp, and I was having trouble hearing on that side. In fact, my right cheek felt hot, as if I'd been slapped. Carefully, I peeled back my undershirt's collar to take a look at my shoulder. It was scraped, a thin layer of skin shredded and lifted, like the outside of an onion. I winced at the sight of it, and Mario helped me to put my shirt back in place. His hands trembled as he did so.

Hail began to pound into us, big pieces the size of marbles. I screamed when they bounced off my shoulder, and was up in Mario's arms at once. He ran under a little outcrop of rock several yards from the river. It was a dry, mossy place. The hail scattered over the rock and came down on our feet, but we were able to keep our heads and bodies dry.

"You're back," I said, sniffing. The smell of the river was trapped in my nose.

"Our regiment is just north of here, on an abandoned sugar plantation. I thought I'd come see you. I can hear the cornets sounding if trouble comes." As he spoke, he kept his gaze fixed on the wound on my shoulder.

"You came to see me?" I asked. My stomach was a knot of tension. I thought I might even vomit again.

"Sí. If that is all right." He picked up a shard of hail. It was the size of a peso. Already, it was melting in his hand.

"Of course it is," I said. I gathered some of the hail, too. At first, we said nothing as we picked up one piece of ice after another and watched them melt in our hands. When he reached across me to get to a perfectly round and smooth hailstone, his arm pressed against my bosom. I held my breath. Mario squared his jaw, the muscles in his face flexing, as he pulled away slowly.

"Perdón," he said softly.

"No hay de que," I answered, but I crossed my arms tightly around myself. "Did you really come back to see me?" I asked.

Mario nodded. I said nothing. I would have, but my throat was full and I was trying hard not to burst into tears. We held each other's gaze for a long time. The storm had subsided, and the woods had gone quiet, save for the rush of the river, which had swollen and grown faster with the rain. I don't even think I took a breath in that space of time. Waves of heat spread over my body as I stared into his eyes. Mario broke first, looking away and clearing his throat.

"I love you, María Sirena. You know that," he said.

I nodded and took a long, trembling breath. The truth was, I hadn't known. I'd been full of doubt, but Lulu had always told me never to complicate a conversation with unnecessary explanations. "During battles," he whispered, "my mission, my real mission, is to come home to you."

I started to cry in earnest now. I couldn't help myself. The soldiers we tended on occasion rarely talked about the war, and we knew never to ask for any specifics about their time spent in the wilderness, about their encounters with Spanish forces, about what they'd sacrificed, what they'd had to do. To hear Mario talk about it now felt so unfamiliar, and I knew what it cost him to do so.

"I want to know I have you to come home to, Sirenita. Every day."

I think I kissed him first, though I can't be sure. The rest of that day was spent testing one another in breathless kissing sessions, broken up by stunned silence. The sun dropped into the horizon. My clothes were still in a soaked heap by the river. The sun had broken through the clouds, drying hair and my modest underthings.

"What will we do?" Mario asked, helping me out from under the little cove. My limbs ached from sitting curled up against him, and I imagined this was what it felt like to be a crab or snail, unfurling from within a rocky carapace to stretch and meet the world.

"What do you mean?" I asked, tucking my hair back in place with long pins that had come undone. My shoulder still burned where the branch had struck me. My face hurt, too, but I was certain that had nothing to do with my injury and more to do with the hours I'd spent with Mario, his fingers digging into my cheeks as he kissed me, holding me in place as if I might flee at any moment. "You and I," Mario began, shaking his head.

I felt panicky. My heart quickened. "I know what you mean to say," I said quickly, the words racing out of my mouth. "But it's a new era. The revolution means to bring us all together, black and white. You said so yourself." I was clutching his hands tightly. Lulu would understand. Wasn't she always making speeches at dinner about equality, about the plight of Cuba's negros, of their heroism in war. She would be glad I was in love with Mario.

"That's all words," Mario said. "My regiment is all black, and in each battle we're assigned to the vanguard. Every time, María Sirena, we're at the front of the line. We're disposable. The white regiments wait for us to plow through the Spanish, and when we're sufficiently tired or enough of us are dead, they come in, machetes in the air. The great white heroes." Mario sat hard on a boulder and looked across the river. His eyes were narrowed, and I thought that he might be on the verge of tears. We were so young—seventeen and fifteen years old—and in moments like that it showed.

"They executed our captain. They said he stole ammunition from one of the white regiments. He didn't! They killed him because we were doing too well, making the white regiments look incompetent." Mario spoke with renewed energy and anger, his brow furrowed and his fists clenched. "They killed him, the bravest military man the Liberation Army has ever seen, because he was black, and we are black, and because of that we aren't allowed to be better than the others. All those battles against the Spanish devils, and it was Cubans who killed him."

"Oh, Mario, I—"

"They blindfolded my Captain then shot him. His last words were, 'Viva Cuba libre,' and still they shot him. They made us watch, María Sirena. They made us watch." Mario broke down in tears then, and sobbed in my arms. I had a feeling he wasn't telling it all. That he was holding back for my sake.

"Your father, Mario. Was it your father?" I asked in a whisper, and he nodded against me and cried harder. Orphaned at seventeen, and yet so strong, I thought. And I was all he had left in the world.

"We'll be together, Mario. You will see, you aren't alone," I murmured into his hair.

He shook his head. "The world won't allow it. I don't care what they're saying about equality, it isn't true."

"My mamá isn't like that," I said. I was surprised to find myself defending her after the fight we'd had. Still, I felt its truth in my heart—Lulu was an idealist, not a hypocrite. She'd stand with Mario and me, no matter what.

"Perhaps she isn't," he said after a while had gone by and he'd composed himself. He looked up at me, his cheeks glossy and tearstained, and smiled. I leaned over and kissed him on the lips, lingering without moving, simply breathing him in, my hero, my young knight, who smelled like leather and iron.

We were frozen that way, as if an artist had trapped us in a portrait, when I heard my name bellowed from a short distance. "¡María Sirena!" came the shout, and following it, I heard a rifle blast.

Mario and I separated with a mighty jump, and there was Agustín, nearly upon us in three quick strides, his weapon pointed at Mario.

10.
The Butcher Does His Work

L ulu and I would see Agustín once or twice a year, and each time, we were surprised he was alive. He'd return with tales from the battlefield—how he'd served under a captain who would have the men carry his rocking chair to each fight, so that he might sit in it, smoke a cigar, and read a newspaper when the fighting started, impressing the Spanish with his nonchalance. The instant his newspaper would tear— either by bullet or debris—then the captain would rise and shout, "¡Viva Cuba libre!" and enter the fray. Another time, Agustín told the sad story of a former slave from El Cotorro, who, returning to that village with his company in order to capture it, took shelter from Spanish bullets in the very house in which he'd been born, and was killed there, a bullet whizzing through a window and into his head. There were many such stories, and with each return, Agustín told a new one. I consumed them all, like fresh bread, gobbling the stories up and begging for more. By then, I'd seen many men come to the tallér, husbands and fathers of the women and children who worked there. None told stories like Agustín. In fact, most did not want to speak of what they'd seen at all. When prodded, they'd grow angry or morose, say something about wanting to forget rather than remember. But for Agustín, the war lived on in his mind like a tragic fixation. Even when he was given a respite from it for a while, he revisited the battlefield again and again.

During his visits, Agustín would stay in the tent I shared

with Lulu, and I was shunted off to stay with one of the women. At breakfast, Agustín and Lulu would sit close to one another. His hand would brush hers as he reached for a plate, or she would lay her hand on his thigh and eat that way, never budging, as if they were making up for lost time by being in constant physical connection. On a few occasions, his visit would quickly turn sour, and we could hear them fighting all across the tallér. One time, when Bernarda was still with us, Lulu had come to breakfast with a red and swollen ear. Though she'd said it was simply an infection, Bernarda picked up a broom and brought it down on Agustín's head the moment he entered the tent. "Desgraciado," she'd hissed at him, and he'd left without a word, confirming for everyone his guilt with his silence. When he came again a few weeks later, he brought violet candies for all the women, which he'd taken from a small Spanish regiment they'd beaten at the entrance of the woods of Manjuarí. He also carried three live chickens with him, dangling by their feet from a cord across his chest. The women of the tallér seemed to forgive his past offense, and welcomed him by making some fresh chicken soup.

On the day Agustín found Mario and me embracing by the river's edge, he carried nothing but an empty knapsack and his rifle. I would later learn that he was low on ammunition. He had spent one bullet already, firing it into the air above our heads. He would not waste another, not even on Mario, who he was looking at with disgust, as if he might vomit. But we didn't know that at the time, and so I wrapped my arms around Mario and closed my eyes tightly, hoping that Agustín would not risk taking a shot if it meant he might hit me.

I heard the safety mechanism on his rifle click.

"Señor, for the love of God," Mario said. He pushed me behind him. I pressed my forehead against his back and sobbed. It was unfair, so unfair, I was thinking, that I would find love and lose it this way. A few feet from us, Agustín looked down the sight of his weapon at us. He was very still, the way he stood when he hunted small game.

"God has nothing to do with this disgrace," Agustín said. He cocked his head, motioning me to step away from Mario, saying, "Go put on your clothes. You dishonor me, and you dishonor this soldier who is about to die."

"No, Papá. Leave him alone!" I squeezed my arms around Mario.

"You would let her die with you, *negro*?" Agustín asked. My breath caught in my throat. What happened to the man who'd defended Macéo, the Bronze Titan? What happened to his grand speeches about equality, about humanity and the future?

Mario undid my grip forcefully. We stared at each other a moment. "No," I said, and made as if to hold him again.

"Vete," he told me, but I insisted, lifting my arms. That's when he took my shoulders and gave me a shove. "Go, I said. It's just as I told you, isn't it? I'm just *un negro*. A throwaway." His lips trembled as he spoke, but when he turned to face Agustín, Mario grew steady again.

They stood that way for a long minute. I'd fallen to my knees, praying to *la Virgen* for protection, except I couldn't hold on to the thread of prayer. The words to the Hail Mary would fail me, the Latin verbs tangling in my mind, becoming other, wrong words. I thought of the mermaid vision and could see her driftwood face before me, compelling me to join her. Perhaps I would. Perhaps I would drown myself after Agustín murdered Mario.

Suddenly, a cornet trilled. The sound made me yelp, and I fell forward, my forehead to the ground. "My company," Mario shouted, turning in the direction of those long, diminishing notes.

Agustín slung his weapon onto his back. "Where is your gun?" he asked Mario, who indicated that he'd left it back in the tallér. Agustín unhooked a machete from his belt and thrust it at Mario. "Toma," he said. "I'll follow you." Then, they were both gone, without a word to me.

The cornets sounded mournfully, and then shots could be heard. Never had a battle come so close to the tallér. I ran back to the workshop and could hear the shouts of men, their moans and screams. Their voices seemed to prick at my back, compelling me to run faster. When I reached the tallér, the women were already in motion. Some were clearing off the worktables for the wounded who were sure to come. Others were gathering the children, strapping packs with supplies onto their small backs, and leading them away from the tallér, away from the fighting. Most were arming themselves.

Lulu put a *pistola* in my hands. It was the same one she'd always kept with her, the one that had once belonged to Aldo Alarcón. She said nothing about my clothes, or about our fight that morning. Instead, Lulu took hold of my hand and led me outside with a group of other women. She ducked back into the tent and emerged a few moments later with a fresh shirt and skirt for me, which she put gently into my hands. "We will defend the tallér," she said as we formed a line in front of our home.

We stood there for the better part of the day. The sounds of the battle being waged close by seemed to amplify in the valley. Vibrant green parrots were rooted out of the trees every so often by gunshot, and their bodies would blot the setting sun. Even then, with the cawing noises overhead and the slap of rifle fire that shook our bones, we were silent, crouched low in our long skirts, our pinned hair coming lose as the day wore on, so that we looked like wild women.

I grew impatient. I was, after all, only fifteen. I said prayers for Mario, and for Agustín, too, and when that bored me, I began to think of kissing. A warmth would flood my body then, startling me, so that I would begin to pray again. So it went, back and forth, for a long time. When Spanish forces finally broke into the valley, we were tired. Some of the women had sat on the ground and fallen asleep.

What came through the brush was a force of only twenty or so men. At the head of them was a man atop a black horse. What I remember most was the placidity of the man's eyes. For a moment, I thought he would greet us warmly, perhaps ask for our assistance, as so many men had done in the past. He held a gleaming saber in one hand, the reins of his horse in the other. Golden tassels hung from his shoulders, and these twitched in the breeze. Bushy sideburns grew on his cheeks, like moss on the trunks of trees. He was not an old man, but he seemed ancient like a tree, as if men such as he was had always existed on the earth and he was only the latest in that long, familial line. His uniform was un-mussed, even after the battle. The pistol in my hand felt cold. I wasn't sure my bullets would find their mark if I shot the gun. The man seemed that impenetrable to me. The men with him pointed their weapons at us. One was a boy, younger than I was. He hoisted a Spanish flag on a short staff and waved it slowly, as if on parade.

The man on the horse pointed his saber at us. "Viva Cuba española," he said, then, he waited. We were supposed to respond in kind, pledging our loyalty to a Spanish Cuba. The women of the tallér said nothing.

"¡Viva Cuba española!" the man yelled. This time, when we did not make a sound, he lowered his saber in a swift motion, and a single shot rang out, hitting a woman named Luisa in the head. The bullet made a cracking sound as it struck her. I cried out, and tasted her blood on my lips.

"¡Viva Cuba española!" he said again. This time, a few of the women answered the call, though weakly. Again, the saber came down, and once more, a woman was shot. This time, death came to the left of us. A woman named Leonora, who was especially good with a needle and thread, gurgled as she lay dying, saying her children's names a few times before she could no longer speak.

"¡Viva Cuba española!" the women began to say without prompting, weeping as they spoke. Again and again they said it. I began to chant the words, too. "Say it, Mamá," I was screaming in between phrases until finally, Lulu spoke, crying the entire time, holding me awkwardly, trying to shield me from the guns.

Though we didn't know it yet, we were in the presence of our greatest enemy, Governor Valeriano Weyler, the man they called "The Butcher." Later, we would learn he was on tour of the island, and had not intended on engaging in battle. His small retinue had surprised Mario's regiment, who'd settled themselves on an abandoned sugar plantation very close to the tallér. Weyler's men had set fire to the barn in which the regiment had hunkered down, and so, though they were few, the Spanish, with Weyler on horseback, were able to come away from that battle mostly unscathed.

Now, Weyler surveyed us, the women of the tallér. Our weapons, which we had not fired, were taken from us. As for my mother's pistola, it was wrenched from my grip and we never saw that gun again. Weyler ordered his men to scour the other tents. "Bring the traitors here," he'd commanded. The women and children were brought to where we stood one by one. Then came the weapons we'd been working on, dumped in a pile in front of the governor. Finally, the goats and horses were shot. I heard their grunts and whinnying, their dying bellows, and I wept. If this is how they treated our animals, I thought, what would they do to us? Then I thought of Mario. *Dios mío*, what would they do to him?

That same night, they lined us up by size, the shortest of us in front, so that the soldiers guarding the governor's back could see us all in one glance. In this way we marched all night, without stopping even once, until we reached the town of La

Cuchilla. I had to carry two children, who'd fallen and would not stand. One was a small girl whom I held in my arms, and the other was a gangly boy of about eight, who climbed onto my back and held me like a vise, his skinny arms choking me. In the end, all the able women were carrying little ones. To their credit, the children did not cry or fuss for food, though our stomachs growled as we walked. The Spanish would not let us stop even to relieve ourselves, and so by the time we reached La Cuchilla, we were all covered in urine and excrement from the little ones, whose diapers were soaked through.

La Cuchilla was barricaded all around with a tall fence of spiked posts. Guards stood at the single entrance to the town. I'd heard of these camps, where Cubans were forcibly concentrated in order to keep villagers from assisting the Liberation Army. People in the camps were called the *reconcentrados*. It was Agustín who had first described these places, cut off from food and fresh water, where Cubans were dying by the thousands of disease and starvation.

"Basta, you're scaring María Sirena," Lulu had told him after she'd heard the story, though it was evident she was frightened, too.

"She should be scared," Agustín had said then.

Now, we were thrown into the camp that was once the village of La Cuchilla. What I would have given for a *cuchilla* of my own, I remember thinking. I would have cut my wrists with it before setting foot into the camp. Already, the effects of the isolation and deprivation were evident. The trees in La Cuchilla were stripped of their bark. Though the fruit trees outside the fenced perimeter were laden with fruit—mango and papaya, guayaba and ciruellas—the trees inside were bare, the fruit having been picked and eaten even before they were ripe. Later, I'd come to learn the tricks of survival—how to eat the seeds of fruit, and how to trap small rodents and skin them, being careful not to pierce the intestines and taint the meager meat. I learned how to follow after horses ridden by Spanish cavalry, picking up grains from their feedbags that had fallen to the ground. And though the Spanish authorities tried to keep us from doing so, we ate the remains of animals that had died of unknown causes.

There was death in every *bohío*, cries of grief coming from every hut. As the Spanish marched us through the village, I caught a glimpse of a female corpse, recently dead, for there was still some color left in her gaunt cheeks, and a baby of about ten months of age, desperately nursing from his mother's exhausted breast. I broke the line trying to reach the baby, and was hit on the back of the head with the side of a rifle barrel.

"Adelante," the soldier commanded me, forcing me to keep marching onward.

They took us deep into La Cuchilla, and then we stopped. "Sit," the governor said, and we fell in worn-out heaps to the ground.

"Now drink," he said, motioning for his men to pass a clay jug of water around. We gulped, water sloshing down our necks and drenching our shirts.

"*Bien, bien,*" Weyler said. I stared hard at him, wishing a seam would open up in the earth and swallow him whole. The truth was, I'd been raised believing in Spanish oppression the way one believes in God. It was unseen, but real. Beyond Aldo Alarcón, I'd had little experience with the Spanish. Here was the face of the enemy, his eyes like black marbles, his hairy hands strong and veined. The saber was back in its sheath, but he kept one hand on it as he spoke.

"I'll need the names of your husbands, as well as their last known locations," he said. I'd expected silence. I'd expected more shooting, and for those to have been my last moments on earth, my life winked out like a candle. But one of the women, a young girl of barely twenty, began to speak.

"There is Roberto Sorral, and Luis Casimiro, and over there

184 · CHANTEL ACEVEDO

is the wife of Agustín Alonso, there is Ignacio Quesada's mother, and . . . " On and on she went, listing the names in a quavering voice. No one moved to stop her, though those near her scooted away as if from a poisonous plant. The girl, whose name I do not recall, did not last more than a week in La Cuchilla. She was found dead one morning, and no one seemed to know how it happened.

The boy with the Spanish flag wrote the names down inside a leather-bound book as quickly as he could. By the time the recitation was done, the sun had pierced the horizon. Weyler turned on his horse and his men followed him. Out the gate he went, and guards closed rank behind, so that we were barricaded in La Cuchilla.

As soon as they disappeared, I tore through the village in search of the baby with its dead mother. When I reached that hut, the baby was gone. The woman lay there, her face a rictus of pain, her eyes open. I looked up. There was a small wasp's nest stuck in the thatched ceiling. A solitary wasp circled it, building its new home. So this was the last thing she saw. *Dios santo*, I whispered. Another villager must have taken the baby, and for that, at least, I was grateful. Though I wasn't sure the baby, having drunk whatever poison had been in his mother's body, would be saved. I bent down to close her eyelids when a hand caught mine in midair.

I turned and saw Mario. "Don't touch her," he said. "God knows what she died of." He pulled me close and held me tightly, breathing hard into my hair.

"How?" I began to ask him.

"I saw the Butcher's horse, and then, the line of women from the tallér. I followed from a distance. The guards at the gate were too busy saluting the governor to notice me slipping into the camp." Mario held my hands against his chest as he spoke. I could feel his heart pounding a strange, fluttery rhythm.

"Now you're trapped here, with us," I told him.

"I couldn't leave you," he said. He gazed at me for a moment, then asked, "Are you allright?"

The question, asked so gently, robbed me of my composure, and I started to cry.

"You aren't hurt, are you?" Mario asked, looking me up and down.

I was about to tell him I was unhurt when I felt a tickle on my ankle, and jerked my leg, turning to stare at the corpse. I'd had the horrible idea that she had touched me. I went cold, and my body shook. Then, I saw that it had been the wasp, flying in lazy circles around our feet, sniffing us out. It landed on the woman's forehead; its long hind legs mingled with her eyebrows.

"Ay," I cried out, and buried my face in Mario's chest. He led me away from that *bohío*. "You're making a habit of saving my life," I murmured against him.

"Quit trying to get yourself killed," he said in exchange.

We wandered La Cuchilla for a while. The residents stared woodenly at us, as if we were just another part of the wasteland they looked on each day. Here and there, a person would nod at us, affirming our existence, and in those people I could still see an aura of hope. At first, we were afraid the Spanish guards would spot Mario, sensing that he did not belong. But they did nothing at all when they rested their gazes on us. To them, Mario was just another man in La Cuchilla, and I was just another woman, both of us trapped.

When we found Lulu she was trying to organize the women of the tallér. She looked like an insolent queen, pointing her finger at this woman, then that one, assigning duties in a tense, determined voice. Spotting me out of the corner of her eye, Lulu spoke without looking at me: "María Sirena, I want you to keep track of the guards. When do they change shifts? Who's in charge of them?"

Tears welled in my eyes. So we weren't giving up! I tried to

186 · CHANTEL ACEVEDO

compose myself as I listened to Lulu giving orders. When she was done, the women of the tallér held their shoulders back. Those who had been sobbing dried their faces. The gestures consoled me, made me feel stronger, though there was a prodding tickle in my throat and a suspicion that this was all an exercise in creating some sort of solace for us, and not a way of saving ourselves. Lulu was keeping us busy, I knew. Perhaps, this was her way of saving us after all. I thought of the residents of La Cuchilla, the ones with the hope in their eyes. I wanted to be like them.

When the women and children dispersed, each to find a soul who would let her stay in their *bohío*, Lulu addressed Mario and me at last.

"You disappear with my daughter for hours. She returns to me undressed, with a bruise like an orchid on her shoulder, and I am supposed to greet you with what? Gladness? Lárgate, Mario," said Lulu.

"I know," Mario said, surprising me. "It wasn't the way I wanted it to be. I didn't hurt her. I wouldn't, ever. But you must know, Señora Alonso, that there isn't much I won't risk when it comes to your daughter. I know all you see is *un negro*—"

"Bah!" Lulu said, waving her hand in the air as if swatting away flies. "*Eso no importa.* But there are decent ways of courting a young woman, and hiding with her in the woods is not one of them." Lulu's eyes flashed in anger. "Consider yourself fortunate that Agustín knows nothing of this."

"This is why you're angry?" I asked her, unbelievingly. "Because I wasn't courted properly. Dios mío, look at where we are," I said.

"I know where we are," Lulu answered me, and turned to stare at the fences.

I reached out and touched my mother tentatively. She tightened against my touch as if I were that wasp I'd seen earlier. At that moment, I could have mentioned Julio Reyes, or the poet. I could have thrown them in her face and then asked her about decency. But I couldn't bring myself to it.

There is nothing more satisfying than having survived a violent experience. I was so grateful for life at the moment, so glad I was not Luisa, with a bullet in my head, or that woman in the *bohío,* her eyes dead and open because no one would close them for her. My joy at finding Mario again ran deep, and the accusations against my mother died in my throat. In fact, after that day, I never once felt that kind of burning, adolescent anger towards Lulu. I was all tenderness for her, my mother, the only one I would ever have in this world. Perhaps it was watching that baby trying to stir its dead mother. Perhaps I had aged in the span of a day, becoming the grown woman I was meant to be.

Mario's face went taut at the mention of Agustín, as if his muscles had formed knots under his skin. "*Está bien,*" I said to him, standing close to my mother still, my hand hovering over her shoulder where I'd touched her before. "He isn't here to hurt us."

Lulu snapped her head to the right, her eyes boring into mine. "What do you mean?" she asked.

"Mamá, there was an . . . an incident . . . in the woods . . . " I tried to explain, wondering how it would all sound to her, how Agustín had found Mario and me kissing, his hand on the small of my back, gripping me hard, and Papá's rifle going off . . .

"There's something you need to know. Both of you," Mario said, interrupting. He spoke with a hoarseness that didn't seem deliberate, but rather, a product of some great grief.

Lulu sat down hard, suddenly, as if she were a mechanical toy that had wound down. She put her hands over her face and took long breaths, as if she knew what Mario was about to say. As for me, I was dumbfounded, unsure why he wouldn't let me tell the story. I thought he was being overly gallant, and for one insane moment, I imagined he was about to ask for my hand in marriage. I could feel my eyes glistening, and I must have looked like a wild animal in that instant.

"El Señor Alonso was killed this morning," Mario said, taking my breath away in a few words. I sat next to Lulu. She wrapped her arms around my waist, and her head fell to my lap.

"Go on," she said, her voice shattered and muffled by my skirt.

Piece by piece, Mario told us the story of my father's death—how Mario's company had taken shelter in a deserted plantation, hiding like rats, how Mario left his brothers in arms to find me in the river, the water closing over my head like a lid, how lightning crackled around us, striking trees with a force unlike anything he'd ever seen before, as if the fingertips of God Himself were grazing the land. He described how my father came upon us in a tender moment, how the corneta sounded, and how Agustín followed Mario back to the plantation, and into the fray without hesitation. He described a barn, where Mario's company stood their ground, emptying their ammunition at a squadron of Spanish soldiers that had amassed on the field out of nowhere. But they were too few. When Mario described the lit torch that one of the Spaniards threw deep into the barn, he traced the arc of it in the sky with his hands, so that Lulu and I might imagine the thing turning end over end as it flew. Then, he told us about my father, how he ran into the barn and stayed behind to fight even as Mario ran away from the conflagration, how the others poured out of the barn like human lanterns—arms and legs afire, torsos blazing, and how Agustín eventually staggered out engulfed in light, every inch of him ignited. He took three steps and fell to his knees. He swayed that way for a moment, then collapsed.

11.
When the Light Fails You

L ulu lifted her head off my lap when Mario finished speaking. "Are you sure it was Agustín you saw burning?" she asked.

"Sí," Mario said. "I'm sorry. Forgive me."

I could feel my mouth hanging open like a door. My father was dead, and we were trapped, *reconcentradas*, left to starve, for that is what the Spanish were doing in these village prisons—cutting these places off, as if they were a cancer growing on the body of Spanish Cuba. In a way, they were. In the tallér we had depended on help from villages like La Cuchilla for supplies. Soldiers stayed in villages overnight. In humble bohíos all over the island, dissent had sputtered to life, foamed and churned, becoming a sea that was sweeping over everyone. Butcher Weyler wasn't stupid. Places like La Cuchilla were the heart of the liberation movement, and isn't that what hunters did? Eat the heart of the animal they killed?

Lulu touched my chin gently, and the shock of the moment dissipated, leaving behind goose bumps all over my body that would not go away for a long time.

"You left your company to see my daughter," Lulu told Mario in a tired voice. "And they were ambushed. My husband was killed." Mario seemed to crumple right before my eyes, like balled-up paper left in the rain. "You are just a boy. You had no business fighting in a war," Lulu continued. "What are you, seventeen? A child, I don't care what others say." Her voice began to rise, and I could see her anger hardening like amber. "Men are at least twenty years old before they even know how to clean themselves properly. In fact, I can see the dirt on your beardless face."

"Please—" he began.

"*No hace falta*," Lulu said, waving him away. "Little boys playing at manhood owe no explanations. You are who you are. Years from now, if we live to see enough days after this damned war, you'll recall your foolishness, how you let your urges rule the day and many men died, including my husband. And what's worse, you involved my daughter in it all. She shares your guilt. All her life she'll have to bear that weight. Her father's death is on her head as much as it is on yours."

"But you don't understand—"

"I understand stupidity. You'll outgrow it, I hope." Lulu turned to me then, and said, "This is finished, María Sirena. Come with me," and she took hold of my wrist. Her hand felt like the strap doctors used to cut the blood off from a limb. My fingers tingled. I was afraid to turn and have a last look at Mario. It was a fear born out of my mother's fury, which was transcendent in that moment. I imagined turning and seeing Mario reduced to ash. I swear I felt his eyes on me, though, like light coming through a magnifying glass—a piercing, damaging pin of light on my skin.

As I stumbled behind my mother, who was sobbing now as she walked, her shoulders heaving and twitching, I thought of what I'd seen at the bottom of the River Cauto. I remembered the mermaid's dry scales, the glint of something golden in them, as if she was once a shiny, new thing that had tarnished. Lulu's hand around my wrist seemed to grow rough before my eyes, as if she were wearing armor. Like a fish, I thought, and gulped the hot air of the afternoon to keep from suffocating on dry land.

Lulu stopped suddenly, and I fell into her, biting my tongue hard and drawing a little blood. "Ay," I shouted, but Lulu shushed me. She ran her fingers through her hair and smacked her lips. With the inside of her shirt collar, she dried her eyes. She fussed with my hair, too, and pinched my cheeks very hard.

"Mamá," I complained, and pushed her hands away.

"Cállate," she whispered at me. Then: "Follow me and say nothing."

I watched as Lulu walked over to a Spanish soldier by the eastern gate. He was leaning against the fence, picking at his nails with a metal file. She approached him so quietly, so cat-like, that he did not notice her until Lulu laid a hand on his shoulder.

The young man leapt, startled, and held out his file like a knife.

"No need for that," Lulu said softly. He had a hard time keeping his eyes on her, it seemed. He would look over her shoulder and she would cock her head to the side, catching his gaze again, summoning him to her. Still, he wavered, as if Lulu were the sun itself, burning his vision.

"Look at me," she said at last. "Look at us," she said, including me, and then the soldier did look, and his eyes were small, coal-like, and utterly disinterested. "We obviously don't belong here," Lulu purred. Such confidence! I mimicked her without thinking, holding my hips to the right a bit, as if one of my legs was shorter than the other, letting one arm hang limply along the side of my body, a pinkie raised ever so slightly, my chin bowed, my eyes up and large. Lulu's posture was one of exhaustion, it seemed to me, wilted and overheated like a flower at midday. And still, it all came together to suggest a kind of ease and that romantic notion of a woman half-sick with love.

"There's been an error, and I believe you can help us correct it," Lulu said, and her left hand twitched and rose in the air, as if pulled by strings, and landed lightly on the soldier's chest, butterfly-like.

The soldier's eyes, black and tearless, finally fell upon Lulu's. I'd hoped to see the same kind of wide eagerness I'd seen in Agustín's eyes, in Julio Reyes's swallowing stare, in the poet's sparkling contemplation of Lulu. Instead, the soldier's eyes looked burnt-out, as if he'd stared at the sun at last and found it damaging.

He slapped Lulu's hand away, and in one fierce move, took her other arm and turned it savagely behind her, so that he held her in a vicious embrace, his nose a finger's width from hers. "I should kill you on the spot, old woman, but I'll let life in the village do it slowly," he whispered, loud enough for me to hear. Then he released Lulu. She staggered backwards, and caught hold of my hand at last after a few desperate swipes.

"Run, Mamá," I said, and we did, our feet pounding the dry dirt. I shivered as I ran, expecting to hear gunshot. Lulu ran behind me, guarding my back, her hands pushing my shoulder blades every so often, so that I felt like a horse must feel when under the reins of an impatient rider.

For the first time in her life, Illuminada's light had failed her.

We took shelter in an empty house. The residents had died, a neighbor told us, of cholera. Lulu went rigid when she heard the news, and forbid me from drinking any of the water the old owners had stowed in ceramic jugs, at least until we boiled the contents. There were stained sheets in the corner of the one-room house. A brown, fetid stench came off of them, and Lulu swept the bundle outside with a broom she'd found. Then, we sat on the dirt floor, cross-legged, in silence. When I tried to speak, Lulu shushed me.

"No, María Sirena. No hables. Not tonight." Lulu stared into the dirt as if she could make a hole with the force of her gaze. When I tried to rise, to stretch my aching legs, Lulu said, "Sit," loudly, as if I were a schoolchild disrupting a class. So I sat. What else could I do? We spent the night this way. It

should have been a proper wake, with Agustín's body in a polished coffin on a stand in the corner, friends from the tallér
around us, bringing us food, plucking a fallen shawl off the
floor and putting it back onto Lulu's trembling shoulders, the
air stirred like a thick soup by handheld fans. At least, that's
what his wake should have looked like, and what I hope mine
looks like someday. Instead, Lulu and I were the only mourn-
ers, and we sat, knee to knee, and imagined ourselves in
another place.

In the morning Lulu was a different woman. I woke with a
creaky neck from sleeping on the floor. But Lulu had sprung
up overnight like a weed, and she was busy cleaning up the
house, deciding what was useful and worth keeping, and what
reeked of disease. When my vision cleared, it was to the sight
of Lulu dangling a calico dress before her, weighing it in her
hands, then leaning forward to put the material against her
cheek and ear, as if it might tell her a secret. The dress was
small. Child-sized.

"What happened to them, in the end?" I asked, thinking
not of living residents, but rather their corpses.

Lulu must have read me the right way. She said, "Look outside. East. At the sky," then began to fold the dress as if she
meant to keep it.

I did what I was told. There, against the blue silk of the sky,
was the constant circling of buzzards. "Ay," I said. "I've never
seen so many."

"The bodies are being put just outside La Cuchilla's
fence," Lulu said, her fingers flying over a small, open box of
needles and thread, picking through it expertly, organizing the
contents into some kind of order. I remembered her childhood, her years spent in a shoemaker's home. Lulu was
breathing deeply, slowly. She was chewing the inside of her lip
thoughtfully as she began to thread a needle with coarse,
brown thread. "I went out while you were sleeping, asked

around. Two hundred have died of hunger and disease in La Cuchilla."

"Doesn't it bother you?" I asked her. I could not stop trembling. Upon sighting the buzzards, I'd had a sudden vision of being eaten alive by them, their black talons hooking into my skin, my heart in a glossy beak.

"Very much," she said, and began mending a tear in the calico dress.

"So what's our plan?"

Lulu shrugged, pulled at the thread hard, so that it twanged like a musical instrument. There were a few needles pressed between her lips, and they trembled as she worked, like the whiskers on a cat. She wouldn't answer me, even after I asked her a few more times. I braced myself for anger. But it wouldn't come. I couldn't summon it. I stared hard at the needles in Lulu's mouth, willing myself to grow furious at her sudden complacency. But there was nothing. It was like I'd forgotten how to breathe. That is how it is with the young. They are pots that boil over quickly, and then, one day, the heat beneath them is turned off, and the anger dissipates, and what's left behind is the person they are to become.

But who was I? Fatherless. Helpless. Imprisoned. Loveless. No. Not loveless, I thought. "I'm going out," I told Lulu, who did not even look up at me. This was new. Back in the tallér, she'd pin me with her eyes, like a butterfly being examined, my wings caught under her stare, and I would have to offer a detailed explanation for my every move. I suppose there wasn't a point anymore. La Cuchilla was fenced in. Where could I possibly go?

She didn't ask me, so I did not tell her that I was going to find Mario. The events of the last two days had taught me one thing—that life was a precarious deal made with an unpredictable god. I felt brittle as I made my way around La Cuchilla, like I might break at any moment. Thoughts of Mario kept me together. As I walked, I got to thinking about the mermaid I thought I'd seen, and then, other watery things—warm currents in the river that pleased you just when you thought it was too cold to go on swimming, the round, brown snails that tugged their shells up and down the banks of the Cauto, the click of stones in the shallow places, like the sounds of a hundred ladies' shoes on a tiled floor. This all made me feel better, somehow, and I searched most of La Cuchilla by lunchtime, having peeked into nearly every window in the village.

In the end, I did not find Mario. He found me. I heard my name being called from a great distance. I turned in all directions, searching for his voice. Then, he started to laugh, and called my name again. "Where are you?" I cried, surprised to hear desperation in my voice.

"Look up," he said, and I raised my eyes to the roof of a bohío a few feet from me. There was Mario, standing on the roof, his face blotted out by the sun.

He moved down to the lip of the roof, swung his legs into the open air, and let himself drop. Like a cat, he landed on his hands and feet, and rose, shaking his hands and cracking his knuckles. He made a funny face, and I knew that the jump had hurt him.

"I'm not impressed," I said, hoping to discourage that sort of risk-taking.

"Ah, well," Mario said. "Next time, I'll jump from the top of that watchtower over there." He pointed at a raised wooden structure at the north end of the village. Inside, I could barely make out a Spanish soldier, his rifle resting on the railing that circumnavigated the little tower.

"It's empty," Mario said, meaning the bohío behind us.

"The owners?" I asked.

"Dead. Like so many others," Mario said. He'd spotted the buzzards in the distance, too, and he'd made up a game in which he'd watch them, looking for patterns in the sky. "They make the shapes of letters sometimes," he said.

"Are they trying to tell us something?" I asked.

"Don't know. I can't read," Mario said, laughing. It was an odd sound in such a place. Across the path from us, a thin man smoking a cigar shook his head, as if Mario's laughter were an indecent thing. When we noticed him looking at us, we grew quiet, and Mario drew me into the bohío.

It was dark and surprisingly cool inside. The ceiling overhead was a dense patchwork of reeds and palm fronds. Inside, the old owners had arrayed their home with very little—a coal stove, a hay-filled mattress and a ratty blue quilt, a wooden box with a few chipped dishes and cups, no forks or spoons to speak of, a single iron pot, and another pot of white porcelain next to the bed. There were no interior walls, no rooms save for the one in which we stood.

"Are you allright?" he asked me. I nodded yes, but I felt my face contort into a mask, and soon, I was crying against Mario's chest. He said nothing, though; if he'd asked me what was wrong, it would have occurred to me first to say that it was Lulu. Lulu was wrong. She'd been so placid that morning, so still. My mother, in my imagination, had always stood out from other women I knew. If they were soft, yeasty beings, my mother was made of iron. Her arms weren't flabby and white, but rather muscular and ropy. Even when bearing the full force of Agustín's anger, there would be a bright charge in her eyes, and when Agustín had calmed, it was as if Lulu had chased down his rage herself, sending it back to wherever it sprouted in him. But Lulu was no longer Lulu, and this is what was most wrong in my heart. It came down to one selfish question:

Who would save me from this situation if not Lulu?

For the first time in my life, I felt truly unmoored. I realized then, crying within the circle of Mario's thin arms, that I'd been a barnacle of a person, clinging to Lulu and Agustín for safety. I remembered that night in Havana, when I broke into an inn to save my mother, and I wondered where the courage had come from. The year in the tallér had softened me further instead of making me strong. I'd grown breasts, and my waist had thinned, and all of those changes disrupted the equilibrium of my courage, had taken so much energy that now I was half the girl I had hoped I would become.

We talked all morning in hushed tones. I kept expecting Lulu's face to appear in the doorway like a sunrise, blinding and angry, but she did not come. We would have been easy to find. La Cuchilla, it turned out, wasn't very big. All day, the buzzards screeched overhead, and we watched them for a while, holding our breath when they all swooped down at once, like a lightning strike with feathers, thinking that perhaps fresh meat had been thrown onto the pile of bodies.

We talked about escape. Mario proposed daring. "We simply rush over the fence when no one is looking," he'd said, reminding me that he was still a boy, just as Lulu had insisted. I was acquainted with escape, remembering how close it had been for us in Havana, how death had been the only open door for us. I lamented the loss of my pistol, though I don't know what I could have done with it against so many soldiers anyway.

It was noon, and my stomach rumbled loudly. "So hungry," I whispered, which turned out to be a peculiar sort of trigger, for Mario laced his hands behind my head and pulled me towards him. His mouth pressed against mine and my lips parted, and then, he was swallowing me whole, one hand still on my head, the other running up and down my ribs, clenching the soft roll of flesh at my waist hard. I could hear myself moaning into his mouth, but the sound felt so foreign, as if some other creature had made it, and I was only the amplifier of the sound.

He released me, gasping, his forehead touching mine. "Perdón," he said. "Ay, perdón."

I thought of Lulu and Agustín in that moment, my brain

betraying me at the worst time. "No," I said aloud, confusing Mario. "No," I said again, and the images of my parents winked out in my head, leaving only black space, and a gnawing hunger that had nothing to do with food anymore, but other, abstract things. I was hungry for love, and for survival and freedom, and in that instant, these things felt very much in reach if I were only to choose the right path.

I led Mario to the bed, which was full of some dry material, with only a few feathers to soften sleep. I lay down and looked up at Mario's dark eyes, which glittered like moonlight on water. His mouth hung open, gasping for air. His chest filled and then collapsed, drowning on land for me. "Ven," I told him, and pulled him close. My voice was a pant, and I was dimly aware of my breath carrying that hungry odor, the sourness of a body empty of nourishment. No matter, Mario's lips touched mine again and I heard him sigh deeply.

I will say no more about it, except this: our love had not been destroyed that day, though the fates had attempted to raze what we had to the ground.

A t noon, Ofelia returns with Mireya. Both women are laughing as they enter the room, each holding a tray upon which plates of congrís and chicken have been piled. Garlic smells fill the space and my stomach grumbles in anticipation.

"This arrived an hour ago," Ofelia says, gesturing to the food that she has put on the bed, inviting each of us to take a plate.

"Who sent it?" Celia asks.

"Fidel, of course," Ofelia answers automatically. We say nothing. Of course our new líder did not send the food. Someone else must have done the cooking. These young revolutionaries sometimes make Fidel sound like Santi Clo, or God himself. I stifle a laugh when I think of our commandante wearing a tall white chef's hat, up to his elbows in chicken fat.

"Who cooked it?" Dulce asks, suspicious.

"If you're asking where the food was made, it came to us from Santa Ifigenia's kitchens. They've set up a food distribution center there. They're delivering food via small boats."

"Ay," Dulce says, startled, and crosses herself. Santa Ifigenia is the cemetery in Santiago, the place were José Martí is buried. "Food of the dead!" Dulce says, and puts down her plate.

"Don't be ridiculous," Mireya chides, her mouth already full of black beans. "Some people rode out in the storm in the mausoleum, and a lucky thing, too. It was high and dry there."

"I would rather die than sleep among ghosts," Dulce says.

"When you die, that's all you'll do," Rosalia says, and we all laugh and eat.

"I heard the soldiers talking," Mireya tells us. "Some people were sheltered in the mausoleum. Others in the cathedral. Some in the Hotel Casagranda," she says, and Celia whistles in approval.

We chat amongst ourselves for a while. Ofelia has stayed to eat with us, and the women are a little more animated for her presence, as if we are all trying to impress the young woman. She's a good listener, and we are warmed from within by the food and her company. When she asks, "What did I miss in your tale, María Sirena?" I am too shocked to answer. I didn't realize she'd heard enough of it to make sense of any of it, nor did I think she cared.

Then, Estrella begins to catch her up, and I hear my story in her voice. She stumbles a bit when describing Mario's family, and Dulce picks up the tale, her own voice tremulous but consistent. Susana takes it from there, then Rosalia pipes in, each of them picking up the trail of the story like those children in the fairy tale who leave bread crumbs behind to guide them home.

Every once in a while, they look to me for clarification, and I only nod, and wave them on. Ofelia has all the right responses, her face revealing shock, sadness, longing, contentment, in all the right places in the story.

They ask me to tell them about Mario again, and I do, lingering long over descriptions of him. "He liked holding hands, you know," I tell them. "If I could see him again, I would hold his hands forever. And he liked to eat chicken soup by the bucketful when we were in the tallér, which was a good thing since that was all we ever ate." The women laugh a little at that. "I would make him soup every day of his life if only I could see him again," I say, my voice breaking a little.

"Did he like to dance?" Estrella asks. "My own Paco, may he rest in peace, he loved dancing."

I shake my head. "I don't think we ever danced together," I say. "But his arms were strong, and his steps sure, and his hips were rounded just a little, just enough for me to rest my hands on the small of his back. I'm sure he would have made a beautiful dancer."

"When did he die?" Rosalia asks quietly. Her hands are folded under her chin like a girl.

"You presume too much," I say. "I haven't gotten far enough in the story to answer that question."

Ofelia collects our empty plates and loads up the trays again. As she works, we all help tidy the room, straightening the bedsheets on the dusty bed, folding blankets, as if we are preparing for guests.

"Another night at least," Ofelia says, pausing a moment to watch us. "The roads are bad. Be patient, señoras. Patient," she says, and we groan and quit putting the room to rights again.

Mireya comes to me, her hand outstretched. "You have my photograph," she says, and I nod, pulling out the picture of Alejandro and handing it to her.

"Gracias," she says.

"My friend, I—" I begin.

"None of that. I can make an uneasy peace with you, but I can't forgive you, María Sirena. I can't. My Alejandro is dead because of you. How can a mother forgive a thing like that?" she says. She is not crying now, nor does her voice waver. Her eyes, too, are locked on mine, and what I see is righteousness and a woman so convinced of her error that she will not be moved.

"I've said it once, and I'll say it until I am dead, I have no idea what you mean," I tell her. For a moment, Mireya seems to be taken aback. Then, her spine goes rigid again, and she stands a bit taller than me. "You and Beatríz might as well have tied the noose around his neck with your own hands," she says, and now her voice does break.

Noose? What noose? "He died of an infection," I say, but Mireya shakes her head and closes her eyes against me, as if I am too difficult to bear.

We have been speaking off in a corner, and when Mireya moves away from me, Estrella, ever cheerful, cries out, "Another story from our lector!"

"No more," I tell them. "Not tonight."

"Ah, we've tired her out," Estrella says. "I have one then," she says, and proceeds to tell a tale about her own youth, one involving roller skates, a steep hill in Havana, a deep sewer, and a bout of ringworm. I tune her out eventually, though the others seem to be laughing, including Mireya.

It's good for them to laugh, I think. Estrella's story breeds another from Rosalia, which is similarly ridiculous, involving a sailor in Havana with a tattoo of Mickey Mouse on the inside of his thigh. Then Susana tells the story of a student who locked himself in a cabinet with a lit bottle rocket in his hands. By the time the sun has gone down, the women have grown quiet again, though none claim to be sleepy.

"A story for us imprisoned women," Mireya says, and I know she means for me to begin again. "I'm tired of laughing, María Sirena. I'm unused to it."

I feel six pairs of eyes on me, and the weight of a story yet untold, and so I speak again.

13

Another Kind of Imprisonment

I t was dark before I reached for my clothes again and slipped them on blindly. I laid a hand on Mario's chest. His sternum rose and fell sharply, prompting me to check his forehead for fever. Just before falling asleep, Mario had mumbled something about the abandoned bohío being our house now, just the two of us, husband and wife. His words were broken up by lazy smiles, as if we weren't reconcentrados, half-starved already, doomed to end up as buzzard food.

"Of course," I'd told him then. Why not pretend? Lulu could have her house, we would have ours, death would come or it would not.

But it seemed I'd awoken with a new kind of lucidity, and as I buttoned my shirt, my tender nipples aching against the material, my legs trembling like leaves in a storm, I'd already made a few decisions about the future, the first of which was the determination not to die in La Cuchilla.

I kissed Mario lightly on the lips, and left the bohío, marveling as I walked at the profound heaviness I felt between my legs, the dull pain deep within, and the sense that I had been disassembled from within and could no longer be put together the same way again. What girl hasn't wondered, after her first night with a man, whether she not only feels different but looks different, too? The village seemed empty at night, and only the screech-screech of frogs broke the silence. The sound was loud, and close, almost as if the creatures were within me, somehow. Every once in a while, I'd disturb a toad in the middle of the road, and it would hop away, making a wet, thudding sound. Later, I'd learn that in the early days of La Cuchilla's reconcentration, people began to eat the toads, and that it went very badly for some. It turned out that the toads' green pustules and glassy eyes were thick with poison. By the time we were taken to La Cuchilla, there were no more cats to hunt the amphibians, and even birds of prey were avoiding the place, abandoning it to the carrion eaters. So, the village was overrun with toads, as if a biblical plague was happening right there in eastern Cuba.

My senses were sharp in the night. Beyond the shrill sounds of small, slimy creatures I began to hear human voices coming from within modest homes. I heard a great deal of coughing. I smelled sulfur, the result of outhouses overflowing. I sloshed through dark, thick streamlets that stirred up even more of a stink. Here and there, the piercing cry of an infant would jolt me, making my eyes prick in sympathy.

When I passed by Lulu's bohío, I heard nothing. Peering through the door, I saw her sleeping shape. I watched for her back to rise, for a breath to enter her body, and when it did, I released a breath of my own. She'd laid out a dozen dresses on the rough wooden furniture of the place. There was the calico she'd been working on before, here and there were broad skirts in dark blue shades, and crisp white shirts. The trunk that had held the clothes was open and turned upside down on the floor. Who knew it had held so much? All of the clothes made the place look a bit like a shop. I walked into the bohío and drew close to Lulu. She was clutching a spool of hibiscus-yellow thread in her sleep. Some of the thread was wrapped tightly around her pinkie like a tourniquet. I unwrapped her finger while she slept, and watched as the blood drained from the tip, the color of her skin fading and becoming rosy again. It was like watching a sunrise in miniature. Lulu stirred, mumbled something that sounded like my father's name. At my back, the dawn broke, and I could feel my neck heating up in the shaft of sunlight that entered the room. I backed away from my mother, vowing to come back later with Mario, to make things right between the three of us, because we were all that we had.

Outside, the villagers were stirring. Many folks were out on the roads, holding tin cups and ladles. They were forming lines at the eastern entrance to La Cuchilla. The sun blazed up before them, and the people squinted against it. The brightness made it so I couldn't tell what they were standing in line for. I walked past those waiting, drawing a few jeers. "Oye, muchacha, the line starts in the back," they were saying, in gravelly voices that held no threat. Finally, I saw what they were waiting for. Two Spanish soldiers were filling the tin cups with a mealy substance that, even from a distance, smelled like rot. The soldiers wore wide-brimmed hats and crisp white uniforms. They served the villagers without speaking, two at a time. They held their heads to the side, as if the smell of the gruel offended them.

"How often do they come?" I asked a woman who was next in line.

She looked up at me blankly, and her moist eyes reminded me of the toads I had seen last night—green and dull. "Only in the mornings," she said, then held out her cup for the soldier on the left. He sloshed the food into her cup sloppily, and some of it landed on her wrist. I watched as she licked the food off her skin until there was nothing left and I was sure she was just tasting the salt of her own body.

My stomach rumbled. My mouth watered. The stuff smelled awful, but my body was betraying me now. I ran back to Lulu's bohío because it was closest, and grabbed three porcelain cups off of a shelf. Lulu did not stir. I waited back in line, and when it was my turn, presented all three cups.

"For my family," I said to the soldiers. "There are three of us."

Calmly, the soldier on the right took all three cups from my hands. His hands were soft when they brushed mine, and I marveled at their smoothness. Then, in one swift motion, he threw all three cups to the ground, where they shattered. Then he stomped the shards of porcelain into powder.

"One at a time," he said in a voice that was oddly musical and sweet. He even smiled. "Try again tomorrow." I was too shocked to move out of line. When a young woman behind me pushed me hard between the shoulder blades, I cried out, and, in shock, pushed her back.

Before I knew it, she and I were on the ground. My hair was tangled in her hands and she pulled and pulled. I threw my knees into her stomach, yanked at her ears. She slammed her forehead into my nose and teeth accidentally, and we parted from one another in pain. The woman cursed me and held onto her forehead, which was streaming blood. My front teeth felt loose, and my nose was tingling. There was an iron taste in my mouth, and I realized with disgust that the blood wasn't my own.

The soldiers packed up the gruel, though the line was still long and their pot was still heavy with food. They said nothing at all, but it was clear that La Cuchilla was being punished for our behavior. The people in line called out to the soldiers, begging.

"My daughter is starving, on the point of death!" one woman screeched.

"Por Dios, be merciful."

"Come back, come back, please," a few pleaded.

Then, when it was clear the day's allotment of food had ended, the people in line turned like a single body to the two of us, still sprawled on the floor. I scrabbled backwards like a crab. A tin cup flew at my head. That was all it took. I was off running, a comet streaking through La Cuchilla. Behind me, I could hear the woman I'd fought yelling, her voice reaching a single high note, an "Aaaayyyyy" of pain, and then going silent.

No one chased me. They couldn't have caught me if they'd tried. I was new to La Cuchilla, not yet diminished by months of reconcentration. My body was young and strong still. I ran until I reached the bohío I shared with Mario, which was on the western edge of the village, as far from the fiasco at the other end as I could go. I tumbled into the house and collapsed on the ground, crying in jags. The world went blurry for a minute, then, I felt Mario's arms around me. He was saying, "Ya, ya," and petting my hair. After that, I don't remember much. He later told me I'd fainted, and that while I slept, I'd talked in my sleep about fighting off sharks in deep water.

I ventured out again eventually. I let my hair loose in the hopes that I might not be recognized. If anyone in the village did spot me as the troublemaker from the morning, they did nothing about it. Perhaps I was recognized. But the heat of the day, and the lethargy that comes with hunger, dampens even the worst rages. Thoughts become unstitched in situations like that. Hunger makes even one's memory go awry, so that by the third week in La Cuchilla, I could no longer remember Agustín's face. By the fourth, I'd forgotten the story of how I got my name. Mario had asked me, and my mind had gone black and stormy. I reached for the story and came up empty.

"Water," I'd said. "There's something about the water."

"Don't talk about water," Mario had grumbled. Fresh water was hard to come by. Thank God for the rainy season, and the bromeliads that caught the rain in their sturdy leaves. People hoarded jugs and other containers with their very lives. The problem was we would leave whatever cups we had out in the rain and had to watch them as they filled. If you left them for a moment, the cups, the jugs, the trays, whatever hollowed-out thing you used to catch water, would be stolen. What was worse, the Cauto River ran, loud and rushing, just beyond the fences, tantalizing and forbidden. While I was in La Cuchilla,

I saw a man rushing towards the river. He'd climbed the fence and taken off. The shots came from somewhere outside the village, I never could pinpoint where. The man reached the river and took a bullet the moment his foot touched water. He fell into the Cauto limply, his arms outstretched, as if he were embracing the currents, giving the water a final kiss. Mario and I watched as his body floated away, tumbling over rocks, his arms flailing. From a distance, he looked like a gull flapping at the surface of the water. Then he was gone from sight.

"At least the buzzards won't get him," Mario had said, and I leaned into him and covered my eyes with his shirtsleeve.

One morning, we watched as a family prepared to baptize their infant. They'd been collecting water for days, and had informed the Spanish of their intentions. The priest arrived one morning in his colorful frocks, flanked by two armed soldiers. The family, mother, father, and grandmother, emerged from their home with a skeletal baby in arms, dressed in a long white embroidered baptismal gown. They were all too thin, and it was like watching a ghostly ceremony, something that was happening in the underworld. The baby cried when the priest poured the sacred water on her head, but she made no sound, as if her vocal cords had shriveled up a long time ago. Her tiny cheekbones caught the sun that morning, like pins of light. When have you ever seen a baby's cheekbones? I fixated on that tiny face, and my jaw ached from clenching my teeth, to keep from crying out, or flying at the soldiers and that priest, who were all flesh and warmth and health. Most of La Cuchilla had turned out for the event, and I noticed how we'd all panted at the sight of all of that water going to waste, even as it cooled the poor baby's head, washing her clean of dust and sin.

What made matters worse for me that morning was the sureness with which I felt that I was pregnant. I had a few weeks at most before the news would no longer be news to anyone in La Cuchilla. I told Lulu first, there in her bohío that had become her cloister.

How can I explain what that small space felt like? She'd draped the clothes she'd found on our first day in La Cuchilla all over the walls, so that the interior of the bohío looked almost like an Arabian tent I'd seen in a book once, layers of colorful fabric closing in on the occupant of the house as if to smother her. Lulu's hands had remembered her days in her parents' shoe shop, and she'd made good use of the needles and thread the old owner had left behind, so that people in La Cuchilla would trade meager supplies for simple repair work. She would repair a seam for a hunk of stale bread, reunite the sole of a shoe to its leather upper for a mushy mango. It was her way of surviving La Cuchilla. Her back grew curved like a moon, and lines appeared around her eyes and mouth where there were none before. Gray hair sprouted at her temples like tiny lightning bolts. Her knuckles broadened and grew stony, like a man's. I began hearing the words la bruja con su aguja, the witch with her needle, and my heart sank when I realized they'd meant Lulu.

I wanted to yell at the people who'd said those words— "Did you know she once killed a captain of the Spanish navy?" or "Did you know that the Poet himself, José Martí, was in love with her?" I wasn't sure of that last assertion, but I wanted to fling it at my mother's offenders anyway, my claims a shot across the bow of their impertinence.

But the truth was, Lulu didn't mind at all. She began to call herself a bruja instead of a woman, and I told her I hoped she really had turned witch, that she might cast a spell and get us out of La Cuchilla.

"Ay, mi'ja," she'd sighed, a pair of needles pressed into the corner of her mouth. "Our story is over, don't you understand?"

I have no theories as to why my mother decided at that moment to give up. Perhaps it was Agustín's death that did it.

I'm not sure. I think of the Spanish soldier who rebuked her on our first day in La Cuchilla, the one who had called her "old," and I think that perhaps that was the final insult. Lulu's vanity and self-possession failed her when she needed them most. It was her best weapon, and it had misfired, blown up in her face, the shrapnel of it piercing her heart.

"Mamá," I said without preamble, "I'm pregnant."

Lulu nodded. Her face was very still. "How did I know it already?" she mused.

"Because you're a witch," I said, hoping to lighten the mood. It must have worked, because Lulu laughed, the needles balanced on her tongue when she opened her mouth. I cringed, prayed that she wouldn't swallow them one of these days.

Our laughter was short-lived, and Lulu was soon in tears. "When you were born," she began, and told me the story of the mermaid again, and of our years in Havana, as if they'd happened long ago and weren't a part of recent history. "From one prison to the next," Lulu said. "My child and now my grandchild, prisoners. Diós mío," she cried, and went back to work, mending the torn sleeve of a man's work shirt, her moist eyes making her stitches sloppy. In the kitchen sat an untouched cup of soup. A horsefly hovered over it, deciding whether or not to take a plunge.

"What do I do?" I asked. My stomach roiled at the sight of the soup, and I wondered at the ludicrous nature of human biology, how such a small thing growing in my womb could turn my body's clockwork in reverse. I was hungry. Why couldn't I eat? Bile rose in my throat.

"There's nothing to do," Lulu said. "Pray. There's that."

"I could try to get out. Get us all out."

Lulu laughed darkly. "You could try," she said. "What about your husband?" she asked. She called Mario my husband, and I let her. Our marriage wasn't made official either by

God or country, but there was no value in documentation in La Cuchilla.

"He doesn't know," I said, and told her I planned to tell him soon. That night, Mario fell asleep with his palm stretched across my flat stomach, and I'd like to think that somewhere deep within he knew what was growing a few inches from his skin, and so I said nothing. I would tell him in the morning, I told myself. In the morning, he would know, and the next time he fell asleep that way, touching me so tenderly, he would imagine the baby we'd made together.

14.
Where Courage Comes From

I woke at dawn to relieve myself, and, as much as I willed it, my eyes would not close again when I lay down next to Mario. I went outside and stared up at the trembling firmament, pink with new light, only a few stars left in the sky. For once, the air was fragrant with something sweet and I realized that the wind had shifted and that the buzzards, always present, were gone. Roosting in the trees at this hour, I guessed, and made a promise to myself that I would wake at dawn from now on to enjoy this false pleasure. In such light, with such fresh air, La Cuchilla seemed like any other village on the island. There was promise in the air that morning, and I filled my lungs with it.

Suddenly, I heard laughter coming from the western gate. A woman's laughter, light and crystalline, like glasses coming together in a toast. I followed the sound and saw that two soldiers were escorting a large group of well-dressed women around the perimeter of the village. I crept closer to the gate, kept my eyes on the ground as if I were looking for something. In the village we all walked this way—our gazes locked on the earth—in the hopes of finding an edible weed, or a lost trinket. Now, all the women laughed at some joke one of the soldiers told, and it was like a burst of oxygen, filling me with energy. I hadn't laughed like that in an age.

In truth, we'd been in La Cuchilla nearly two months. But it felt like years, and my body was beginning to show it. There were hollows in my cheeks where once there were none. My elbows were growing knobby and wider than my arms. But my breasts were full, and my teeth were still white, and my hair had not begun to fall out, as I'd seen happen with other villagers.

It seemed the women were on tour. There were about twenty of them, as far I could tell. It was early, and the women were yawning, their fingertips fluttering before their open mouths, their well-trimmed nails white like seashells. I could hear the soldiers explaining daily life in La Cuchilla, how and when food was distributed, the role the village had played in supporting the Cuban rebels, the recent battles nearby, Butcher Weyler's return to Spain, all of the news of the last few weeks exchanged easily, as if these things were happening elsewhere.

"There are women and children in the village?" one of the women asked. She had a tender voice and wore a straw hat with a red ribbon tied around it. The ribbon trailed down her back. She spoke with a Spanish accent, lisping delicately around certain words.

"Even the children helped the rebels, sneaking out food to them and such," the taller soldier said. The woman who'd asked the question sighed and tilted her hat over her eyebrows, then clasped her hands together at her waist. Her lips were moving, and I thought she was muttering a prayer.

Her sympathy sent a surge through me. There was a chance here, I thought, and once my mind fell upon it, I seized the moment. When the group had turned their attention away from where I'd stood, I ran for Lulu's bohío, my feet pounding the dirt.

"Mamá," I called, "wake up, wake up!" Lulu rose from her bed unsteadily, blinked at me, and rubbed her eyes, like a child. The gesture unnerved me for a moment, and I launched myself upon my mother, hugging her so hard that I thought I might hurt her.

"What's the matter?" she asked, patting me all over as if she might discover an injury on me.

"We're leaving," I said. "Quickly, are there clean shirtwaists here?" I asked, looking around the room at the clothes strung all over. I explained my plan as I searched, plucking a hat from a hook on the wall and undoing a belt that was looped around a bolt of oilcloth. We would change into better clothes, approximating the look of the women on tour, and then, we would simply join the group, blend in. What would two more women be in such a large group? Surely, Lulu and I had not yet taken on the look of the reconcentradas. Surely, we weren't that far gone.

As for Mario, perhaps if he lingered by the gate, pretending to scavenge in the weeds for something to eat, if he timed it just right . . . These were my frantic thoughts as I pulled dresses from the lines strung across the room.

Lulu dressed me, taking my old, worn clothes and folding them carefully as if she meant to keep them. There was no mirror, but I could tell we'd cobbled together a passing outfit. The straw hat on my head had no ribbon, but perhaps no one would notice.

"Now, your turn," I said, and began to look for clothes for Lulu.

Lulu shook her head. "You've a better chance of going alone," she said.

"Mamá—"

"Look at me, María Sirena," she said, and I looked, for once I really looked, and I saw that my mother's eyes were dark and bottomless. In them I saw haunted shapes; in the flit of her eyes, darting from side to side as she watched me watching her, I saw nocturnal things sprouting and growing tendrils. A ferocious oblivion had overtaken my mother, and I saw that she no longer cared to live even outside of La Cuchilla.

"Go, mi'ja," she said.

"What about Mario? I can't leave him," I said.

Lulu shook her head.

"I can say goodbye, at least," I said, desperation beginning to nip at me. Fate was sharpening its blades, I could feel it. "An hour then. Just an hour with him," I begged.

"Mi vida, no, it's . . . "

"Five minutes, Mamá!" I cried, thinking of all the places Mario and I had littered with kisses and sweet words, and of the baby that would grow strong in Mario's presence, the way I had grown strong.

"Enough!" Lulu said, pinning my arms down at my sides. "You have a chance now, and you must take it. One day, you'll look upon this moment and all you have suffered in this war as a series of distant marvels, and it will only hurt a little to remember them. You will think, 'I was lucky and blessed to get out of that place alive,' and the sting of goodbye will be gone."

I shook my head, closed my eyes and moaned. "That will never happen."

"It will. I promise you, mi amor. Save yourself and your baby. Go."

There was no point in trying to coax her. Lulu had never been the kind of woman one could cajole, anyway. "I'll come back for you," I promised, defeated. We were talking as if my plan would work, and I was glad for the pretense. Otherwise, I would have faltered.

I told my mother that I loved her, and she held me and wept into my hair.

"Begin again," she sobbed. "Begin your life anew, mi vida."

"Tell him I love him," I tried to say, though the words sounded mangled.

"He'll know it, I promise you."

"And if I'm caught?" I asked, trembling all over. I have never shaken so hard in my life, not even when Butcher Weyler was shooting women to my left and right. I felt closer to death in that moment, saying goodbye to Lulu, than I ever had.

"You won't be," she said, and it was as if I were a little girl again, being told a lie by my mother, one I believed wholly and without dispute. It filled me with courage, and I closed my eyes and imagined that I was Lulu, the woman who had traveled to New York City and met with rebels there, who had married a man she did not know for his principles, who killed another and suffered no nightmares afterwards. What was courage made of? I wondered at this, peering at Lulu, who tucked my shirt in and straightened my skirts. Just thinking about all my mother had done made me feel braver. The girl I once was felt nearer to me, as if I could reach out into the past and stroke her cheek.

Lulu followed me as far as she could. I drew close to the touring women. When they rounded the corner of a small plaza at the center of the village, I folded into the back of the group, adopting their shuffling steps. The women were nurses, it turned out, and they'd been brought to tend to the recon-centrados. News of conditions in the camps had gotten out, I heard one soldier say.

"There's talk of the Americans entering the fray," a woman near the front of the group offered, and the tidbit rippled through the women, until they were all commenting on it. They walked in pairs, arm-in-arm, making me think of braids, rope, and other knotted things.

The one with the red ribbon, whom I'd found and stuck close to, was the only solitary woman. I held my breath, slipping my arm behind her elbow as if it belonged there. She allowed it, and turned to me, saying, "The Americans are agitated. I read it in *Ecos*. Have you seen the latest edition?"

"No," I said, and kept my face hidden in the shadows of the hat. I hadn't seen a newspaper in over a year. I shouldn't have said anything at all, because the woman turned her face sharply, her nostrils flaring. While she smelled like flowers, the scent coming off of her in the morning heat in mighty wafts, I could only imagine what I smelled like. My last bath had been in the Cauto, on the day that Mario saved me from drowning. It felt so long ago, as if that day belonged to another time before this one, or as if Mario and I were merely characters in a historical play.

"Say no more," the woman whispered. I halted, making her stumble. "Walk. Can you walk? Look at your feet. You are ill, do you understand? This heat is too much for you."

I nodded, and leaned into her, stared at her hands linked with mine. My dirty nails beside her trim, pink ones shamed me, so I curled my fingers to hide them. My heart pounded and I could hear it above all the other sounds of La Cuchilla as the village rose from sleep. The woman must have heard it, too. She whispered, "It's nearly over," patting the top of my hand.

But reason can abandon even the calmest head in moments when death is nearest. When the woman said, "It's nearly over," I had a mad thought that she was going to turn me in, that I had given myself up as an escapee before ever having escaped. So, I began to unstitch myself from the woman, struggling to get my arm away from her.

"Don't be stupid," she whispered through clenched teeth. I saw that she was trying to smile as she spoke, and that her eyes were fixed on the soldier before us, who had stopped talking all at once.

We froze in place, all of us—the soldiers, the pairs of women, and the two of us. "¿Qué pasa aquí?" one of the soldiers asked. I hadn't noticed, but we were outside the gate now. I chanced a look behind me and saw Lulu and Mario in the distance. Lulu had her arms wrapped around Mario from behind, and he was struggling against her. When he looked at me, I turned away, hoping he would listen to my mother, quiet down, and let events unfold as they would. Fate was firmly in charge. I let my body soften, dropped my head onto the woman's shoulder, and was very quiet. I spoke to Mario in my head, saying something like, "Please be good. I love you. Diós, how I love you. I'll come back for you. Take care of my mother," on and on as if I were praying to God Himself, or to the soul of a dead man. Perhaps Mario's two deceased brothers, the Marios who came before him, heard me, because the woman at my side said:

"My colleague has taken ill. It's this infernal heat. You've spent far too long on this tour and now, look! One of our finest nurses is incapable of doing her work today." Her voice carried far, startling the buzzards in the trees so that they began their hideous hissing. The birds had no songs to call their own, but they grunted and hissed all day long.

"What is that?" one of the nurses asked, pointing, as the flock of birds rose into the sky and began their circling.

"Buitres," another nurse said, folding her hands over her mouth.

"So many," they began to wonder, pointing at the place in the distance where they'd begun to do their spirals. "What are they eating?"

The shorter soldier clapped his hands three times, and the women stopped discussing the birds. "The tour is over. You all need rest before your work begins, and this one needs medical attention," he said, pointing at me.

My eyes closed, I felt myself being led away. "Up," I heard the woman who'd saved me say, and I opened my eyes to see a carriage before me, big enough for just the two of us. Around us, the women were being loaded into other carriages, as well as an open wagon. "They let us have this one to ourselves. The others are afraid you might be contagious," she said, smiling at me the way one smiles at a child.

My hands shook, and I laced them together to still them. "You're a reconcentrada, aren't you?" she asked.

I nodded. "Poor thing. Here," she said, and pulled a small candy from her purse, unwrapping it for me and holding it up to my mouth, like a piece of communion wafer. She laid it on my dry tongue and watched as I sucked on what turned out to be a honey-filled sweet. She was observant, and I'm certain had she had a piece of paper and something with which to write, she would have taken notes on me, the way scientists observe the behavior of wild things.

"What's your name?" she asked.

I considered keeping it to myself. I did not trust her yet. Her accent grated at me, and I'd already taken note of her bony wrists and long neck, plotting out ways I could subdue her if I needed to. "Your name?" she asked once more. "Else I'll give you one," she offered. "We are only a few miles from the field hospital. If we're going to concoct a story for you, we'd better start now."

"Why have you helped me?" I asked.

The woman studied me a moment longer. She drew a man's pocket watch from the waist of her skirt, eyed it, ducked her head out of the carriage and peered down the dusty road, then sat down again. "We have some time, I suppose," she said, and then answered my question.

15.
The Birth of Carla Carvajál

Have you ever heard of New York City?" she asked me. I nodded. I'd, in fact, been in New York City, I told her, though I was in Lulu's womb at the time. She laughed at that, saying, "Then the city is in you. I knew I liked you."

Then, I asked her if she'd ever been there. The woman laughed again. "Querida, I was born there." When I raised an eyebrow, she twittered away in American-inflected English, and I stared at her as if she'd grown another head.

"My mother is from Madrid. My father is an Irishman from a place called Pittsburgh. Have you heard of that city?" I shook my head. "No matter," she said, waving her delicate hand in front of her face. "I'm a journalist, and this war is the best thing that's ever happened to my profession," she said.

My left hand rose to my lips as if it had a will of its own and stayed there. Who was this woman? She seemed to be delighting in our war with Spain, as if the events of the age were a gift just for her, tied with a ribbon to match the one on her hat, or an experiment to examine so that she might bask in her findings. I was quivering now, my fear replaced by anger. My rage grew molten, and tears came to eyes.

"Oh, now I've upset you," she said, and drew an embroidered handkerchief from her purse. I took it and wiped my eyes, happy that the white cloth came away grimy. I hoped I had ruined it. "I'm on your side," she said. "I may have been formed in a Spanish matrix, but my blood runs red, white, and blue, I promise you."

Did she mean the Cuban flag, or the American one? I wasn't sure. Nothing made sense in the presence of this woman. Just that morning, I had been starving in a reconcentrado camp, and now I was riding in a leather-upholstered carriage, clutching a fine handkerchief, my mouth still slick with sugar.

"I am writing a report on Weyler's reconcentrado policy. My editor said I wouldn't be able to manage it. He said, and I quote, 'If you get yourself executed by the Spanish, or eaten by one of those Cubans, don't come haunting me.' I told him you Cubans weren't cannibals as far as I could tell, and that I technically was a Spaniard, on my mother's side at least. My Spanish is better than good. I had you fooled, didn't I?"

Yes, fooled, I thought. I looked miserably out of the carriage windows. I jumped when she touched my knee. Her face was soft now, and her eyes had lost that intense stare. She was no longer observing me the way a hawk catches a mouse with her sight before she digs her talons into its back. She was just a woman now, and her brow was creased in worry.

"I haven't answered your question. I couldn't leave you there. You look so young to me. What are you, eighteen? Nineteen?"

"Fifteen," I said, and she sighed and patted my leg again. "Let me take care of you. We'll say you're a novice nurse, sent to the field by your father, an uncompromising Cuban farmer from Santiago who swears allegiance to Spain. That should do. Just make sure to say, 'Viva Cuba española,' every so often and you'll pass."

I could feel my stomach roiling now, protesting the candy. Nausea filled my mouth with an iron taste, and I bit my tongue against it.

"Oh, is it so hard to pretend to support the Spanish? In your heart you are still a rebel," she said.

"It isn't that," I said, holding the back of my hand to my mouth.

"Are you really ill?" she asked, flattening herself against the back of her seat. "I've heard about the diseases that rage in the camps. Dysentery. Cholera. Diós mío, what's wrong with you?"

"Pregnant," I said, choking, and then I really did vomit out the window. When I sat down again I felt better, and hungrier than ever.

Now it was her turn to be stunned into silence. She scanned me again with her hawkish eyes, lingering long on my midsection, counting full moons in her head, I'm sure. "We'll come up with a story for that, too," she said at last.

We rumbled along without speaking, the woman's eyes locked onto me the entire ride, memorizing the look of me, I was certain of it. What words would she use to describe me, I wondered. Thin, I thought, looking at my elbows. Ordinary, I knew, thinking of the smooth planes of my face, the shape of which was more round than anything else, and of my hair the color of an old coffee stain, and my eyes just as watery and without depth.

After a while, she asked, "Who's the father?" I did not speak, because the words would not come. Thinking of Mario deflated me, and I thought if I spoke I would start crying. Already, I could feel my face tensing, growing ugly with the effort not to weep.

"No, no, you don't have to say," she whispered, and I knew she was imagining some ugly moment for me in a dark, muddy bohío. A rape. Incest. It was all over her face—pity bordering on fear. She was writing the story even as I sat before her.

"I love him," I said at last. "He's just a boy. A rebel. He's a hero and my husband," I lied, and touched my stomach.

She smiled. "Have you thought of a name?" she asked.

It was a curious question, and not the first one I would ask of a girl in my position. "Name?" I repeated.

She nodded.

"Mario. Like his father. Mayito," I said. It was the first time

I'd given it any thought, and the name came unbidden, without thinking, really.

"That is sweet. And if it's a girl?"

"I don't know," I said. Again, I hadn't given any of it much thought. Boy, girl, names, none of it seemed to matter while in La Cuchilla. But now, with the green Oriente hills outside, and the reverberation of the carriage wheels and clop of horse hooves, and in the hands of this capable woman, these things took on greater importance. "What's yours?" I asked.

"Blythe Quinn," she said. "But they know me as Blanca Lora around here." She winked at me. I told her I couldn't pronounce her real name anyway. Then, I told Blanca Lora my name, and she said it wouldn't do. "Carla Carvajál," she dubbed me, and I nodded in approval.

"It's the name I'll use when I write your story."

"Gracias," I said.

Years later, the name Carla Carvajál would return to me in the haze of smoke when I told the cigar rollers my life cloaked as fiction. She was the author of the tale, I told them, as if it were all a fantasy. In my heart of hearts, I wished it really had been untrue.

16.

Of Small and Significant Persons

As Blanca Lora promised, the others stayed far away from me, afraid that I'd caught some kind of jungle disease. Some of the nurses were Spanish, and for them the island represented a final frontier. They were the upstart daughters of wealthy families, unwilling to allow themselves to be married off, seeking their own paths in the world. Most of the nurses were Cuban-born, and sympathetic to the Spanish cause. They, too, were the kind of young women that did not fit the typical mold, who nurtured romantic natures (though of the monarchic kind). There were, at the time, parallel field hospitals in other places around the island, staffed by American and Cuban nurses, run by a woman named Clara Barton, who'd garnered some fame for herself as a wartime nurse and volunteer. Her name, among others, fell from Blanca Lora's lips as if she knew these people, and for a long time, I thought she regularly consorted with Theodore Roosevelt and J.P. Morgan and Fanny Brown.

Blanca regaled me with stories of New York City, but more than that, she asked questions. A thousand questions or more she put to me as I "rested" in a bed in a curtained corner of the field hospital. She wanted to know about La Cuchilla, of course, and whether I knew the names of the soldiers in charge of the place (I did not), and how many in the village had died (I wasn't sure. "Many" was my answer), and all about life in the tallér (which I described with such longing for those days that

Blanca sobbed at my bedside and told me I was a born story-teller.)

Once I recovered, Blanca introduced me to the other nurses. My backstory as a Santiaguera with a rigid father was swallowed like a juicy bit of fruit, and when Blanca revealed my pregnancy, explaining that my condition was the product of a violent rape by a vengeful Cuban rebel, the others treated me like a glass figurine, giving me the smallest of jobs to do and bringing me food all of the time—buttered slices of bread, figs and a glass of milk, mashed bananas and rice—so that I fattened up quickly, my cheeks filling out in time with my belly.

Blanca's story had angered me, though. She'd applied a sensational gloss over the narrative my expanding body was telling, which was, in truth, one of love and devotion. How I missed Mario. And Lulu, too. At night, I dreamed they were with me at the field hospital, that we'd switched sides in the war and that Mario now spoke with a Spanish lisp. I would dream him up beside me, conjuring a vision so real and pleasurable that I would wake gasping and shuddering, afraid that the other nurses would notice the way love possessed me, even in the dead of night.

There was this, too: when Blanca spread the story of how I came to be in such a condition, more than one concerned nurse asked me, in tones hushed and deliberate because I was a creature to be pitied, whether my assailant was un negro, one of the dreaded mambíses, those machete-wielding warriors that the Spanish soldiers feared, the ones who threatened to take this paradise of a colony and turn it into another Africa.

"Sí," I told them, and their faces would freeze, their worst fears confirmed. What was I to say? The baby would be born in a few months' time, and he would not be fair. He would be like Mario, and these women would loathe him for that.

Were they capable of hurting my baby? Of taking vengeance on my behalf? I thought so, though I also thought them gentle, especially when tending to the wounded soldiers. Their hands were like butterflies hovering over gashes and split skin. Their mouths made only shushing sounds, and some of them hummed softly, soothing hurt men the way infants are soothed, by filling their eardrums with a continuous sound, mimicking the rush of the womb.

Would they hurt my baby? I wasn't sure. They never referred to him as a baby. The child was "it" and "my complication," and the head nurse, a woman named Andromeda, called him "the issue" with an arch of her eyebrows. Andromeda was aptly named, as there were constellations of moles up and down her arms, in strange patterns. So, I made plans to leave a month before the baby was due. My strategy was only to head back through Oriente province, in the hopes of stumbling upon another tallér somewhere.

I didn't tell Blanca Lora my plans. Anyhow, she had moved beyond me as her pet project. She would travel with medical units to the reconcentrado villages every chance she had.

"There isn't much we can do to help there," she would report to me. "Everyone is starving. Medicine can't cure that. I'm heartsick over it, Carla," she would say, having adopted my new name so fully I'm certain she forgot my real one. I was also certain that she wasn't as heartsick as she claimed. Each night, Blanca Lora would sit, poring over pages filled with figures that mimicked letters, but, upon inspection, were only squiggles and dashes. "Shorthand," she told me once, as if I knew what she meant.

"Have you been back to La Cuchilla?" I asked her, desperate for news about Lulu and Mario. Underneath the palm of my hand, the baby squirmed, and I squeezed a little knob of flesh beneath my skin, felt the retreat of a tiny limb, then resistance again. The baby fought back each time I intruded in its space, and this filled me with joy.

"Yes."

"Is it bad there?"

"It's bad in all the villages," she said, then dropped her voice and covered her pages with her hands, "but this can't last. I overheard a captain saying that the Cubans had them retreating all over the island. The Spanish can't fight guerillas."

"Freedom," I said as if it were a prayer.

"This is what 1776 must have felt like back home," Blanca Lora said with a smile, and I returned the grin, having no idea at all what she meant.

So, the days went, with Blanca Lora talking with me in whispers when she could, and that nurse, Andromeda, following me around the hospital, reprimanding me for bandaging a soldier's wound too tightly, or for sitting on the edge of an unoccupied bed when it felt as if my back would snap in two. Once, she eyed me for a long minute, then, asked, "Where are your parents from?"

"My father was born in the Canaries. My mother in Oriente Province," I answered.

"Where are they now?" she asked.

"My father is dead," I told her without thinking.

"I thought he was a landowner. I thought he sent you here to stay with us, to do your part for Spanish Cuba?"

"I meant my grandfather. My grandfather is dead," I said lamely, keeping my eyes trained on the floor. Andromeda said nothing else, only reminded me to sweep the supply closet sooner rather than later, and to check the splint on a certain Lieutenant Torrejo two beds over.

Every few days, Andromeda would check my pulse and palpate my belly, her eyebrows forming a deep V of consternation. I would tolerate her touch only by counting her moles, which were countless. Sometimes, she spoke of "the issue" and what was to be done with it.

"I will raise him, of course," I told her.

"Raise him," she echoed me, but in that clipped way of speech that was solely hers. When she gave orders in the hospital, it was as if a telegram had come alive and was speaking, dropping articles and the flourishes of sentences. "Clean pans," she would bark, and the other nurses would scurry, cleaning the pans with hands gone raw and cramped. Andromeda's speech. Blanca Lora's shorthand. I was living in a world of abruptness and efficiency, and so I should not have been surprised when my plan to slip away in the night, back towards Dos Ríos, in the hopes of finding a new tallér, amounted to nothing. The clock in the field hospital, it seemed, moved faster than anywhere else in the world, and my body responded in kind.

My son was born early by my count. I had carried him for eight full moons, not nine. But he was big enough and screamed his first sounds while I was still pushing him out. I could say more about the pain, I suppose, but I don't remember it. Rather, I can't name it or describe it. I recall shoving Andromeda's hand away from mine; I could bear no touch in that moment. I can describe for you the feeling of a needle piercing my arm at one point in the ordeal. It was like a bee sting. But the agony of birth is an artful thing—it slinks down deep into a woman's brain, so deep it is later impossible to retrieve. It is like trying to describe the flavor of an avocado. It's buttery texture one can name, but the taste? It escapes expression.

I will just say that Mayito was born at night, just as the sun dipped into the horizon line; that I held him through the hours of darkness, examining his hands, which were like pink starfish; that the quality of his skin reminded me of my girlhood, when I played with potted aloe plants, running my fingers along the smooth, green shoots; that when Mayito's eyes fluttered open, they were gray, and while I never liked the color, I found myself suddenly enamored with it, wishing I had closets full of gray dresses and gray shoes and hoping that my hair would turn just that shade of gray some day; that I kissed the top of his head so often through that night that my mouth hurt from puckering; that his hair was soft like cobwebs, and I imagined tiny spindles in my body, weaving the fine silk; that his breath was sweet, ay Diós, so sweet, like an unripe melon; that his mouth around my nipple was strong, and he would shake his head like a shark tearing at flesh as he drank, but I did not dare wince or make a sound, but only held him closer and clucked into his little cup of an ear, pouring into that tiny vessel the songs Lulu once sang to me, "*Duérmete mi niño, duérmete mi sol . . .* "; that his nose whistled in his sleep; that the skin around his wrists and ankles was flaking off, shedding a waterlogged layer; that I called him my coconut, my little god, my small saint, my sky, my heart, my love, all in succession; that, God forgive me, I imagined the next day with Mayito, and the days after, and the two of us growing old together.

I was young. Even after all I had seen, and all I had lost, that night I believed in a future with my son. I fell asleep holding him, his round bottom a perfect fit in the palm of my hand, his head, still elongated, egg-shaped, hard and warm in the crook of my elbow. The last thing I remember is the sweat collecting between the skin on his back and the skin on my arm.

When I woke up at dawn, Mayito was gone. Andromeda sat at the foot of my bed, writing something down in a notebook with rough, brown pages.

"Where is my son?" I asked carefully. Underneath the sheets, my hands were making fists, opening and closing like crab claws.

"The issue has been resolved," she said, then struck the notebook with her pencil, making one furious dot at the end of a sentence.

17.
The First Surrender

I remember rising from that bed the moment Andromeda turned away from me. I remember coming up behind her so quickly that she did not hear me. I can still remember the texture of her skin under my hands, the wrinkles in her fat neck, how I squeezed and screamed in her ear, and how she peeled my fingers away from her the way one peels a banana. She was calm, even then. She bent over and picked up her notebook, made a few notes there, her eyes darting to me often. She coughed, lightly, as if a piece of meat had gone "down an old road" in her throat, as we used to say. I sobbed and huffed in bed, asking, "Where is he? Where is he, please?" But now she sought to punish me, and so went mute, only writing in her damned notebook for a moment before leaving me.

I wanted to get up and find him. I listened hard for the sound of a baby's cries. I sniffed the air for him, like a dog, and could not detect his honeyed scent in the air. "Mi niño, mi niño," I wailed until Blanca Lora stood by the curtain that divided my bed from the others in the field hospital.

Blanca Lora rushed to my side. "Oh, I know," she said, pulling me close so that my ear lay flat against her breastbone.

"Where is he?" I asked.

"I'll show you. When you're stronger, I'll show you," she whispered.

"Take me now," I insisted, pushing Blanca Lora away and kicking at her.

"I hid him away for you. Somewhere these women can't

find him. You should have heard them whispering after the baby was born. They saw the way you cooed at him, and they didn't believe for a minute the story I concocted for you. 'She must have loved the father,' they said. Another said, 'That girl is a rebel, I promise you that. She stinks of it.' They huddled together, heads down like hens picking at their own waste, thinking of the best way to be rid of the baby and you. 'I'll take care of it,' I told them, and they handed the baby over to me. I have taken care of him, Carla, but you must trust me."

I listened to her and wanted to believe every word, for in her speech there was the promise that my baby was alive and waiting for me.

"Just take me to him, please, Blanca Lora. I've lost everything," I cried and fell upon her breast once more.

"I will, soon. I have to go," she said, and planted a kiss on my forehead. "There's been an explosion in Havana Harbor. An American ship. And here I am in Oriente province, missing it. Mark it down, Carla, President Roosevelt will swarm this island before long." Blanca Lora was vibrating with excitement.

"My son," I said, gripping her wrists and staring hard into her eyes.

"I haven't forgotten him. He's safe and not far, I promise you. Get strong. You'll see him soon," she said, and kissed me again. Then she was gone, walking so fast her backside wiggled and her hair bounced. Blanca Lora cut a springy, cheerful form as she wove around the beds of the field hospital, disappearing from my view.

In the days that followed, the other nurses treated me no differently from any other patient. They did not, of course, meet my eyes, though I searched their faces for signs of betrayal. Which woman had slipped Mayito out of my arms? Which one had first uttered the plan to do away with him? It was a good lesson to learn—evil did not make a mark on a person's countenance. There was no wildness in the eye that spoke of mischief, there was no reddish tinge on guilty hands, there was no nervous laughter between them, nor did they chew their lips anxiously. There was only calm among the nurses of the field hospital, and when they said, "Viva Cuba española," to one another in the passageways, there was a lilt in their voices, as if they were used to singing instead of speaking.

Andromeda no longer came to see me, and I wondered whether I had actually hurt her and whether she was now afraid. I hoped so. Every day without Mayito was like a day without a limb. I was crippled. I could barely feed myself. Sometimes, an air bubble or some other gastric movement would pinch me from within, and for a second, I would think it was Mayito, still in my womb, kicking, and my hand would fly to my belly to touch that ghost baby. It was only a second of confusion before I realized the truth, but each occasion reenergized my grief at having lost him, and I would weep in bed and pound the mattress with my fists, my cries joining the moans of the soldiers around me, the ones who lay injured just past the curtain.

I was the only female patient in the place, and so was kept in isolation. It was just as well. I detested the soldiers. All of them. I hoped that the man who had thrown the torch that set my father on fire was here, limbless, perhaps, oozing all sorts of stinky fluids, dying a slow, reeking, painful death. Twice, a soldier peeked through the curtain to get a look at me, and both times I threw a bedpan at the face. On the third try, the man spoke quickly, saying, "I heard them talk about you, the nurses. They suspect you're a spy for the Cuban Liberation Army. Is that right?"

He was young, and his skin was yellow, like an old piece of parchment. Yellow fever had run rampant among the Spanish, and the field hospital was full of the worst cases. When the skin took on that strange color, everyone knew the case was a bad one, that the black vomit would soon follow, and most likely, death would come.

"No, I am not," I said to the soldier, who grew braver, and stepped out from behind the curtain. He was sick, but strong, and I thought that perhaps he was mending, and that the color would fade from his skin, soon.

"Who are you, then?" he asked. "We all heard your baby being born. We saw when that nurse took him away in the night."

"We?"

"The other boys. All of us saw. We're sick with the yellow fever, but we have eyes and ears, still. We know what you did to that one nurse, saw the marks your fingers made around her throat."

"I was crazed," I said quickly. "Not myself. I want my son back, you must understand."

"She deserved it, I'm sure," he said, smiling, and taking another step forward. I pulled my blanket further up my body.

"You don't sound like a Spaniard," I commented.

"I'm not. Cubano hasta la muerte. And fighting on the wrong side of things," he said quietly.

He grinned at me, and I couldn't tell whether he was toying with me or not, trying to trap me, draw me out so that I would confess who I was. Perhaps Andromeda had set him up for this. "Why are you here?" I asked, keeping the subject on him.

"My father is a Gallego. He also happens to be seventy years old. I was born in my parents' old age, like a character out of the bible. Bueno, the old man tried to enlist. I took his place, but like I said, I'm fighting on the wrong side of things." He coughed every once in a while into a dingy handkerchief, and wiped his mouth carefully. He swayed a little when he finished speaking.

"Sit," I told him, and he pulled a low wooden stool out from under my bed and sat, exhaling, his shoulders slumping. "What's your name?" I asked once he was settled.

"Gilberto Torres," he said. "And you are Carla."

"How do you know my name?"

"You're our sirena, didn't you know?" he said. Gilberto was bold. Sick as he was, he flirted without hesitation, his brown eyes fixed on my face as if he'd known me always.

"Sirena?" I repeated, stuck by the sound of my real name. It had been months since I'd heard it.

"Sí. We're like the lost sailors in stories, the boys out there and I, and you're la sirena that draws us in, keeps our hearts beating. The other nurses have faces like horses. But you, ay, sirena," he said, and clapped a hand against his breast and pretended to swoon. It wasn't too far off the mark, as Gilberto already looked close to fainting anyway. There were dark circles under his eyes and that steady little cough. Suddenly, I thought he might not live.

"Go rest," I urged him.

"Where is your husband?" he asked, leaning forward a little now.

"I don't know," I said honestly. How I wanted Mario with me now, instead of this young man, however sweet Gilberto was turning out to be. That would be my next step—retrieve the baby, and take him to Mario and Lulu. We would be a family again, even if it meant being reconcentrados.

Gilberto began to cough violently. His chest heaved, and he fell off the stool. I clambered out of bed and went to his side. He gripped my forearm and squeezed, then vomited a thin trickle of black fluid. "Here, here," I said, pulling a corner of my bedsheet and wiping his chin.

"Perdón," he kept saying, and I told him it wasn't anything, that we've all been sick before.

"I plan on seeing the end of this conflict," he told me. I didn't know if he meant the war or his illness, and I wondered whether I had triggered something brave and stubborn in him with my pity.

"Of course, Gilberto."

"Call me Gil, and after this war, should you need a friend, find me in Placetas. My father owns a cigar factory there. Torres Reál Cigars. Don't forget, promise?" He extended a shaky hand and I took it and told him yes.

"Good. Good. I'll leave you to your adventures, sirenita." Then, he rose and walked slowly back to his cot among the other sick soldiers.

Three more days went by quickly, while I stayed in that little space. I was not put to work, but I could not rest. My mind reeled with possibilities, and every question I asked about my son, about my future, went unanswered. Once, a pigeon flew into the hospital, and it roosted in the beams above my bed. I watched it for days as it hobbled to and fro on the thick wood, the violet feathers on its cheeks and neck picking up the light like glass. I grew to feel a kind of kinship with the bird, so that when I awoke one day to see it had gone, I lost my breath and felt as if I were going to choke to death, or swallow my own tongue.

It was in this distress that Andromeda found me. She gasped, dropped her scribbling pad, and shook me hard, so that I sucked a great gulp of air. We stared at each other for a long moment. Something shifted in her gaze, I thought, as if she were seeing me for the first time. "Get up," she said softly, and handed me my nurse's clothes, the ones they'd assigned me when I first came to the field hospital. "Dress," she ordered, more harshly this time. Then she left me to do so.

It is a wonder what clothes can do. In bed, I had felt achy from the birth of my son. My limbs were heavy like mallets, and my head felt as if someone had shoved cotton into my ears and nose and mouth. Everything was dull, and I could focus only on the pain in my body and the piercing sorrow regarding my son. But dressed and standing, the physical hurt seemed to diminish. As for the other injury, the one to my heart and soul, there was no remedy.

"Bedpans today," Andromeda said. "After lunch, laundry."

"Sí señora," I mumbled, taking note of the bruise on her neck, faded but still there after two weeks, just beneath her ear. It looked like a pale green orchid, flowering out of the dampness of her skin.

"In the evening, General Gasco is coming to tour the facilities, see the soldiers," Andromeda said, touching the bruise on her neck lightly with two fingers. "I'm certain he'll want to speak with you, Carla." Then she smiled. For the first time since I'd been in the field hospital, Andromeda smiled. She had bright, straight teeth, which were large and square. The top and bottom rows touched, so that there was something simian about her grin that frightened me.

"Sí, señora," I said again.

"You are not my prisoner, Carla," Andromeda said. "If you are able, I expect you to work."

I nodded and worried my fingers against my stomach.

"Did you notice," Andromeda asked, her back turned to me as she wrote a bit in her notebook, "the bird that was trapped in the hospital?"

"Sí, señora."

"It flew away, you know. It found a way out. Finally, after so many days. I'd thought it was a very stupid bird, but I was wrong," she said. Then, Andromeda left me alone.

Perhaps it was an invitation to be like that bird, I thought. It was possible that Andromeda was warning me, in her way.

I searched for Blanca Lora. If I was leaving, I was taking her with me, and she would have to take me to my son. She wasn't among the soldiers. She wasn't in the kitchen, or outside among the nurses who were washing linens in tin tubs with lye soap. "Have you seen Blanca Lora?" I asked a few nurses, and they shook their heads. I grew desperate as the day wore on. I overheard talk among the soldiers about General Gasco's visit, and once, when passing his cot, Gilberto gripped my wrist and said, "You must leave, sirenita. Leave today. Now," and then his eyes had rolled back, revealing yellow orbs without an iris, like twin suns. I checked his pulse before leaving, felt it strong and galloping, then proceeded to the back of the field hospital. On my way, I stole a small handsaw from a table in the operating room. It was still rusty with blood, but it was compact and fit under the waistband of my skirt.

I would find my son even if it meant I had to kill someone.

I was nearly to the back entrance of the field hospital when I heard someone call my name. I froze, afraid to turn around.

"Carla Carvajál, come with me." It was Blanca Lora, wearing a travelling jacket over a long brown skirt. The hat with the red ribbon was back on her head. She clapped a hand on my wrist and tugged me across the road and just past a stand of flamboyán trees. The trees were not in flower, but the giant seed pods hung, dry and clacking in the wind, just above our heads. The noise rattled me, and I kept glancing at the entrance to the hospital, unaware that Blanca Lora had been saying something.

"Listen, will you?" she said, pinching my face between her thumb and forefinger. "I've received a telegram from my editor. They're stirring up for war back home. I've been assigned to Havana, to meet the American consul."

I swatted her hand away from my face. "You promised you'd take me to my son," I said, afraid that she was abandoning me for the city.

"I'll do better than that," she said, and led me on a rocky path parallel to the road until we could no longer make out the hospital. "Up here," she said, moving through the trees and back onto the road, where a carriage waited, hooked up to a giant black horse covered in scars, as if someone had whipped it. The wounds appeared old, and the animal snorted at us when we approached and showed its teeth.

"Apocalyptic, isn't he?" Blanca Lora said before ushering me into the carriage. A slender man in a white shirt and dark pants spoke to Blanca Lora in rapid English. Then, he drove us away, clipping the tortured horse with a short whip so that it galloped as fast as it could go. We bounced on our seats inside the carriage, our heads hitting the velvet ceiling every so often.

"Where are we going?" I shouted over the noise of horse hoofs and the clatter of wheels.

"Another hospital. This one is run by the Liberation Army. Used to be a tallér of the sort you remember."

"And my son is there? He's well?"

"He's there. So is your mother." Blanca Lora went very still when she said all of this, and I should have understood that something was wrong. Instead, I wept joyfully into my hands.

"Where? Where is this place?"

"It's north, in San Agustín," Blanca Lora said, only her lips moving as she watched me.

I felt like leaping from the carriage and running the rest of the way. San Agustín, my father's name-saint! My father was watching us from above, I was sure, guiding our little family, reuniting us. Such were the thoughts I had as we rumbled through the war-scorched countryside, passing burnt sugar fields and ragged men marching through swampy pine forests. I'd forgotten that I had given thought to my father in the after-life already, in the months after his death, and had decided that he was likely not in Heaven.

"Carla, your mother—" Blanca Lora began.

"Ay," I said because I knew at once that something had gone terribly wrong.

"She's ill. Very ill, darling." Blanca Lora did not look me in the eyes as she spoke, but instead, looked at a spot at my collar, as if I had a stain there.

"Is there hope?" I asked.

"I am not certain. I'm not really a nurse, you see," she said, and smiled just a little. She reached out and held my hand, and we traveled the rest of the way like that.

We rode hard for a few hours until we came to the tallér in San Agustín, which was larger than the one I had lived in with Lulu. There were no tents, but a proper building with coral walls, bleached white in the sun. There was even a small lawn, where soldiers lounged on the grass, their wounds wrapped in clean linens.

"How is a place like this possible?" I asked, thinking of what had happened to our tallér, how Weyler had shut us down, killed our women, moved us all to reconcentration camps.

"The Cubans are winning the war," Blanca Lora said. "The Spanish are in retreat throughout the east. And now, with the Americans thinking of joining the fray, talléres like this are of little concern."

"If we're winning," I said, running my hand along a sharp coral wall as we entered the tallér, "why are the Americans coming?"

"You know that Cuban saying about picking low-hanging mangoes, don't you?" I understood and asked no more questions. Even if I'd had more of them, the sight before me would have rendered me mute.

"Lulu," I said, for she was directly before me, in one of the beds nearest the entrance.

"Wait," Blanca Lora said, trying to stop me and failing. It was a halfhearted attempt on her part, like trying to keep someone from jumping off of a high place—she was afraid I would take her with me, plummeting into a terrifying emptiness.

My mother was sick. My mother was dying. I heard a nurse somewhere say the word "typhoid," and I saw at once the rosy bloom all along her neck. They'd put her in bed naked, covered in a scratchy sheet that was pulled over her breasts. Her shoulders were bare, and dotted in pink spots. The hollow of her neck was a dark, shivering pit, her pulse racing just beneath the skin there.

"Mamá," I said, and searched for her hands in the mess of sheets. I took them in mine and squeezed lightly. Lulu was in a fever dream, and her hallucinations had deposited her somewhere in the past, for when she spoke it was to Agustín, and she was saying, "The baby needs new bottles. She needs diapers, and gold earrings for her ears. Where are you, Agustín? Where have you gone?"

I felt Blanca Lora's cool hand on my shoulder. "I went back to La Cuchilla two days ago, once I knew I was leaving for Havana. I'd heard the Spanish had abandoned the village, and that the people inside did not leave. Like animals trained to love their cages, they did not leave. I wanted to surprise you, Carla. I wanted to bring them here, like I brought the baby, and have you join them. But I found Lulu in her house, sick as she is. There were clothes everywhere, hanging like curtains. I've never seen a thing like it. She was burning up, Carla. Just burning up."

"How long?" I asked without letting go of my mother's hand. Lulu was saying something now about boots ("Put them away," she kept crying).

"How long?" Blanca Lora echoed me.

"How long had you known that La Cuchilla was liberated?" I was afraid of the answer. I knew the progression of typhoid. Four weeks, from beginning to end. From the looks of it, Lulu was in the third week of the disease.

"About a month," Blanca Lora said. "There was no way you could travel, Carla. Not with the baby."

I took a deep breath and tried to forget about the saw still hidden in the waistband of my skirt. "Where is Mario? And the baby? Where is my baby?"

Blanca walked around and sat on the other side of my mother's bed. "Oh, Carla."

"That's not my name."

"Mario is gone. I asked for him, and they said he enlisted with the Spanish."

"That's a lie," I said. I could not imagine it, my Mario in Spanish uniform.

"I'm not lying to you," Blanca Lora said sadly.

Lulu opened her eyes and saw me. Her mouth formed my name but no sound came forth. She smiled, and I saw that one of her front teeth was missing. I wept, squeezing Lulu's hands as if trying to pump blood into them, the way one works a bellows.

"One of the villagers helped me transfer your mother into a carriage. He was gentle, and informative. He said Mario had struck a deal with the Spanish shortly after you left. He would enlist because their forces had been greatly diminished, and in return, Lulu would be set free. Of course, those kinds of promises are easily broken . . . "

What had happened while I was away? What kind of bond had Mario and Lulu forged? He, who had lost his mother so young, had found Lulu. And she, abandoned by her child, for that is how I thought of my departure now, had found a son to love. Had they taken refuge from storms together? Had they talked about me and about the baby? Had they imagined a future where we could all be together, or had they despaired? This was the story I told myself, the way I imagined them in that place while I changed bedpans and held down Spanish boys having their limbs sawed off, and delivered a baby who was taken from me.

"Where is the baby?"

"Next door. There are a few children here. Orphans mostly."

I rose at once, eager to see him, but Lulu held my hands tightly. "No te vayas," she whispered.

"Mamá, the baby is here. Let me see to him, and I'll come

242 · CHANTEL ACEVEDO

back. You can hold him, when you're stronger," I said. Her eyes fluttered, and she began to pick at her arms, pinching her skin and hissing. It reminded me of one of those times when we were marching the countryside with Agustín, and Lulu had stepped on an anthill. The creatures had crawled up her legs and torso, and spread like Chinese fireworks over her arms, and she'd picked at them in just that way. Agustín and I had helped, of course, and later, had put cool compresses on the welts that formed on her body.

But there were no ants here. Nothing crawled upon my mother but death, for I had seen such delirium before in typhoid patients, and it meant that the end was closer than I had thought at first.

I tried to still her hands, but they jerked away from me. She clawed at her eyes and moaned. "Help me," I said to Blanca Lora, and she held onto one of Lulu's hands while I held the other.

I hailed one of the nearby nurses, and she brought me water, which I tried to give to Lulu in small sips. Dehydration, delirium, a body gone poisonous—the typhoid fever was running its course and I was helpless to stop it.

She was like one of those buildings from Cuba's pirate age that have fallen into ruin. They're in Havana, mostly, and their airy balconies and wooden shutters speak of another time, when there were cannons upon the walls along the sea, and men out there who made a life out of pillage. When they crumble, they're clouded in dust, obscuring the wreckage. Foamy, like a great wave crashing, the debris hangs in the atmosphere for a moment before cresting and falling. After the air clears, the broken building reveals its treasures—copper wiring glitters in the sun, steel rods shine like swords, and the possessions of the people who lived inside become new again in the open air.

This is what it was like watching Lulu die. She was broken

and ugly at the height of her illness. Feverish, red-faced, and delirious, she had become the witch she had conceived herself as back in La Cuchilla. Her hands were claws. Her feet curled in on themselves, too, as pain ratcheted through her body. But somehow, her voice grew softer and more beautiful, huskier than it once was. Her eyes, filled with tears, shimmered as if her irises were laced in tinsel. Her eyes and mouth became windows to the woman within, and inside, she was beautiful.

When her eyes rolled back into her head, I backed away, a terrible thought crowding my head. "Mayito. I need to see him," I demanded, thinking of my son sleeping so near this kind of infection.

"The next building over," Blanca Lora said, and led the way. I followed. Even when Lulu called my name, I followed Blanca Lora instead. I replay that little moment in my head often. I've dreamed it myriad ways—Lulu says my name while trapped in a coffin, or gurgling the syllables underwater, or mutely, from behind a thick piece of glass. Again and again I see her in my imagination calling to me and I always go towards my son. Lulu would often tell me that I would know the sum of love and grief when I had children of my own, and so it was. I know, too, that Lulu would run to me, always, no matter who called her name. This guilt is monumental, as is the certainty that I would do it the same way again, given the chance.

I followed Blanca Lora first to a washstand, and I scrubbed my arms and neck with lye soap, my skin turning red from the harsh treatment. Then, we entered a squat building behind the place we'd just been. Inside, a few children played with wooden toys—tops and rolling carts and even a small wooden bicycle without pedals—on a tiled floor. In a crib were three sleeping babies, and lying in the center, with his legs draped over those of another infant, was Mayito.

I lifted him up without concerns about waking him. He did

wake, in fact, and howled, his face wrinkling and grimacing. I kissed his cheeks and forehead, and held him close to my body. Mayito quieted, and rooted around for the milk I no longer had. "Mi santo," I told him. "Mi rey." He was, indeed, like a tiny saint and king to me. Already, I was under his spell, small as he was.

"Gracias," I said to Blanca Lora through my tears. She touched my shoulder and patted Mayito's head. "How did you manage it?" I asked.

"I was the one who took him from you as you slept. I'd arranged things here in this tallér just after I met you. I simply could not trust Andromeda and the others," Blanca Lora said.

"What were they going to do?" I asked, clutching Mayito tightly.

"God knows," Blanca Lora said, "but I wasn't about to let them show us. I told Andromeda that I would handle 'the issue,' as she liked to put it."

I kissed Mayito, and said, "Mm hmm." Then, I kissed him again. I could not stop myself.

"She didn't even ask any questions, for goodness' sake. For all she knows, I threw the baby into the river," Blanca Lora said.

I looked up, aghast. Just the thought of it made me teary, and Blanca Lora apologized, and called me "darling" as she was apt.

"It's safe for you to take him to Lulu," she said. "I've asked the nurses. As long as she doesn't touch him, it's safe."

I nodded, but wasn't eager to leave the safety of the nursery just yet. So, I sat in a rocking chair and rocked my son, singing him songs until the sun began to set.

Later that evening, I introduced Mayito to his grandmother, who couldn't focus on him. I sniffed his head, and fed him from a bottle when he cried out. He was changed. Bigger, he curled his hand around my thumb with purpose, drawing it to his mouth as if to eat it. His eyes no longer crossed when he stared at my face, but instead, he gazed at me sleepily. His long lashes begged to be touched, and I did so, with the back of my fingers. Mayito looked like his father, and this made me cry in silence and send prayers up to guard his safety.

All the while, Lulu was restless, moaning and smacking at imaginary creatures on her body. She finally grew still at dawn. Only her eyelids fluttered upon her face like moth wings. The baby was asleep, snoring softly, his rib cage showing itself with every exhalation. The tallér had grown quiet, and in the calm I began to count Lulu's breaths, wondering how many she had left.

PART III

1.
What Lulu Wanted

S top that," Lulu said suddenly, and I startled and gripped her hand.

"Mamá?"

"You're counting. I can hear you. It's making me nervous." Lulu's chin trembled as she spoke.

"I'll stop," I promised, and felt her face, which was still burning. I peeled the warm, damp cloth from her forehead and replaced it with a fresh one.

"I feel better," she muttered, and tried to rise. I should have been glad to see her sudden burst of energy, but it saddened me. I'd seen it so many times at the field hospital. The spirit rallies, one last gust of life blows through, and then, the patient dies.

"Perhaps you shouldn't," I said.

Lulu pushed my hands away. "I want something for you," she said quietly. She touched Mayito's head and smiled. I waited. In my arms, Mayito began to stir.

"Mamá, you should rest."

"No, I want something for you." Her voice was husky. "I wish I had a dish of honey for you to taste. That way, when you think of me, you will also remember something sweet. My father, que en paz descanse, once told me that Jews gave children a taste of honey before teaching them about God. Did you know that la Virgencita likes offerings of honey?"

Lulu began to cough, and tried covering her mouth with her hands. But they twitched at her sides with the effort to raise them, and her eyes filled with tears.

"Mamá," I cried, and rested my head on her chest. I could feel her lungs rumbling with something thick and foul. Then, I felt her hand on the back of my head. Mayito mewled between us, and I sat up. When the coughing fit subsided, Lulu spoke again.

"We kept dessert plates filled with honey next to the little statues of la Virgen in our house and in the shoe shop. Ants would often drown in the stuff, and my father would then clear the honey away, wash the dish and fill it again. He used to wear a scapular around his neck, underneath his crisp shirts. It was soft like leather, and I used to fall asleep in his arms with the scapular tight in my grip, or else, I'd pass it over my eyes and cheeks and I imagined the thumb of an angel touching my skin.

"My father's last words were, 'My scapular, my scapular,' which a doctor had removed from him during an examination, and which, my father believed, was a token that guaranteed entrance into Heaven. I remember putting the frayed ribbon around his neck, and arranging the images of Christ and his Mother on his heaving chest. He fingered the leathery squares blindly, having to grope for them before catching them in his weak grip. Then, he began to scream. My father died screaming, a hoarse, screeching sound, like a rodent in a trap. What kind of payment for a lifetime of devotion is that?"

A nurse came and took my mother's temperature, glanced at the reading, then gave me a frown, the expression spreading across her face rapidly. Everything felt as if it were moving too quickly—facial expressions, the ticking of a clock on the wall, my mother's breaths. It was as if the shock of her death had already happened, and the world was trying to catch up to it.

With effort, Lulu touched Mayito's cheek. "The baby's father—" she began. A frown spread slowly across her face.

I felt a space open up in my chest, a hollow feeling. "What about Mario?"

Lulu swallowed hard, then said, "He gave up his freedom for me. They promised I could go if he joined the Spanish. But they put a uniform on him and swallowed him up, leaving me to die."

"He'll find a way out," I said to Lulu. "He's smart, and strong. He's—" But Lulu shook her head.

"I saw him when he went. He was already half-dead with sadness. A broken man has no business fighting a war."

The pale moon of her face was very still and her dark eyes unblinking. "We're all dying," she said. "Even the stars and the sun. They'll wink out one day. Nothing a human can think up can stop death when it comes."

"Mamá, don't talk that way," I said.

"I want something for you," she told me again.

"What is it? Tell me," I urged her, but her fingers began to flutter rapidly, and the convulsions began. Nurses ran to join us, and they held my mother down, gripping her in their strong hands. Lulu's gaze was fixed on the ceiling, and I looked up too, asking for a blessing. "Pray, Mamá, pray," I whispered, thinking that if she joined me in this, if we both asked jointly for a miracle, then our prayers might be answered.

In the end, Lulu neither cried nor struggled much. She trembled a bit after it was all over, then was still.

2.
A Story New to Me

I've come to the part of my story I cannot tell. All con-
fessions come to their decisive moment, the part of the
tale where one can choose to lie and save face. It is like
standing at a precipice. One need only take a single step into
nothing and then, the fall just happens. There is no stopping it
then.

I tell the women, "I'm finished. I can't go on." They don't
say anything. Dulce is drying her eyes with the collar of her
housedress. Susana is staring at me with her mouth wide open,
revealing three dark metal caps on her back molars.

"Of course you can go on. It's what we do. We go on. Learn
how to live with the suffering we're dealt," Rosalia says in that
squeaky voice of hers.

She and her healthy twin sons can go to hell, I think, and I
am about to say something along those lines when Mireya says,
"Isn't that the point of all of this, to share your story with us?
So let's hear the rest of your great, tragic tale." She watches me
with a single arched eyebrow.

There have been only a few moments in my life when I have
been so blinded by anger that I seem to have lost possession of
my mouth. Once, when Beatríz was fourteen, she called me
una estúpida because I had refused to buy her a dress with a
coveted pink crinoline. Right there, in the middle of the third
floor of El Encanto Department Store, I launched into a ten-
minute declamation about the abuses of daughters, the
impunity of fourteen-year-olds, ingratitude, selfishness, and

ugly fashion. There have been other times, but I have not felt this way, the words pushing past my lips in an angry torrent, in a very long time.

I tell her, "Let me say what I've been meaning to say for the last ten years, ridícula—all of your dramatics and for what? Some invention of your addled brain," I say. "My Beatríz left your son ten years before he passed. A decade. What did that break up have to do with his death? Nada. Nada. God only knows why He took your son. An infection can happen to any of us. Rosalia talks of living with our suffering, but you, Mireya, have not lived in it. You have wallowed in it, consumed it, let it get you drunk with stupidity and self-pity." I open my mouth to say more when I feel someone physically shove me back into my seat. Had I been standing? I realize that yes, not only had I stood up, I'd looked down on Mireya as I'd raged, my finger wagging in her face. Now, Mireya is sobbing, and Ofelia (it was Ofelia who pushed me down), is saying, "¡Basta! ¡Basta! We have to be good compañeras to one another. You're behaving like children, all of you!"

I remember once going to a bullfight in Havana with Gilberto. I watched the bulls in their pens with fascination. Gilberto had won a pair of tickets in a raffle, and so we dressed up in our Sunday clothes, packed a meager lunch, and attended the bullfight. We even shouted, "¡Toro!" now and again, taking sides with the black beasts. How they huffed, their snorts rumbling through the stands, and blowing out plumes of dirt roiled up by their massive hooves. Theirs was incessant motion. Even when a bull was killed in the arena, the ones in the pens stamped and huffed, and bumped the door of the pen with their giant foreheads, eager to get out. That is how I feel now, I think. Like a great bull. It doesn't matter that I am asking for the hurt that is sure to come. Mireya might as well be holding a red cape for me. I tremble, coiled in frustration as I watch her weep.

I can feel it—the sides switching. The women have surrounded Mireya, childish, whiny Mireya, and are patting her hair and telling her everything will be fine. Even Susana has joined them, and she is holding up a cup of lukewarm lemonade to Mireya's flaccid lips. Every so often, one of them looks at me, the way Lulu did when I had been naughty and was caught.

We are quiet for a moment, only the sounds of Mireya's sniffling breaking the silence. I am hopeful that Ofelia will choose to remove me from the room. Damn this confession, I think. These women are no friends of mine. Perhaps, if I still have a home to return to, I can tell Panchita my story. She can regale her grandsons with it once I'm dead, and they can tell their wives. One of them, I've heard, is a professor in the University of Santiago. She could write it all down. And the cigar rollers, they've heard parts of the story, with different names, of course. Perhaps my story has already been told, thousands of times, perhaps this has all been a big waste of—

"I found him. I found him," Mireya is saying, and we all stand very still and listen.

"Found who?" Dulce asks.

"I found Alejandro hanged from an exposed beam in the kitchen. He punched through the ceiling to get to it, and he used the laundry line for rope. I found him. No one else. And I brought him down and called his name. He was alive, you see, but hurt. 'My legs,' he said. 'My hands,' he said, and I knew he could not move them. In the hospital, he caught an infection. 'Beatríz,' he said at the height of his fever. Her name was the last word he uttered. It was an infection. I told no lie," she says.

Mireya looks past Susana, who is blocking her view of me, and lifts a finger to point, shakily, in my direction. "It was a decade since she left him, yes, but he never forgot," Mireya says. "And Beatríz told him that you had convinced her of the error of loving my son. You turned her head, and he, he . . . he put his own head in a noose. Perhaps, María Sirena, you know a little something about remembering the dead. We've all had to listen about the ghosts of your family for some time now. We all have ghosts. And none of us forget them," Mireya says, and for once, I agree with her.

I sit stunned into silence. The pain in my center sharpens, and I think—*so little time.* "We all have our ghosts. You're right, Mireya." I stand and go to her. I am thankful, suddenly, that she has kept this secret. Beatríz never knew, and she will never know, not if I can help it. Mireya lets me wrap my arms around her, then, slowly, I feel her arms at my back, squeezing tight. "Tell us about Alejandro," I say. "I am so very sorry. Tell us a funny story from his boyhood. Make us laugh, the way you once made me laugh, Mireya," I say, and realize I am weeping.

Diós, I'm tired. So tired. The walls of this room feel like they are thickening, trapping us inside as if we are in a cocoon, and outside, a creature is spinning, making the walls congeal, waiting for us to turn into some new beings at the end of our confinement, or to die and make an end of it. This is what a baby feels like before its birth, I think. Surrounded, muffled, made sleepy by the unending darkness. The word comes to me without warning—entombed. I shudder.

"Is this Mayito?" Estrella asks, holding up the picture frame that has been in my pocket all this time. It must have fallen out when I embraced Mireya.

"Sí," I say, and take it back, hiding it again.

"Looks like a newspaper clipping," she says. "Was your son famous or something?"

"No. He wasn't famous."

"Why was he in the newspaper then?" she persists.

"I don't want to go on," I say, and mean more than just answering Estrella's questions, more than just the story. "I'm tired," I say. "Let Mireya tell us a story. Come, my friend. Please."

Mireya shakes her head. I start to protest, but Mireya shakes her head again.

"Hurry up," she says. "We don't have much time left." The waters have been receding, and already, we hear a different kind of noise from outside. Hammers are pounding away, and car horns are honking. The roads must be clearing. She's right. We won't be here, together, not for much longer.

"Not much time at all," I say, and finish what I've started.

3.
The First Mistake

I fell asleep shortly after Lulu died. Blanca Lora happened to walk by and saw us, like a Renaissance sculpture—my head on my mother's stomach, the baby nestled in the crook of my arm, and Lulu's face, as white as marble. Mayito cried when I shifted him, and I squeezed my eyes tight

In the days that followed the women learned that I already served as a nurse and they put me to work in the tallér. They heard, too, of my time in that other tallér in Dos Rios, which had become well-known after General Weyler's attack. I did not realize it then, but one of the women had escaped from the tallér in Dos Rios, and had watched as Weyler ordered the deaths of our compatriots, then marched us to La Cuchilla. She told the news of our capture and the story had spread like pollen on the wind.

"Tell us what happened, María Sirena," the women would ask me, and I would repeat the story for them. This happened each day, so that Mayito, whom I carried in a sling across my chest like an Indian, would settle and go to sleep once he heard me describing the scene of our ruin. That story was his first lullaby, and I am sorry for it. I now wish I had filled his ears with a different kind of story, one full of hope instead of despair.

I lived in that tallér for five months. Mayito was a big baby, his thighs fat like sponge cake, and his smiles were shiny, easily given things. He was sitting by himself by then, too, and I thought him the most gifted of children for that skill alone. "He's beautiful," I bragged at every turn, "and not just because he is mine," I would add, qualifying the boast.

I thought Mayito and I could go on this way indefinitely. The tallér was safe, the work was satisfying, and there were always plenty of other women around to watch the baby for me while I worked. He was the doll of the place, and more than once, I'd discover that someone had dressed him like a girl, or put ribbons into his curls, or set him on a large, friendly dog that lay about the place waiting for scraps, just to watch the baby riding the gentle beast. Mayito was loved, and I was happy for the first time in an age.

The news regarding the war was good, too. We had nearly beat the Spanish, and the Americans, having joined the fight, had sounded the death knell for the Spanish cause. Now, American soldiers came and went in the tallér, and Blanca Lora was among them often, though they called her Blythe Quinn, or Miss Quinn. She had a way with those blond boys, making them laugh and clip her chin with their knuckles playfully. They'd sneak peeks at her notebook, and steal her pen, and she would chase them around the beds, which were mostly empty now that the winter was here and the cases of typhoid and yellow fever were diminished.

It only took ten weeks for the Americans to finish what we started. We celebrated our independence only briefly. Already, there was talk among the women regarding the interference of Washington in Havana affairs. Wasn't this our war? Why were the Americans deciding what happened next? They had fought for ten weeks. We had fought three wars over decades.

I tried explaining this to Blanca Lora, but she shook her head and told me I didn't understand.

"You have bigger problems," she said. "The tallér is going to be shut down. Where will you work? Who will take care of Mayito?"

I hadn't given it a thought. I was only seventeen, orphaned, husbandless.

"Perhaps you can come to New York? There's work to be had. Opportunities abound, Carla!" Blanca Lora said.

"I can't leave Cuba," I mumbled, though I could not come up with a reason why. After all, hadn't I been born at sea? What claim did the island have on me? I had nothing left. True, my mother was buried not far from the tallér, and Agustín's ashes, for I imagine his body having burned down to cinders, floated on Cuban breezes. Only God knew what had become of Mario. Corpses, and a loveless future, were all I had left.

Blanca Lora shook her head and gave me a soft kiss on the cheek. "Think on it," she told me. "I'm leaving in a week."

Seven days later, I let her leave. It was hope that did it, kept me pinned in place. Soldiers often appeared in the tallér, boys who were once thought lost resurrected. And we witnessed reunions that would move a statue to tears. Mothers embracing their sons, wives their husbands, children their fathers. Perhaps there was hope that Mario would return to me.

Blanca Lora hugged me hard and said, "Remember my name, Blythe Quinn, should you ever find yourself in New York City." She handed me a piece of paper with her name and a foreign address printed in neat letters and numbers.

"María Sirena Alonso, not Carla Carvajál," I told her, and she laughed and said of course she would remember the real me.

Then, she was gone, and letting her go was my first mistake. I watched her slim figure board a carriage bound for Havana. She thrust her arm out of the window and waved her straw hat at me. The hat's red ribbon trailed in the breeze for a long time like a flag of surrender before she disappeared from sight.

4.

The Second Mistake

S oon, it became clear that the tallér would be closed for
good. There were no more soldiers to tend to, no more
work to be done. I spent the days with the other women,
learning to crochet long, sloppy chains of yarn while the baby
slept, and trying not to think of Mario, or Lulu, or of anything
but the needle in my hands.

Then, a soldier stumbled into the tallér, dragging his left leg
behind him. We rushed towards him, happy to have something
to do. He let us take care of him, allowed us to discover his
wounds. I mapped them out on his body, like a cartographer,
drawing lines with a damp sponge across a scar behind his ear,
connecting that to a fresher scratch on his collarbone, stopping
for a moment at a coin-sized wound on his chest, soothing a
flowering bruise at his hip, and ending at his leg, which was
full of shrapnel. I thought of a globe that used to sit atop the
dresser in Julio Reyes's own room, back in the Havana of my
childhood. How I used to make it spin. How I dug out the
island of Cuba with a sharp pencil, and how Julio Reyes had
pretended not to notice, to spare me the punishment Lulu
would surely mete out. The world was small and hollow and
covered in paper when I was a child.

"What's happened to you?" I asked him in a quiet moment.

"I don't want to speak of the war, señorita," he told me, and
he said the same to any of the women who asked him.

But over the course of that first night in the tallér, the soldier's wish was proving difficult. He awoke from what must

have been a hellish nightmare, screaming. Once, he sat upright and shouted, "To the wall! To the wall!" then he stopped, looked around, and fell asleep as he sat.

In the morning, over breakfast, we sat around him as he ate, and he told us about the reconcentration camps all over the eastern end of the island, of the skeletal children who haunted his dreams, and the twisting bodies of vultures over each camp, like flags marking the place where the soldiers of the Liberation Army were to go next.

"I am the very last soldier, I think," he said. "The last. All the rest are well at home, their uniforms hanging in their closets, or they are dead."

One of the nurses patted his arm. Another took his breakfast tray away. I sat very still, registering the impact of what he had just said.

The last soldier. The others all dead, or safe. And me, alone in the tallér, waiting in vain.

There was no hope for Mario, I thought. For days I repeated this to myself and my body always tensed when I thought of it, of never seeing Mario again. I would imagine him in a field, his dark eyes somehow pale and lifeless. I thought ceaselessly of shallow graves, and of his strong fore-arms withering away to the bone. I would tremble and swal-low hard to keep from crying. After a while, the bouts of trem-bling ceased, and a weakness of my body took over. *Perhaps there is a chance . . .* I would think for a moment, then grief would come and I would avert my face if anyone was nearby. My nature once leaned towards hope, but no longer.

In the days that followed the soldier's appearance and recu-peration I felt somehow more alone than I had ever been. The tallér would soon close. I had nowhere to go. I imagined the island like a map. I let my mind wander over the hills and val-leys, down the snaking rivers, through jungles and onto open beaches. Then, in that space between wakefulness and dreaming, I shot out over the ocean, north, following the trail my parents had made sixteen years earlier at my birth, past lighthouses and rocky shores and arriving at New York City, with those buildings I'd only seen in sketches in the newspapers, and men and women in long coats.

I rose and practiced saying her name a few times—Blythe Quinn, Blythe Quinn. When the opportunity arose, I would know what I had to do.

The day after Christmas, a group of Americans arrived at the tallér. There were five men, and two women, who carried black books in their hands with half-filled pages. There were rows of numbers on the paper, and they scribbled incessantly in those books as the men spoke. Among them was a Sergeant Landon, who seemed too young for such a title. His hair was a brassy color, and his eyes were two blue buttons. He was very tall, far taller than Mario or Agustín had been. He wore the dark blue uniform of his rank, with a sharp-edged cap with light blue piping above the black leather hatband. He held the hat in his hands, twirling it playfully as he spoke with a chaplain who had come with the group of Americans. Sergeant Landon and the others walked through the tallér, pointing here and there at the ceiling, peering out the windows at the vast tract of land that surrounded the tallér, and avoiding the eyes of the women there, the ones who had called the tallér home and who now stood with their backs against the walls, wondering what would become of them.

I do not count myself among these women. I would not simply wait for a future to develop slowly before me like the seasons. I would force tomorrow's hand.

I had picked up a little bit of English from Blanca Lora. I heard the Americans talk about real estate, and I heard the word "tobacco" again and again. The tallér would become a processing plant, American-owned by the looks of it. I followed the men as they toured the buildings, and they ignored me. Mayito was asleep in my arms. I listened, picking up what I could, and watched the scribbling women. I had found a savior in Blanca Lora, an American woman, and I hoped for another chance, counting on kindness and generosity of spirit as a national trait among these northern creatures.

"Señores," I called out once the men reached the courtyard. The breeze was cool and parrots squawked in the palms. I addressed Sergeant Landon first.

"New York. Blythe Quinn. We go," I said, hoping he could string together what I meant.

"What's this?" Sergeant Landon asked, wrinkling his nose at Mayito who had woken and smiled at the blond man.

"We go New York," I said. "Miss Blythe Quinn. Amiga mía," I tried again. "You take. You take."

The chaplain pressed forward and stood next to Sergeant Landon. The women scribbled furiously, and I wondered what numbers they were deriving from this exchange. Mayito tugged at my hair.

Sergeant Landon stuffed his hand into his pants pocket and drew out a piece of bread, still soft from the morning. He held it out to Mayito, the way one presents a bit of food to a wild animal, and like a wild thing, the baby snatched it fast, and stuffed it into his mouth in one motion.

"No, no," I said, taking the bread from him. He was too young for it, and I feared he would choke.

"Hungry," Landon said, and I pretended not to understand that particular word. I waited for Mayito to smile at Landon, which he did, darling boy. I pushed towards Landon again, saying, "Take New York. Blythe Quinn." I had the little piece of paper ready in the palm of my hand. "Mira," I said, pointing to the address Blanca Lora had given me before she left.

Landon and the chaplain conversed for some time, and they seemed to be in disagreement over something. All the while I repeated, "Blythe Quinn," her real name, and, "New York City", and I gestured by touching Mayito's chest, and then reaching out to touch Landon's. He jumped back at that, startled, and the women of the tallér who had been watching laughed. Landon's cheeks reddened.

I heard him say the word "Manhattan," which Blanca Lora had mentioned as her home, and I smiled. It was working. We were going to leave the island, and perhaps, perhaps, the cold and the distance would sap me of affection, draw Mario and Lulu and Agustín's memory from me like a leech draws blood.

"Come," Landon said, and reached out for Mayito. I let him take the baby. My God, I let him take the baby, who watched this enormous blond man with such interest. Landon handed Mayito over to one of the scribbling women, who took the baby and bounced him on her hip. I thought, *look, they are kind, these American women*. He took the paper with Blanca Lora's address on it from me. His fingers were hard and rough as they brushed against mine, reminding me of bamboo stalks. He put the paper into a pocket on his breast. Then, Landon and the rest of his retinue turned to leave the tallér.

I followed them, shouting about my meager things. "I have only a few clothes. And the baby's things. Give me but a moment to collect them," I said in Spanish. The group of Americans paused, turned, and gave me strange looks.

"Money," I heard the chaplain say. It was another word I understood.

Landon drew out a ten-dollar bill from another pocket. He flattened it against his thigh before giving it to me. I shook my head and gave it back. The chaplain sighed, and drew a five-dollar bill from somewhere, added it to Landon's money, and handed it back to me.

"Perhaps they want you to secure your own passage to New York," one of the women said quietly from inside the building. They'd been watching.

"Sí," said another. "It's money for a ticket."

I faced Landon. "We go together or we don't go at all," I said, gesturing for my son.

"What's all this about?" asked another man striding across the tallér towards us. He wore a suit and vest. A golden pocket watch swung against his belly. He'd asked in Spanish, and before I could answer, Landon whirled, smiling broadly, and chittered away in English with the man. The two embraced, pounded one another on the back, and talked about things I did not comprehend. Soon enough, they both turned to look at me, and at Mayito, still in the arms of one of the American women.

The man introduced himself to me. "Gustavo Bernál, a tu servicio," he said. Short, stocky, but gallant, Bernál brought my hand to his lips and placed a warm kiss on my knuckles. "You are in need of help, I can see," he said.

"My son and I—" I tried to begin.

"Your son? Yours?"

I always forgot what others saw first—the differences between Mayito and me. "Sí, all mine," I said, trying hard to keep frustration out of my voice.

"Que bonito," Bernál said. "His skin is like café con leche."

I did not like this man. But he was the only translator around at the moment. "Señor, I have here the address of a friend in Nueva York. She has promised to take my son and me in, to help us make lives for ourselves in América."

Bernál turned to Landon, and the two conversed some more. They both laughed a great deal, punctuating their sentences with mirth. I wished they were less jolly, more serious. So much depended on this moment, and I didn't find a thing about it funny.

"Can he help us? Can you?" I interrupted. "We have no means of passage," I went on. "We have no way of getting to Blythe Quinn at the moment, and our moment is a very desperate one. We cannot stay here."

"These are desperate times for all Cubans right now, despite our victory," Bernál said, very serious. "I mean to convert the fields behind this place into a world-class sugar farm, and here, where you stand, señora, will be the machinery to process the sugar. So, you are quite right. You and your son cannot stay here."

"Help us," I blurted.

"Sí, of course," Bernál said. "I am a helpful man. Sergeant Landon suggests a two-part immigration. He can easily take your son with him. Many American soldiers are bringing with them orphans from the reconcentration camps. They are a generous people, you see."

"Mayito is no orphan," I argued.

"Of course not. Mayito? A sweet name. An apodo for Mario, sí?" I nodded. "Bien, bien. Once the boy is settled in New York with your friend Blythe Quinn, she can begin the paperwork to bring you, as well."

"Paperwork?" I asked.

"When it comes to America, the entire country runs on paper, and the people earn a living from the work it takes to move it about. A curious place, you'll soon see," Bernál said.

"I will wait with my son here for this paperwork," I said.

"That might be a challenge, to draw up papers for two Cubans," Bernál said, rubbing his chin. "As I said, so many orphans are leaving the ports now. It seems to be what the Sergeant has in mind."

"I'm only seventeen. And I'm an orphan, too," I said.

"My darling, you are no child." Bernál's eyes betrayed him for an instant as they took in my body and lingered in places no gentleman would dare look.

"I wouldn't do it," Teresa whispered behind me.

"But what is she going to do otherwise?" another woman said.

"Basta," I said to them both. I was so tired of struggling,

running, having to make decisions. All my life had been this way, and now, finally, someone was offering to help make things easy. Mayito would go, and I would soon follow, and we would learn how to navigate a big city like New York, and move papers about if necessary, and start anew. I could see it— the snowfall, the shadows of skyscrapers, the things I'd seen in books would make Cuba seem small and insignificant, and for once I would take a free and hopeful breath. It was settled. Fear would no longer be the weakness that undid me. I was seventeen and unsophisticated, and thought I could dig about in my soul for the mettle I needed, and that it would be enough.

"Take Mayito New York?" I asked Landon. I still held the money he'd given me.

Landon smiled. "Yes," he said. "Yes, that's it."

I took a long, trembling breath. It would only be a short separation. "Sergeant Landon," I said, cementing the name in my memory. "C.L. Landon," I read on his badge.

"Christopher Lewis Landon, that's right," the Sergeant said, and I repeated it. They laughed at my accent.

"They shouldn't laugh," Bernál said. "You speak English so well."

"Thank you," I told Bernál. "For your help."

"It is nothing. And when the plantation is up and running, you will work for me as you wait. Yes?"

I nodded again, unable to speak. Bernál said a few more words to the American retinue, and they shook hands with him, looking to me every so often. The moment was now, I told myself. Blanca Lora had set me on my feet again, given me a path to tread. I would follow it, no matter how hard it would be in the moment.

Mayito began to cry, and it was as if my soul had grown a small voice separate from my body.

Then, they all turned to leave. The woman carrying Mayito

handed him back to Sergeant Landon at the man's request, and he lifted the baby onto his chest, looking over his shoulder, so that Mayito was higher than he'd ever been. He turned his small, wet face to the sky and marveled at it. I watched him go. Mayito did not lower his eyes to look at me. I watched until he was out of sight. Even then, I watched the place where he had just been, the air shimmering there, still trembling from his presence.

I did not remember until later that night, while I wept for my son, that Landon had carried away Blanca Lora's address with him, with Mayito. I hadn't told them Mario's last name was Betancourt. I'd forgotten to tell them he liked his milk warm, but not too hot, that he fell asleep by pulling my hair across his eyes, and that he'd just learned to clap for me, his little palms making the softest smacking sound in the world.

5.
Confessions

There is a silence so profound it rattles the soul, makes one feel displaced, as if one has been born again into a new life, unrecognizable from the one that came before. It's a feeling that lasts only a moment, but is unsettling, like a bad dream. That is the kind of silence I meet when I finish speaking. My voice is raw and my head is pounding.

"Here," Susana says, and hands me a glass of water.

"You went to New York, then," Dulce says, and it is a statement, not question. I can see in her eyes that she wants this to be true. They all do. Some of the women are crying, and I know they have imagined themselves in my place, handing over their children to strangers. They shudder at the thought. They think: there but for the grace of God. Or else: I would never. Pity and disdain mingle in their features. It's a toxic mix, and the women whom I have grown so fond of over the course of the storm seem strange and unknown to me again, the way they did those first moments on the bus ride to Casa Velázquez.

"I did not," I say.

"But why?" Rosalia squeaks. "It was all settled."

"I never saw Gustavo Bernál again. Whatever plans he'd had for the sugar farm never materialized," I say.

"Blythe. What of her?" Susana asks.

"I did not hear from her again. Not until it was too late, anyway." I answer the questions automatically, as if I've answered them a thousand times before. It all ran like an old record through my mind. "Why? What happened? How? Por Dios, what have I done?" again and again, without pause, each night, for decades.

"What did you do with the money?" Mireya asks. She is quiet about it, as if the question shames her.

"I fed myself. It didn't last very long, in the end. The money wasn't enough for passage to New York on any ship I could find," I say. "I sent a few letters to Blanca Lora. A few. I lost count. I—" I stop there.

They are quiet again, and I notice that the rain has stopped completely, and that the sun is piercing the windows and illuminating the room in ways I had not noticed before. A yellow stain blooms on the ceiling and it looks as if the storm has damaged the roof. There is a mouse hole in one of the walls, and tiny, black droppings outside of it. The wall, too, is stained yellow. I think of that smart mouse that knows it's best not to foul one's home, that such things are left outside, and I wonder at myself, having revealed so much in this small room, polluting the space with my confession.

"What became of Mayito?" Susana asks. "You never saw him again?"

I shake my head, and, trembling, I draw the picture frame from my pocket. I do not let the women look at it for long. Instead, I take apart the frame. The page of newsprint behind Mayito's picture is folded tightly to fit the frame. I undo the fold carefully, afraid that it will disintegrate in my hands. A separate sheet of onionskin paper comes loose as I lay the newsprint flat on the dusty bed in the center of the room. A fine, faded scrawl fills both sides of the onionskin paper.

"It's from Blanca Lora. She translated the article. Her article," I say. "This explains why I didn't go to New York. This is why I'm confessing to you all now, because I can't live another moment carrying this shame on my own." I wince, and have to grip my sides with both hands. "The envelope with this," I say,

gesturing to the article, "found me in August." I squeeze my eyes
shut and Susana flies to me, trying to take hold of my shoulders.
"No. I deserve this," I tell her through gritted teeth. Dulce
shakes her head at me. "I deserve worse than this," I say, looking at her hard, and then, when the pain passes, I begin to read.

A CUBAN MASCOT
Blythe Quinn Witnesses
"Butcher" Weyler's Reconcentration Camps

*You will Learn Here About Wretchedness and Squalor in Cuba—
How the Wickedness of Spain Abuses Poor Creatures—The
American Soldier Who Befriended a Cuban Negro Infant—The
Generosity of Members of the Manhattan Club*

Quite recently I had the idea that a woman undercover in
Cuba would possess an advantage over any other who might go
to this tumultuous island and attempt to report what he saw. I
speak fluent Spanish, and my accent is inflected in the Galician
way, and so, I passed easily for a Spanish nurse. In Cuba, I was
witness to abuses by the Spanish armed forces upon the simple
Cuban people that I may never shake from my mind. What did I
see that so rocked this reporter to her very foundations?

I will tell you.

General Valeriano Weyler, he whom they called "The Butcher,"
proved to be aptly named. We have all read with great interest of
the reconcentrados, those unfortunate villagers in the Cuban
countryside, who were, because of their support of the Cuban
Liberation Army, sequestered in their own homes, left to die of
starvation and disease.

To such a place my duties as a nurse led me. One village in particular, named La Cuchilla, or "The Knife," was among the most
miserable.

I witnessed a woman no older than forty, dying of yellow fever,
left alone in a small hut that the Cubans call a "bohío." Flies gathered at the corners of her mouth, and her eyes were swollen shut.
She was one of many in such a condition.

I saw a child, of no more than five, sitting up with the bodies of her parents in her bed. She had laid a hand on each of them, and it took several nurses to tear her away from their cold forms.

The Spanish would take the bodies and dump them not far from the village, so that they formed a great pyramid of death, and buzzards circled the place day and night, blackening the sky.

All this happened in the name of Spain, to thousands of innocents, and in defense of that nation's terrible army.

One Woman's Misery

I was able, through wile and subterfuge, to rescue one young woman from La Cuchilla. She was unmarried, and with child. I could not help but imagine her in New York City, where lost girls such as she was would find refuge in places like Magdalen's House, where she might be reformed.

The young woman's name was Carla Carvajál, and she had fallen in love with a hero of the Cuban Liberation Army, a freed slave and courageous son of Cuba. She posed as a nurse in the Spanish field hospital where I worked, and proved herself to be both a talented caretaker of so many wounded and ill Spanish soldiers (all of whom were her enemies, though they did not know it) and a marvelous storyteller, as well, as is true of many Cubans, for whom it seems the knack of weaving a tale comes naturally.

She bore a half-negro son shortly after her rescue. I took pity on Miss Carvajál, and on her son, and arranged a safer place for them to stay. The Cubans were willing to look the other way when it comes to women who have started on the downward path. The Spanish are far less tolerant, and indeed, there was talk among the nurses in the field hospital of disposing of the infant, as one would rid a house of a rodent.

I would have arranged for Miss Carvajál and her son to accompany me to New York, but she declined my offer, proving once again what I have known all along—that one can only seldom rescue another being, be it war-struck women or stray animals, and that the role of a reporter is one of objective observation and not interference.

A Delightful Turn

How delighted then was I to learn that Miss Carvajal had decided that the best course of action for her future and her son's was to submit the child to rearing by the most upstanding of men—Sergeant Christopher Lewis Landon, chairman of the Manhattan Club.

It was during a meeting of that illustrious group of New York men that I discovered the happy turn of events. The war being over eight months now, the Manhattan Club members were gathered to celebrate and I had been invited as well, to capture the event in print. After dinner, which consisted of calf's liver with bacon of such delectable quality that this reporter can taste it still and feel absolute satiety, the housemaid brought forth a light-skinned negro child, of about one year old. They set him down, and introduced him as Fourth of Landon, named in honor of our nation's independence day.

"Go on, Fourth of Landon," Sergeant Christopher Landon said, "show them what you know." Then, the child clapped his hands, and proceeded to untie the laces of all the shoes of the men present. Then, with a dexterity that is characteristic of his race, he tied each and every shoe with a perfect loop.

"Where did this marvelous child come from?" I asked. "Where are his parents?"

Sergeant Landon relayed the curious origin of Fourth of Landon.

A Son of Cuba

"We met a young Cuban woman while on tour of a Cuban field hospital in Oriente. She was desperate for someone to take the child off her hands, and specifically, to bring the child to New York City. Curiously, she had gotten hold of your name, my dear Miss Quinn. Where she came by it we could not have guessed, as your time in Cuba was secret to all. How disastrous it might have been for you, had she revealed your identity while the war waged! We had no one among us who spoke Spanish at first, and so, much of what she was saying was unclear to us except this: that the child should come away with us," Sergeant Landon explained.

"I told my companions, 'It's the Fourth of July, isn't it? And we've just captured Siboney, haven't we? I'm feeling patriotic. Yes, I am. And, well, the Manhattan Club needs a mascot.' Then, I gave the mother a generous amount of coin, and told her, 'The boy will be a mascot to the greatest club of men in all of America. He'll be my little friend. He'll be safe and fed and educated. He'll be American,' and she seemed pleased. He's the brightest little chap I could ever imagine."

I knew at once who the babe was, and I rejoiced that he had found a home. I told the marveled celebrants of my time with Carla Carvajál, and the role I played in the child's rescue.

"His mother remained in Cuba then?" I asked, and was told that she had happily taken the money and stayed behind, advised by a certain Cuban investor named Gustavo Bernál, who happened to arrive at the scene at just the right moment, and translated the mother's wishes to Sergeant Landon.

"His English was terrible, the poor chap. But he did his best by the woman and the boy, alleviating her fears," Sergeant Landon told me.

While I am delighted at the happy turn of events for the boy, I would have liked to see Carla Carvajál again, and to have shown her New York, as I had promised on more than one occasion during the war.

Nevertheless, the child Fourth of Landon is a testament to the good work our men accomplished in what is now a free Cuba, and his presence in Manhattan is a joy to those who know him.

Today, there is a cry of gladness that resounds over that tropical place, so far from New York. "¡Viva Cuba libre!" It echoes there and here, in the halls of Manhattan's salons and in the mouths of all who believe in liberty.

I finish reading and clear my throat. I am shaking all over. "I sold him, you see," I say to them. "Like a slave, I sold him. His father was a slave once, and now he, he—"

Rosalia is weeping openly, while Mireya stares and stares. Dulce has placed her withered hands over her eyes, as if she might block out the pictures I've planted in her head. Susana holds my hand and says, "No, you must not think that."

"What then?" Ofelia asks. She has been standing in the doorway for a while, and I noticed her mid-story. Every so often, another soldier would come and chat with her in whispers, but she remained, neglecting whatever duty she had to listen to my tale.

"What do you mean?" I answer her without looking up.

"I mean what happened next? Where did you go?" She sounds vulnerable for the first time, her voice raspy as if she's been shouting for days. The skin under her eyes is shadowed, and her clothes hang limply on her, as if she's lost weight over the course of the storm.

"Why does it matter?" I ask.

"It matters," Ofelia says, coming fully into the room and sitting before me. "You survived, didn't you? War and bloodshed and horror. And yet here you are." There is something desperate in Ofelia's eyes. I wonder why the epilogue to my story means so much to her. What does it matter? My story is simple.

I sold my son. The end.

"There has to be more than just sorrow," she whispers intently, and I see in her a wish unspoken—a hope that her life has not amounted to the wearing of olive green uniforms and barking at old women.

I do not tell her about the long days afterwards, how I was transfigured into a mute thing, finding work on farms and in hot, greasy kitchens up and down the province, nor do I mention a disastrous month in 1912, where I sat on the sand day in and day out, carving faces out of driftwood and trying to sell the pieces for pennies. I leave out the times I sat in the dark, counting money, trying to scrape together enough for a passage to New York and always falling short. I say nothing about the painter from Bogotá, who gave me a typewriter in exchange for posing in the nude for him, and how I learned to type while sitting in a park, the heavy machine resting on my thighs. I am sure that Ofelia does not want to hear about other things I did to survive, trading parts of myself for paltry change. The men I slept with were like boys trading marbles, this for that, and I would oblige, because there was nothing else for a girl like me. By the time I remembered Gilberto, and his offer, I had become quiet, like a doll made of felt—I was played with and made no sound.

"There was Gilberto. My Gil. I found my way to him, to Placetas. He was well, and the yellow fever had left no mark on him. He made me a lector in his father's cigar factory, and this is where I told the men snippets of my story, written by a woman named Carla Carvajál. When they asked me what the book was called, I would say it was *The Distant Marvels*, and they accepted it as true. I learned to forget Mario, and to love Gil. I miss them both. There is Beatríz still, who lives in Havana. She promises she'll visit me at Christmas. Is that what you wanted to hear?"

Ofelia nods and squeezes my hands. "Sí, it's something," she says, and leaves us again.

The women break off into small groups, leaving me alone. I think of the little sloops that used to sit in Havana harbor when I was a child, how Lulu and I watched the big ships go, leaving behind these small vessels, tossed in the troubled water. I think of them, and feel myself swaying a bit, as if I, too, am bobbing up and down on the waves. Susana sits by my side and says only that she is sure the others will not forget my story.

"Maybe it will even get to Mayito, wherever he is," Susana adds.

I nod and smile at Susana, who accepts my smile like a gift. But I know it is a pale copy of real happiness I've just handed her. The hope she wants for me—that my son still lives, that somehow, by some miracle, this story will reach his ears, will roll like a pebble through a pipe, tumbling, growing smooth and fast and true—is a kind of fiction.

We listen as the women talk to one another. They are weaving new tales now, of their own children, of the men they love.

I catch a bit of Rosalia's story, of the man who cheated on her, how she wrote on the windows of his car with red house paint, "How many putas can one man sleep with?"

Snippets of Dulce's story come to us whenever she raises her voice: she had a psychic once read her palm, and on her hand the woman saw that Dulce's only daughter would cross an ocean alone, and she left for Miami two years ago and hasn't come back.

Estrella and Celia are in earnest conversation regarding their twin boys. They trade stories about youngsters who completed one another's sentences as children, and now, as men, have married witches in disguise, who keep Estrella and Celia apart from their grandchildren.

Mireya speaks the loudest, and she is telling everyone that she, too, loved a poet once, but he drank a whole bottle of aguardiente on a dare in his youth, and when sobered, he could no longer write poems. So, bereft of his gift, he had nothing but harsh words for Mireya, and she left him.

We listen to one another until midday. The sun burns bright in a cloudless sky, as if the storm has propelled every single cloud in the Caribbean to some other part of the world. The sky looks bare and scoured.

Ofelia comes in and announces that our stay in Casa Velázquez has ended, and that buses will be arriving soon to take us all home.

I am glad. My ears are beached cockleshells full of stories instead of sand. I am bursting with them. I listen for my own story, and find it curiously missing. I can no longer remember the exact color of Lulu's hair, or the smell of Mario's breath in the morning, or what hunger, real hunger feels like. I cradle air, holding my arms as if an infant rested there, and find I can't recall how much my son weighed at birth, or whether he was born in the morning or the night. Perhaps what was once important is no longer so. Other stories are flickering in my imagination, pushing, wind-like, insistent. I want to sleep in my own bed and dream the stories alive.

There is also this: I want to go home to Maisí, and see what damage the winds have wrought.

6.
Tending What We Can

Ofelia leads us out of that room which has been my confessional. It is late in the afternoon, and Casa Velázquez has a musty smell now, like paper steeped in water and left to dry. We trudge down the stairs and the steps give softly under our feet, bending with our weight. I notice a jagged brown line on the wall, about a foot over my head, and realize it is a water line. The others have noticed, too, and now we are all running our fingers along the length of it, following it out of Casa Velázquez. It reminds me of the veins visible inside my arms and in the backs of my legs, and I think that this desiccated artery along the walls is an omen. The pain in my midsection flares and fades, flares and fades, and I ignore it as best I can.

Once outside, we stand in the sun, blinking like moles. There is so much debris in the roads I have a hard time thinking that the bus can get through it. I spot umbrellas and lawn chairs, gray tarps wrapped around lampposts, a drowned dog and a man poking it with a cane. All of this is in sight, and the sky above us is blue and spotless, mocking the ravaged earth with its beauty. The sun bears down on my neck and the place where my skin touches the chain I always wear burns. I adjust my necklace and sigh.

"¡Esto es un sol africano!" Mireya shouts to the sun, wiping her brow with the back of her hand.

The others nod in agreement. Yes, it's an African sun, I suppose, though none of us has ever been to that faraway place. I turn to look at Casa Velázquez one last time and think about the slaves brought here in my father's youth, the ones who had sneaked sideways glances at the sun back home, felt it hot on their bodies, and carried those rays of light in their skin. What did they think of the rearrangement of light here in Cuba? Was it all that different from home?

We hear the bus before we see it, rattling down a side street and blowing the wreckage of the storm out of its path. It rolls to a stop before us and the driver, another soldier, waves us on.

"Bueno, damas," Ofelia says, her hands on her hips as she faces us. "It has been a pleasure." She smiles, but her eyes are tired. The women take turns hugging her before boarding the bus. Susana gives Ofelia a quick kiss on the cheek, the way friends who are sure they will see each other again do. I am last, and I wrap my arms around Ofelia's shoulders and pat her back.

"I could barely get you on that bus," she chided me, still in my embrace.

"I'm glad you did," I told her, releasing her, and turning to go.

"Oye," Ofelia says, and I turn. "If he knew, he'd forgive you. I'm certain of it."

I don't know if she means Mayito, or Mario. Or perhaps Agustín, who did not fare well in my story. Maybe there are other men I've defamed. The poet. Gilberto. It doesn't matter. I want to say that I am not so sure, that none of them would forgive me, but my throat has tightened up, and I know that if I speak, I will cry.

Ofelia stands up straighter and takes her eyes off of me. She assesses the bus, the women who have propped open the windows and stuck their faces out for one last look at Ofelia and Casa Velázquez. "Consider tomorrow's dawn a new beginning, comadres!" she says in that commanding voice again. I had forgotten how masculine her voice was, and how I'd thought she was a man at first, when she shouted at me from the other side of the door to my house back in Maisí. It is as if the sun-

light has caused her to revert to an earlier state. She is all soldier again.

I take my seat as we begin to pull away, and I listen as the
women sigh. God knows what they're thinking.

Susana has saved a seat for me. "Aquí, María Sirena," she
says.

I settle in. The driver is a man. His uniform is pressed well,
and the creases stand out on his thighs like tiny mountain
ranges. It speaks of his devotion, I think, or else, of his wife's,
proud of his rank and station in life. He does not flip on the
radio, even when a few of the women ask for the distraction.
He simply puts up one finger and shakes it at us, as if we were
a caravan of children accustomed to being pointed at, made
obedient with a single gesture. I do not like his face. Every feature offends me. If Mario and Gil's faces were softly painted
visages, in muted colors, made blurry by my affection for them,
then this man was carved out of granite. He is all pale angles.

"What's your name, hijo?" I ask out of curiousity.

"Cresencio," he says after a beat. Even his name is a sharp
thing, and I decide that it is best to nap, and to ignore this soldier who will never be one of us.

It is early in the evening when we drop off Mireya. Her
house has weathered the storm well. The windows look to be
intact, and only a palm tree has fallen in her yard. I remember
her house with such fondness. Those were the days, when I
could show up unannounced, and she would greet me with a
hug, a cup of coffee, and a morsel of savory gossip we might
chew on like dried meat. I wonder if our last few days in Casa
Velázquez have returned Mireya to me, if, perhaps, I might
visit her again.

"Bendito séa Diós," she utters as the bus comes to a stop and
her house comes into view. "Adiós, todas," she says, addressing
us all. The tumult in my throat as I see her begin to go surprises
me.

"Mireya," I call out, my voice hoarse for reasons unknown.

She turns, walks up to me swiftly, as if she is about to do an unpleasant thing and wants it over with quickly, and lowers her pale face towards mine. An unexpected kiss against my cheek, and then, her soft hands around my own, undo me.

"Ay, Diós, I've made my friend cry," she says, laughing quietly.

"We'll see each other soon," I say.

Mireya leaves the bus, shuffling towards her front door. The driver does not wait for her to enter her house, which is bad form and everyone knows it. We turn in our seats and watch Mireya's tiny figure recede in the distance, fumbling with her keys. Susana's eyes are better than anyone else's and she announces, "She's inside," and the rest of us exhale in relief.

This happens again and again—the driver drops off one of us and drives away in a rush. The rest of us turn to watch, to make sure of one another's safety. This is how we tend to one another, I think. We are old. Should one of us need a new roof on our house, for example, we are helpless to do anything. But this watching, training our eyes on one another until the last moment, this we can do. What if I am the last one on the bus? It is likely, considering the location of my house at the end of the world. I am used to the feeling of going untended. It will be fine. I will get into my broken house, or else I will stand in the ruins until I can no longer do so. And then? There has always been an "and then" in my life. Today will be no exception. I can feel it in my stomach, where the pain is, and in my heart and mind that this is not my last day.

We're at Rosalia's house when I realize I haven't been keeping track of where these women live. I would have liked to stay in touch with some of them. I have more in common with these women, I realize, than I do with anyone else in the world. We are bound together by fear and memory, fastened by the common mysteries of motherhood, made familiar to one another in the shadow of a monstrous storm. Before disembarking, Rosalia says, "Mis amigas, que Diós las cuide," and we thank her. She rushes to her front door, which has been blown open, and she straddles an upturned urn in the doorway, one that once must have held a fern or a boniato plant. Rosalia waves at us as we go.

Estrella and Celia, mothers to twins, live on the same block. The discovery that their homes are still standing sets them panting with joy, and they disembark together, twinned themselves. They point at one another's houses, which have been spared the worst of the storm.

Dulce lives nearest me, in Maisí, and we're headed to her house next. The town is in tatters. We drive the roundabout in the plaza, and I realize that the statue of Cristóbal Colón is missing. Then I spot him, thrown off his pedestal a few yards away, having rolled onto his face.

"His hand, look," Susana says, pointing at a broken part of the statue—Colón's hand, still gripping a rolled map, lies in the grass.

"Ay, Maisí," I say.

The bus pulls away from the plaza and into the neighborhoods closest to the sea. Here the destruction is palpable. The air tastes sour and a fine grit hangs in the atmosphere. Houses have been blown off their foundations, and here and there, cars rest up on trees, having floated there when the water was high. We ride in silence and can hear the slosh of the bus tires treading through still-flooded streets. When we arrive at Dulce's house, the bus driver opens the door and doesn't help her out. Susana and I do, and watch, horrified, as the water reaches Dulce's calves. Her house is flooded, and when she opens the door, we see furniture floating inside, bobbing in murky waters.

Susana and I take turns embracing Dulce. "I'll check on you tomorrow," Susana says, and Dulce begins to weep.

We leave her there and as we step onto the bus the driver starts to pull away.

"For God's sake," Susana yells at the driver as we stumble to our seats.

Then, we hear Dulce shouting, "Ay!" and watch as a snake swims around her ankles, making "S" shapes and rippling the water.

"Come with us!" I yell to Dulce out the window, but the bus driver is accelerating.

"You can't leave her," Susana cries, and he lifts a finger again.

"Lift that finger again, cabrón, and I'll bite it off," I tell him, but the soldier says nothing. Susana yells back at Dulce that we will come for her, and she nods, holding herself.

Susana's apartment building is next, and there is a commotion here. Residents are lined up along the sidewalk, but there are two policemen keeping them away from the apartment.

"Unsafe," we hear them say. The building looks fine, but I catch a strange smell in the air around it.

"Probably a gas leak," I tell Susana, and her eyes fill with tears.

"I'm so tired," she says, pulling off her scarf for the first time. She rubs her scalp, which is patchy with hair here and there. She covers her face with the scarf and weeps.

"She's coming with me," I tell the driver, and we are off to the farthest corner of Maisí, to a place I think might have been devoured by the sea.

I can imagine what this place must have looked like during the storm—the rooms dark even during the day, the mango tree in the front yard lashing the windows, the waves of seawater sprinkling the house at first, like a baptism, then growing, swelling, becoming unhinged jaws and swallowing my home. There is seaweed on the roof of the house, and on the little concrete path to the front door, there is a dead fish, yellowtail it looks like, though it has gone pale and gray. In the sunlight, the windows glisten and I realize it is salt that has dried on the glass.

Though briny and foam-washed, my little cottage still stands. Susana is helping me off the bus when I see something else that surprises me—a car, parked on the side of the road, its engine humming. I squint to make out the driver when the car door opens. My daughter, Beatríz, steps out of the passenger side. She holds a flat brown purse close to her body. She fishes in it for a moment, takes out a bundle of pesos, and hands it to the driver, a man with a cigar stuck in his mouth. A bloom of smoke obscures his face. Beatríz clears the car, and he drives off, splashing mud and muck onto my daughter's legs.

"¡Coño!" she curses, then looks up at me, her face filling my line of sight. Seeing her again, after all these months, reminds me of her birth, how her tiny face saturated my vision, so that I was blind to everything but her features. It was the same with Mayito.

Now, I think, now I might just die of happiness. I feel the knot in my stomach distinctly, as if it has become a living organism of its own. It is as if the tumor, or whatever it is that is killing me, has quickened.

"Beatríz," I say, and feel myself falling. The picture of Mayito, back in its frame now with Blythe Quinn's article, tumbles from my pocket. "Mi foto," I say, and then all goes dark.

7

The State of a Daughter's Heart

I have come to. Except I have not. It is still dark, and I cannot pry my eyelids open. But I can listen, and what I hear is this—the mechanical trilling of gears of some sort, the scuffle of hard-soled shoes on tiled floors, the tinkle of metal in a room far away, the sluggish cough of another person, and a woman's voice, fading in and out, saying something about a room and a bed.

I am in a hospital. I can smell it, too, the alcohol in the air, and the scent of stale rice and beans left over from the lunch hour.

This paralysis is a curious sensation, and I'm sure of a needle placed in my hand, delivering whatever cocktail is keeping me in the dark. I test my voice, but I can manage only a little squeak. Then I feel a hand on mine, and Beatríz's voice saying, "Ay, Mami."

"Is she waking up?" Another voice that I recognize as Susana's.

"The doctors say she will once the I.V. runs out. They ran so many tests last night," Beatríz says.

"I'm familiar with the process," Susana says and I can picture her face in the instant—saturated with sadness, puffy eyed, grim-lipped.

"I'm sorry," Beatríz says.

They are quiet again. I long for them to talk. Again, I squeak, and there is Beatríz's hand on mine.

"My father died when I was a little girl. He was cutting my hair, and then, fuácata, he was dead. Just like that."

"Your mother told us. I'm so sorry."

Once more, there is silence, and I can imagine the expression on Beatríz's face, one of surprise and irritation at me for telling stories to strangers.

"And now Mami. Look at her," my daughter says.

I can feel them looking, and I want to shake my head, tell them both to get their fill while they still can. Anger bubbles in my throat. This desperate feeling, this anesthetized wakefulness, offends me, as if someone has slipped a quiet hand into my purse and stolen my wallet.

After a moment, Susana speaks. I hear her ask, "Does the name Mayito ring a bell?"

Shame and terror course through me. I want to weep, to rise, to clamp my hands over Susana's mouth.

"No," Beatríz says, lifting my hand now as if she is examining it. "Should it?"

Susana laughs, high and false. "Oh, no. It's just I have a friend in Havana. I thought you might know him."

"Oye, chica," Beatríz says, "Havana is a big place."

They are quiet, and I feel myself settling down. I feel like a root, underground in a dark, damp earth.

8.
Of Promises Kept

She comes in a dream, I think. I am in my room in my cottage in Maisí, and though I strain to hear Beatríz and Susana, the house is silent. Every light in the room is ablaze, and the bulbs sputter, risking explosion, as if her presence is a charge of energy. She herself is a ray of light, engulfed in brightness too harsh to gaze upon. But her face is a shadow that holds her features in place.

"María Sirena," she says.

"You've come for me," I tell her. "I kept my end of the bargain," I say, feeling courageous now, in the end. "Tell me you've kept yours."

Her face shifts, and now she is Gilberto, masculine, straightnosed, as handsome as he was on the day he died. The smell of tobacco fills the room. "Let me tell you a story," she says.

"There once was a faceless girl, one without a reflection. Neither mirror nor slow river nor shard of glass could capture her face. It would slosh about on surfaces like an ice cube. And yet."

I feel myself nodding. Her face shifts again, and now she is Agustín, and her hair becomes a lick of flame. When she speaks, the room grows warmer. Now she is Blanca Lora, and her speech becomes accented and slippery. The pink tip of her tongue peeks between her teeth on voiceless syllables. She becomes Lulu next, and I want to speak, to yell, "Mamá," but Lulu is gone, her mouth a trembling "O". The face blurs and becomes Mario, who covers his eyes with his hands and disappears, too, fast, as if he can't bear to look upon me. At last, she settles on a countenance that is at once familiar and strange. It is Mayito, and he is a man approaching old age. His face is round, his cheeks dotted with freckles, like Lulu's. These appear on the bridge of his nose bit by bit. His lashes grow before my eyes, long and curly like Agustín's were. His chin is Mario's. His nose and ears and eyebrows come from places unknown, though I recognize the shape of his fingernails, which are like Beatríz's, and I wonder who that ancestor might be with the perfectly square nail beds.

"Mi hijo," I say in a whisper. Mayito nods.

When he speaks it is in a deep voice that is strangely familiar to me.

"I will know you," he says. "I will know you when you come to me at last, and you will be cloaked in a new countenance."

Mayito melts away and reveals her again, brighter now than before. "I have kept my promise," she says.

I wake and know I have dreamed my last dream. Beatríz hears me coughing, and she and Susana rush into my room.

"Ay, Mami," she says, and lays her chest down upon mine. I smile at the inherited gesture. She cries without a sound.

I want to say something, to mark these moments with final words, but my voice is shattered. In the corner of the room, a small lamp burns brightly. Susana catches me squinting at the light.

"I'll turn it down," she says, and stands.

"No, déjalo," I manage, and Susana sits, worrying her scarf in her hands. Her cheeks are rosy, and I'm certain now, looking upon her, that she will be cured and live a long life. She is young. Perhaps she will have children. Perhaps she will tell them about my son. I can imagine her children up north, searching for Mayito; for them, he will be a legend, merely one of their mother's stories. Perhaps they will find him and tell him something about me. Perhaps he will recognize me in them somehow.

It grows clear to me that something has shifted. The pain, yes. That has radiated outward and tingles my skin, making Beatríz's head on my chest a strange sensation, like ant bites everywhere. But there is something else that has loosened, and I realize it suddenly, that what had been tormenting me has lifted.

"I loved. I have been loved," I whisper.

"¿Qué?" Susana and Beatríz say in unison.

"And forgiven," I want to add, but I can't say it again, though I try. I was loved by Lulu and Agustín, in his way, and by Mario and Gilberto, and by my children, even Mayito, who must have imagined the mother he'd had once, and may have guessed that he had been given up unwillingly. He must have held me in his heart, unknown as I was to him. He may even have felt me, so many miles away, whenever I gazed upon his picture, like a benign pressure in his head.

"Amor," I say, though it sounds more like "no, no." Beatríz cups my face in her hands. Susana shakes her head.

"Mamá, como te quiero," my daughter whispers, proving what I already know—that there can be no safe place, no body that does not grow ill at last, no escape from death or absolute shelter from storms. But that love, in its full measure, is a kind of swirling tempest, too, and in its eye, there is stillness and comfort and peace.

I close my eyes and picture the sea, calm like a plate. I imagine floating upon it. There is no wind to churn the waters. There is only the sunlight. There is only a story I try to tell myself to pass the time, about a mermaid, and a girl, and love building upon love over the course of a life.

ACKNOWLEDGMENTS

This book is dedicated to my mother, Marta Quinn, and my grandmother, Maria Asela "Tita" Garcia. But I'd be remiss in not also acknowledging the ways other mothers have shaped my life, including my madrina, Acela Robaina , my "Titi" Aris Concepción, and my mother-in-law, Josefa Acevedo. These women make up the strong, beating heart of my family, and they have loved me deeply and honestly always. If the mothers in this novel know how to love, it is because I had incredible models.

I am grateful to Europa Editions, and especially my editor Michael Reynolds, in ways I cannot express. An editor who will come to the heart of Alabama just for a visit with an author is a treasure. Thank you, Michael, and thanks to everyone at Europa for taking such care of this book.

My agent, Stéphanie Abou, arrived in my life at a time when I needed nurturing and encouragement and a champion for this book. She has been all of those things and more. Mil gracias, querida.

Writer friends who have given me their time with close readings of this book when it was still in progress include Hallie Johnston and Emma Bolden. My heartfelt gratitude to you both. Much of this novel was written in the home of Ash Parsons, who let me sit on her couch and write on it so often that I was convinced no other place but her sofa held the "magic" I needed to write. For this, and for her support in so many innumerable ways, thank you, Ash. Thanks, too, go to Rachel Hawkins, for inspiring me to be bold, make the hard choices, and always reminding me of the importance of laughter. To Julianna Baggott, you are incredible in a million ways. Thanks for having my back.

I finished the book shortly after attending Las Dos Brujas, a workshop run by the inimitable, talented, and encouraging Cristina Garcia. It was the final dose of inspiration I needed, and I am grateful to the example Cristina has provided for me and for many Latina writers, laying down pavement again and again.

For their support both financial and collegial, and the space and time to write and teach, I'd like to thank Auburn University, the Department of English, the College of Liberal Arts, and the Alabama State Council on the Arts.

Jana Gutierrez, a colleague at Auburn University, translated, in a way far more elegant than I could have, the José Martí epigraph used in the book. Thank you, Jana.

For their love and encouragement, I thank my husband, Orlando Acevedo, and my daughters, Penelope and Mary-Blair. They are my world and I adore them.

Finally, I wish to honor the memory of my mentor and friend, the writer Lester Goran. Were it not for Professor Goran, I am certain that I would not have become a writer of books. He called me a writer before I believed it and I am forever grateful for his guidance and friendship.

ABOUT THE AUTHOR

Chantel Avevedo, "one of the most versatile and exciting writers of her generation," says *Pure* trilogy author Julianna Baggott, is the author of *Love and Ghost Letters*, winner of the Latino International Book Award, and more recently, *A Falling Star*, winner of the Doris Bakwin Award. She studied writing at the University of Miami with the late Lester Goran. She is an Associate Professor of English at Auburn University, Alabama, where she founded the Auburn Writers Conference and edits the Southern Humanities Review.

Q & A with Chantel Acevedo

Your heroine María Sirena is an oral historian, and your book almost has the feeling of a folk or fairy tale. Does a tradition of oral history influence your writing?
Absolutely, and the source is a very specific one. My mother and I lived with my grandparents when I was growing up, and my grandmother was (and continues to be) a wonderful storyteller. Every lesson came with a cautionary tale about some child or other in Cuba who had died quite tragically and, often unintentionally, comically. And she told stories about her own childhood in Cuba, where she was the youngest of nine. She is a magnificent storyteller.

How did you decide which words and phrases worked best in Spanish?
It's not so much about the specific words as it is about giving the reader *a sense* of the language. I think a lot of it has to do with instinct, and in speaking with other bilingual writers who use code-switching in their books, it seems we all have an inner ear for those moments that call for a switch.

What kind of research did you do to write *The Distant Marvels*? Are any of these anecdotes or events drawn from your own family's stories?
I spent a lot of time in the library and online learning about the Spanish-American War. That's where I started, but the research had such an American perspective on what was actually a really long war and not Roosevelt's "splendid little war" as it was perceived in the States, that for a while I

thought I was at a dead end. It wasn't until I started finding pictures of the reconcentration camps that the research gained traction for me. From there, I learned so much about what Cubans call the War of Independence, and the book started to take shape. My own family history doesn't play a role in the story at all, but the character of Mayito is based on a brief article I found early on, about a "reconcentrado" child who was "adopted" by an American soldier and made into a mascot of the Manhattan Club. They renamed him Fourth of Wilson. For a long time, I looked and looked for more information about this boy, even finding a book of minutes from Manhattan Club meetings of the era. But he disappeared into history. Fourth of Wilson, whatever became of him, was nowhere to be found. So, I invented Mayito first, then his mother, as a way of recapturing that lost boy for myself. I was a little obsessed, to be honest. Maybe a better historian can someday tell me about the real Fourth of Wilson. I'd love to know.

What about the Cuba of María Sirena's time survives in present day Cuba? Is there an essential Cuban-ness that transcends time?
Politically, the end of María Sirena's life is also the beginning of Castro's rule in Cuba. That's still true, of course, which suggests how long Fidel, and now Raul, have been in charge. But more generally, I think the patriotism of the 19th century Cuban rebels was motivated by a love of country that is infectious. Today, that love of country spans the political spectrum and exists both on the island and in the diaspora. And in the most beautiful sense, at least among exiles, that love has meant that now, with three generations in the United States, Cuban-American children are nevertheless bilingual, can sing along to Beny Moré's music, and recite José Martí's poetry. Naturally, the effect is diminished with each generation, but it's still there, still resonant.

María Sirena has a complicated relationship with the idea of America. As a Cuban-American writing in English and in the United States, can you describe a little bit of your relationship to both countries and identities?

Gustavo Pérez-Firmat wrote this wonderful book called "Life on the Hyphen," which seeks to answer this question. I feel very much like I live on that hyphen between Cuban and American. On most days, I am not enough of either one. I speak Spanglish more than anything, and as I'm typing this, I'm wearing an *azabache* for luck and a pink Timex watch I got at Target. My youngest is napping downstairs, with an *angel de la guardia* attached to her crib, while my oldest watches an American sitcom on cable. I'm currently sitting in my house in Auburn, Alabama, and we recently visited the Country Music Hall of Fame in Nashville. Tonight, I'll make *picadillo* for dinner. And so on. The complexity these days comes not from living on the hyphen, but from identifying as a Cuban when the Cuba-that-was has changed so much. Now, when I visit Miami, I no longer recognize the slang that the new exiles are using, or the songs they're listening to. And, I imagine that once Cuba becomes a democracy, which is bound to happen, there will be another shift. What will it mean to call oneself an "exile" when there is nowhere to be exiled from?

Telling her life story saves the women of Casa Velazquez and allows María Sirena to leave this world unburdened. Can you talk about the power of storytelling in your own life?
Having grown up in Miami, surrounded by Cubans, the power of the stories told by all of those friends and relatives has had an immeasurable effect on my life, and my sense of myself as a Cuban-American. Whatever we did, ate, said, how we behaved, all drew comparisons to Cuba, and with those comparisons, came the stories. They had the gloss of nostalgia, of course, but sometimes, the darkness would seep through, and then there would be a sharp edge of realism in the stories. I often get asked if I've ever been to Cuba, and the answer is no, I haven't. I'd like to go, and I have this crazy notion that I could find my way around Havana by instinct. This, I realize, is a ridiculous thing to think, but it's a feeling I cannot shake. What is that? That's the power of story.

María Sirena tells her story so that people might remember her after she's gone. Is this reasoning part of why you write?

It really hasn't been about that, though now that I have two beautiful daughters, perhaps my answer is changing. I'm glad that they'll have these books they can put on their shelves, and these stories they can go to and find pieces of themselves in, learn something about the places where their ancestors came from.

Is history inescapable, or do we need to make an active effort to preserve, learn from, and remember it? Or can both things be true at once?
We absolutely should all be in the business of preservation. When I think about the ancient library of Alexandria burning down, I feel a really deep loss. Seriously, I do. What is human history if not the passing on of stories, that most fundamental kind of communication? We stall out without stories of the past. I'm utterly biased, though. I'm obsessed with history, with museums, with little-known facts. I don't believe in reincarnation, but if I *have* had other lives, I was most certainly a Classicist in one of them.

Do you think it's possible to learn from history, or are we fated individually and as a society to repeat our mistakes and triumphs?
It's entirely possible to learn from history, both good and bad. Hitler was inspired by the reconcentration camps in Cuba, for example. If we could apply human history to some kind of scientific theory, then the trajectories of past events would suggest future paths along the same lines. That's a sad view of it, but science also tells us that when things are in motion, they keep going until some other force gets in the way. We're that force, aren't we? History is the instruction manual, for those of us paying attention. And thank God, some of us are always paying attention.

For discussion

1. María Sirena's mother Lulu had the spirit of a true revolutionary, but as a woman, lacked the social position to fight for the cause. What does *The Distant Marvels* suggest about the place of women in history?

2. Why is Agustín so determined to keep Lulu and María Sirena in his life when he expresses so little affection for them?

3. After living a strangely sheltered life as a child prisoner, at the age of fourteen María Sirena is thrown into a world of conflict. Is there a singular moment in the story when she becomes an adult, or is it a gradual transformation?

4. How has motherhood shaped María Sirena, softened or hardened her remembrances, and changed her perspective on herself as a younger woman?

5. Does María Sirena ever get the "cosmic justice" that Dulce claims the world lacks? What might that justice be?

6. Do you think it was reasonable for Mireya to blame María Sirena for her son's death?

7. What is the relationship between María Sirena's ailing physical body and her vision of herself as a young woman? What does *The Distant Marvels* suggest about the relationship of the physical body to the life of the mind and the spirit?

8. How does the Casa Velazquez serve as a metaphor for the dramatic changes taking place across Cuba?

9. What aspects of *The Distant Marvels* recall the form of a fairytale or an epic?

10. What relevance does storytelling have in contemporary life? Is it a way to preserve valuable history, or a way of obscuring the cold facts of history?

11. Is it possible to look objectively at one's own history? How objective or subjective is María Sirena's tale?

12. What does *The Distant Marvels* suggest about the relationship between the individual and history? How much of an individual's life is shaped by the history that precedes them, and how much power does an individual have to shape their future?

13. At the end of *The Distant Marvels*, do you think that María Sirena has forgiven herself for what happened to her mother, Mario, and Mayito? Did she ever deserve blame for their fate, and if so, does she deserve forgiveness?

Find out more at www.europaeditions.com